Twisted Lies

by

C.B. Clark

Twisted Lies

Cover Art by *Debbie Taylor*

The Wild Rose Press, Inc.
PO Box 708
Adams Basin, NY 14410-0708
Visit us at www.thewildrosepress.com

Publishing History
First Edition, 2021
Trade Paperback ISBN 978-1-5092-3861-3
Digital ISBN 978-1-5092-3862-0

Published in the United States of America

A shape materialized out of the gloom...tall, lean, dark...infinitely terrifying.

She whimpered, pivoted, and fled out of the house, stumbling over hidden roots and rocks, crashing into trees, fighting through the clinging prickles of wild raspberry bushes.

She ran until her chest heaved and her lungs burned as if they were on fire. Her heart pounded with such ferocity she feared it would burst from her chest. Too exhausted to run farther, she sank to the cold, damp sand, curled into a ball, and closed her eyes.

Her pursuer's labored breathing pierced the late-night air. "Maggie!"

Risking a peek, she opened her eyes and shuddered.

He loomed over her. "Why are running from me, Margaret? I'm here to help." His glower fixed on her; his gaunt face twisted into a parody of a smile. His thin lips shifted upward, teeth gleaming in the glow of the flashlight he carried.

She scuttled behind a washed-up log, her small hands scrabbling in the soft sand, tangling in the crackling strands of dried seaweed and broken shells.

His fingers wrapped around her shoulders, his nails digging into her tender skin as he dragged her from her hiding place.

She opened her mouth to scream, but her throat was too tight, and no sounds emerged.

Praise for C.B. Clark

TWISTED LIES is award-winning author C.B. Clark's seventh novel published by The Wild Rose Press. Her first novel, MY BROTHER'S SINS placed first in the Melody of Love Romance Writing Competition. BROKEN TRUST placed second in the 2017 Best Romance Novel Critters/Preditors & Editors Reader's Poll. BITTER LEGACY, BROKEN TRUST and SECRET BETRAYAL are out in audible.

"C.B. Clark takes readers on fabulous adventures."

~Top pick, Night Owl Reviews, 5 Stars

"Ms. Clark has done a fantastic job with yet another spellbinding story."

~Reviews by Crystal, 5 Stars

"BROKEN TRUST was an amazing mystery. Read this book in a few hours because I couldn't put it down."

~PRG's Reviewers' Choice Award 2018

Dedication

This work would not be what it is if not for my ever-supportive editor, ELF, and the staff at The Wild Rose Press. Thank you for making my dreams come true.

And of course, to Lin, my beta reader with the sharp eye.

Chapter 1

Twenty-one days.
Twenty-one days sober.
Other people talked about abstaining from alcohol in terms of months or years, but in the three years since her drinking started impacting her life, the longest Athena Reynolds had been dry was seven days.
So, twenty-one days was good.
Damn good.
Abstinence was an ongoing battle. Every hour, every minute, every agonizing second of the past twenty-one days, her body ached with a bone-deep desperation. She'd made it that long, but today, the thirst was like a beast inside her, screaming to be fed. Her hard-won sobriety was about to end. She craved a drink. Now. She'd never wanted one more.
Sinking onto the couch, she smoothed the crumpled envelope on her lap and reread the address label. Her stomach knotted. Someone knew her real name, and that she lived in the bustling foothills city of Calgary, Alberta.
How was it possible? After all these years? The past she'd been running from had found her. The nightmare was back. The envelope fell from her shaking hands. Her legs wobbled as she rose and stumbled out of the living room and down the short hall to the kitchen.

Afternoon sunlight streamed through the window above the sink. The cozy kitchen, with its walls painted a cheerful butter yellow, and the well-scrubbed laminate countertops, gleamed. The steady hum of the refrigerator and ticking of the antique clock on the wall were the only sounds in the silent house. The pungent smell of fried onions and roasted garlic, from last night's homemade spaghetti sauce, hung in the air.

The efficient kitchen, with its breakfast nook and view of the tidy, fenced backyard and the rolling, grassy foothills and snow-crested Rocky Mountains beyond, was the reason she'd bought the small rancher. This was her favorite room—the place she sought refuge when life overwhelmed her. How many times had she sat there in the evenings after work, sipping a glass of chilled white wine, watching the birds at the feeder on the back porch, breathing in the sweet smells of flowering Saskatoon bushes, regrouping until she was ready to face the world?

These days, her drink of choice was a cup of herbal tea or unsweetened apple juice. Alcohol was off the table…had been for twenty-one unendurable days.

But today, all bets were off.

The brown-paper-wrapped bottle sat on the counter taunting her. She'd read the letter, then rushed down to Larry's Liquor Outlet on the corner and bought a twenty-sixer of vodka. The alcohol called to her with the siren song of a mermaid, leading her, like the sailors of old, to certain destruction.

Otis, her mixed-breed rescue dog, padded into the kitchen, his nails clicking on the tiles. He leaned his large hairy body against her legs, offering unspoken comfort. His long pink tongue lolled out, and he licked her hand.

"Hey, boy." Never taking her focus off the mesmerizing bottle, she scratched him behind one floppy ear, threading her fingers through his rough coat.

His tail thumped the floor like a bass drum.

Giving him a final pat, she crossed to the counter and ripped the bag off the bottle. She crumpled the brown-paper wrapping into a ball, then tossed it into the sink. The brand was one she hadn't tried, but the taste or quality didn't matter. She wasn't going to sip the vodka.

Not a chance.

A single, quick gulp, and she'd drain her glass. Then she'd pour the rest of the contents down the sink. She just needed one drink…one stiff shot. Twisting open the bottle top, she poured several ounces into a glass tumbler.

Don't do this!

The command bellowed through her like an edict from above.

You're throwing away twenty-one days of sobriety.

Her stomach twisted, and her brain whirled with the coping strategies she'd learned from the four AA meetings she'd attended. Stress was a trigger. She needed to calm down and take control. Closing her eyes, she focused—breathing in through her nostrils and out through her mouth. Slow and steady, just like she'd been taught.

Again, and again.

Really? This mindfulness crap was supposed to work? Who were those AA people kidding? She opened her eyes and spotted the full glass. In that second, the battle was lost. The booze called, promising instant gratification. She needed a drink more than she needed her next breath. Grabbing the tumbler with both hands, she lifted the glass and gulped.

The vodka slithered down her throat, coiled in warm anticipation in her stomach, and seeped into her bloodstream. The familiar, tart, citrusy taste settled on her tongue like an old friend. A tidal wave of comforting warmth swelled, filling her body, relaxing and exhilarating at the same time. She slugged down the rest of the drink and wiped her mouth with the back of her hand.

She'd go back on the wagon tomorrow, attend an AA meeting, voice her regrets, and all would be well. Everyone had relapses. Today was hers. Lord knew, she had plenty of reason. She picked up the bottle, held it over her empty glass, and poured.

Her cell phone rang, the tinny peal piercing her brain like a dentist's drill. The bottle slipped from her hand and landed on the tiles with a thunderous crash. Shards of glass sprayed across the room. Liquor puddled on the floor. The sharp bite of alcohol filled the small kitchen.

Otis barked and bounded into the room.

"Get back, boy." She gestured for him to sit. "Stay."

He stopped inches from the spilled liquor and glass splinters and sat.

Cursing under her breath, she tore off a handful of paper towels and crouched on her hands and knees. She ignored the earsplitting ringing and mopped at the spilled liquor. The call was probably from work.

Three weeks prior, her boss, Frank Schuster, at the prestigious law firm of Schuster & Corbin in downtown

Calgary, had called her into his office. Apparently, her drinking problem wasn't a secret anymore. Her co-workers had noticed her all-too-frequent absences and tardiness, and the quality of her work was suffering.

All things considered, Frank had been pretty decent about the uncomfortable situation, but he insisted she take a paid leave of absence while she got her *problem* under control. The underlying threat was that either she stopped drinking, or she'd be fired.

Hell, if gaining control of the beast that had taken over her life was that easy, she'd have quit long ago. But she needed her job, and she promised him she'd seek help and be back at work in a month, two at the tops. He wished her well, and she packed up her desk and drove home. A woman from the law firm's human resources department called her every week or so for an update on her recovery. Her mouth twisted. Wouldn't HR be happy to hear of her most recent relapse?

A sharp, stabbing pain shot through her hand. "Ouch!" She winced and studied her palm. A tiny splinter of glass was embedded in her skin, and a thin trickle of blood seeped from the wound. She sank onto the floor and leaned back against the cupboard. Blood dripped from her cut, mixing with the vodka in a pink-tinged puddle. Tears burned her eyes as she looked from her bleeding hand to the spilled vodka, unsure which upset her more...the wasted alcohol or her oozing wound.

Otis trotted to her side, somehow avoiding the wet floor and broken glass. He licked her face, lapping up the tears.

She buried her nose in his furry neck, inhaling his comforting doggy smell. He plopped on her lap, his heavy body crushing her legs, and she rubbed his belly, tangling her fingers through his coarse gray hair.

The sting in her hand pierced her desolation and guilt. The small cut had stopped bleeding, but she should remove the sliver of glass and clean and bandage the wound. And then she'd go to the store and buy another bottle.

Why not?

The damage was done. She'd broken her twenty-one-day record. One more drink wouldn't make a difference. Ignoring the inner voice warning her she was destroying her hard-won sobriety, she shoved off Otis's dead weight and hauled herself to her feet.

The phone rang again.

Throwing her hands up in the air, she swung to the counter, grabbed the vibrating phone, and hit Cancel. Blessed silence filled the air like the sweetest of symphonies.

Otis barked and scratched at the back door, his thick claws digging new furrows into the scarred doorframe.

"Hold on, boy. Let me fix my hand, then you can go out." Shifting to the sink, she twisted the tap and held her injured palm under the cool running water. The tiny sliver of glass washed away, and she turned off the tap and dried her hand with a paper towel. Sliding open the drawer beside the sink, she fished through the jumble of twist ties, screws, nails, and other junk, and tugged out a crumpled cardboard box of bandages. She removed a bandage, used her teeth to rip off the paper covering, and smoothed the thin plastic bandage over her wound.

Otis barked again. Tail wagging, he perched on his

hind end, staring expectantly at first her and then the door, his request more than clear.

Exercise was supposed to be another coping strategy for staying sober. Maybe a walk in the fresh air would help dull her insatiable thirst, and she wouldn't have to buy another bottle and hate herself even more. "Okay. Okay. You win, boy. Let's go for a walk."

Otis's mouth curved in a lopsided grin, and he danced in a circle, his tail wagging.

She dodged the damp patches and shards of glass on the floor and grabbed her coat and purse, plus Otis's leash, from the hook by the door. Shrugging into her wool coat, she flung open the door.

Otis shot through the opening, bounded over the small porch, and raced across the lawn to the back gate, barking in high-pitched excitement.

Chapter 2

They crossed the busy street and entered the green belt. She chuckled at the dog's antics. Otis was three years old, but even though he'd grown from a tiny pup that fit in the palm of her hand to over a hundred pounds of shedding fur and slobber, he still acted like a puppy.

The siren call of alcohol faded as she strolled along the wide gravel path past budding green ash and trembling aspen trees. She inhaled the rich scents of rain-washed earth, growing plants, and spring. Unhooking Otis's leash, she freed his squirming body.

He bolted to the base of a tree and barked.

A squirrel scampered up the thick trunk and chittered noisily, taunting the dog from the safety atop a branch.

If she let him, Otis would happily spend hours waiting at the base of the tree in hopes the squirrel would forget the dog was watching and return to the ground. She called him and strode down the path.

Nose to the ground, tail wagging, Otis followed.

The trees deadened the sounds of traffic, and she could almost forget she was in the middle of a busy, modern city. Birds flitted through the trees, and the afternoon sun filtered through the branches and shone warm on her shoulders. The fresh scents of rising birch sap, melting snow, and…dog dung?…hung in the warm spring air. She lifted her foot and grimaced. The sole of her sneaker was coated in brown, foul-smelling dog feces. Muttering under her breath, she scraped her shoe on the grass.

Otis blasted ahead, chasing a new intriguing scent.

She didn't worry about him running loose. The trails were usually deserted at this time of day. The young urban mothers wearing the latest yoga gear, pushing their strollers filled with squalling babies and followed by a gaggle of straggling toddlers, didn't make an appearance until the afternoon. Runners and power walkers waited until after work to get their exercise.

She used to be part of that after-work crowd. Before her world fell apart, three times a week, she'd switch from her high-heeled pumps and power suit to a T-shirt, leggings, and sneakers, grab Otis, and together they'd run along the park's kilometers of paths.

That was before—before her heavy drinking made doing anything more than sinking on the couch with a bottle of wine or a glass of vodka too much of an effort. But since she'd been home on leave, she'd been doing well, getting out and walking Otis almost every day.

Until today.

Until the letter showed up in her mail. Her good intentions had gone south after that. She searched her coat pocket. Damn. She'd left her cell phone at home. Two missed calls from work could be explained. Three…not so much. She wasn't independently wealthy. She needed her job, needed her boss to know she was trying her hardest and had every intention of getting healthy and back to work. Even if her actions today proved that was a lie.

Loud, frantic baying jolted her out of her dark thoughts. Her heart stuttered as the barking ramped up another decibel. Definitely not Otis's *I saw a squirrel!* bark. Something had the dog nervous. A bear? Not likely, not this close to the city. "Otis, come!"

The high-pitched barking increased in volume.

She hurried down the trail. *Please don't let it be a skunk.* Otis's unforgettable encounter last spring with a skunk flashed before her. He'd come running back to her, his tail between his legs, whimpering and stinking to high heaven. She'd hauled him home, wrestled him into the bathtub, poured six large cans of tomato juice over him, and hosed him down. Even then, he'd stunk for weeks.

She sped around a bend in the path and skidded to a stop.

Otis ran to her, whining and racing in frenzied circles around her legs, threatening to trip her.

She grabbed his collar and held him close. "What is it, boy? What's wrong?"

He whimpered and licked her hand, straining to break free.

A muttered curse sliced through his anxious whining, and she looked over his head.

A man was sprawled in the middle of the path, a bicycle lying on the ground beside him.

Releasing Otis, she hurried over to the injured cyclist. "Are you okay?"

"I…I think so." He sat up, undid the chin strap, and removed his bike helmet, revealing thick, dark curls cropped close to his head. Grimacing, he rubbed his right shoulder. "Is that your dog?"

"My dog? Why would you—" *Oh no.* Her heart

sank. "What happened? Did he cause your crash?" Dogs were supposed to be leashed and under the control of their owners. It was the park regulation. "I'm so sorry." Was the man injured? Was he angry? Oh Lord. Would he sue? She slid a glance at his bike.

The front wheel of the expensive-looking, high-end road bike was bent.

She bit the skin on the inside of her cheek. How much would the wheel cost to repair?

The cyclist rose to his feet and brushed clumps of grass and mud off his form-fitting, black spandex bike shorts. His broad shoulders and muscled forearms stretched the tight fabric of his black, long-sleeved shirt, revealing the dips and swells of well-toned muscles. His muscular, tanned calves, sprinkled with dark hair, extended beneath his shorts, and his feet were encased in red and black cycling shoes.

She gulped and looked up...way up.

Sweet Jesus.

Mid-thirties, maybe? His rugged face was tanned as if he spent a lot of time outdoors. Thick black eyebrows arched over honey-brown eyes rimmed by long dark eyelashes. Instead of the anger she expected, he smiled. Tiny laugh lines bracketed his generous mouth. His white teeth gleamed.

"Is this your dog?"

She gulped. "I'm...I'm sorry. Did he run in front of you? Is that why you crashed?"

Otis padded to the man, sat on his haunches, and lifted one monstrous paw and waved it in the air. He cocked his ears, put on his adorable puppy face, and whined piteously as if begging forgiveness.

The man crouched and petted Otis's velvety head.

11

A sucker for attention, the dog flopped on his back and exposed his hairy stomach.

The cyclist chuckled and scratched the dog's belly.

Otis wriggled ecstatically.

"It's not his fault." The hunk looked up and met her gaze. "I was going too fast. I should have been paying more attention." He shrugged. "I wasn't expecting this handsome fellow to chase a squirrel across the path in front of me. So, I guess we should blame the squirrel." He patted Otis. "Isn't that right, boy? It was that big, bad squirrel's fault."

Otis's tail beat a rhapsody.

"I'm so sorry. I should have had him on a leash, but he loves to run, and…" Under the heated power of his golden eyes, she lost track of what she was saying.

"Don't worry. I'm fine." He grimaced and jerked his thumb at his damaged bike. "Can't say the same about my ride."

"I'll…I'll pay to have your bike fixed." She fumbled for her purse and fished out her wallet. Removing several small bills, she held them out. Her face heated at the paltry amount. "This is all I have with me, but I can—"

"Keep your money. The bike's a rental. I paid extra for insurance, and that should cover the damage." Rubbing his hip, he limped to his bike and crouched. His shorts tightened across a toned butt and muscular thighs.

She swallowed, her mouth bone dry. "Are you sure?"

"The wheel's not bent too bad." His grin widened. "The bike shop should be able to repair it."

Otis, his swishing tail raising a small dust cloud,

12

sat at the cyclist's feet, adoration shining in his expressive dark eyes.

The man rubbed behind the dog's ear. "What's his name?"

"Otis."

"Otis, huh?" He ruffled Otis's hair under his chin. "How are you doing, Otis?"

Otis's entire back end wagged. More dust rose in the air.

The intriguing stranger laughed, and a dimple popped out on his lean cheek. "He's a handsome dude. What breed is he?"

She shrugged, struggling to think under the power of that devastating indentation. "I…I don't know. Heinz fifty-seven, I guess. I found him as a stray when he was a puppy. No one claimed him, so he moved in with me. That was two-and-a-half years ago. We've been roommates ever since."

One dark brow arched. "He's your only roommate? No husband or boyfriend?"

"No…ah…there's no one else." Butterflies danced in her belly. He was one fine-looking man. No doubt about that. No doubt at all.

He stood and stepped closer, holding out his hand. "I'm Russ."

She stared at his hand. Long, tanned fingers, large knuckles, a sprinkling of dark hair. Her heart sped up a notch. No ring. There was a God. "My…my name's Athena."

His callused palm and fingers tingled against her skin. A whiff of the light, lemony tang of his aftershave filled the air.

His eyes were the color of rich, melting taffy.

Sparks of gold ringed the outer irises. "Athena? You're named after the ancient Greek goddess." He grinned, and his dimple popped out. "The name suits you."

She swooned. She honestly swooned. "I…" Giving up trying to speak in coherent sentences, she contented herself with drinking in his every jaw-dropping, curl-your-toes inch.

He waved his free hand at the surrounding forest. "This is my first time here. The park is sure pretty." His gaze wasn't on the trees and wildflowers. He was staring at her, his meaning obvious.

His shameless flirting amped the heat searing her cheeks to a raging inferno. "You…you don't live near here?"

"No. I'm in town for business. I live in West Vancouver." He shrugged, and his shirt tightened across his broad shoulders. "It's such a beautiful day, and after being locked inside for meetings these past few days, I wanted some fresh air and exercise. The concierge at my hotel told me about this park. I rented a bike and—" He grinned boyishly. "—the rest is history."

She chuckled, actually laughed out loud. Amazing. A weight lifted off her shoulders. How long had it been since she'd laughed? "Beaton Park is pretty special."

The steel guitar twang of an old-time country-and-western song split the air as a cell phone rang.

His cell phone, though for the life of her she couldn't see where he kept it. His cycling clothes were so tight the bulge of even a small phone would be visible.

Releasing her hand, he slid a cell phone out of a hidden pocket on his upper sleeve. He glanced at the screen, and his mouth tightened. "Sorry. I have to get this." Turning away, he spoke into the phone. "What's up? Tell me you found her."

A trill of unease tickled down her spine, and she eyed the attractive stranger. Was their meeting an accident? Or had he somehow arranged it? Was he connected with the letter she'd received? Even though she knew that was impossible—she hadn't known she was going to be in the park that morning—her good mood vanished, replaced by her usual wariness.

Grabbing Otis's collar, she attached the leash and dragged his resisting body away from the all-too-handsome stranger. The sound of Russ's deep, resonant voice faded as she and the dog hurried down the path.

Chapter 3

She unlocked the back door and stepped into the kitchen.

Otis burst past her, scrambling across the slippery tiles to his water dish.

The bite of alcohol fumes slapped her in the face. The pile of sodden paper towels lay on the floor, and tiny shards of glass sparkled in the sunshine streaming through the window. She heaved a heavy sigh. No magical cleaning fairy had made an appearance while she and Otis were out.

Her cell phone rang, the plastic case vibrating across the countertop where she'd left it. Grabbing the phone, she studied the call display. Punching the Answer button, she raised the phone to her ear. "Aunt Clara, how are you?"

"Hello, dear."

"What's up?"

"I just got back from Palm Springs. My flight arrived this afternoon, remember?"

Guilt flooded Athena, and she smacked her hand on her forehead. She'd promised her aunt she'd pick her up at the airport, but in all the stress she'd forgotten. "Oh, Aunt Clara. I'm so sorry. I forgot."

"That's okay, dear. I got a ride share. I know how busy you are."

Clara's statement hung in the air.

Athena grimaced. Her aunt was well aware Athena's days were spent watching television cooking shows, surfing the Internet, walking Otis, and struggling with her sobriety. She'd had plenty of time to meet Clara at the airport, but no energy to defend her forgetfulness, so she kept silent.

"How are you doing?" A note of concern crept into Clara's usually cheerful voice. Her mother's sister was Athena's only surviving relative. Athena, as a young, grieving orphan, had moved in with her aunt after the tragedy that changed her life.

Those first months living with Clara had been a nightmare—for both of them. Athena was a traumatized twelve-year-old, reeling from the shock of her parents' sudden, mysterious disappearance. Clara was a single woman with no commitments, and she liked to travel. Her carefree lifestyle ended when Athena was thrust upon her doorstep, but she'd welcomed her niece with loving arms and showed remarkable compassion for the emotionally bruised and battered girl.

Athena would never forget those dark months. Inconsolable and immersed in her unimaginable loss, she'd lived in a world colored in shades of gray and black. Clara's boundless patience and unconditional love broke through the walls surrounding Athena and helped her heal. Realizing her aunt was speaking, she shoved the painful memories away and forced herself to listen.

"Palm Springs is beautiful. You'd love it…everything's so green and lush. It's hard to believe I was in the middle of a desert."

"Did you manage to get in much golfing?" Even though she suffered from arthritis, the elderly woman was an avid golfer and spent most of her days on the golf links.

Clara chuckled.

Athena closed her eyes and let the familiar, warm sound wash over her like a comforting blanket.

"I was out every day. I'm finally getting a handle on my backswing." Clara cleared her throat. "But I didn't call to talk about my adventures. What about you, dear? How's everything?"

Athena made a face. Even though Clara hadn't said the exact words, *everything* was about one, single thing—her drinking. "Fine. Just fine." The blatant fib tasted bitter in her mouth.

Clara clucked sympathetically. "Hang in there. You're doing your best. You'll get this under control, and before you know it, you'll be back at Schuster & Corbin."

Her throat thickened at her aunt's unfailing confidence. She had Athena's back even if her faith in her niece wasn't warranted, especially not today.

"What's wrong, dear? Something's bothering you, I can tell." Clara's concern radiated down the line.

Athena rubbed the back of her neck. Her first inclination was to lie again, but Clara was her biggest supporter on this difficult journey to sobriety. She deserved the truth. "I...I had a drink today."

A heavy silence, sparked with faint static, filled Athena's ear. She visualized Clara's mouth set in a disapproving line.

"Oh, my dear. What happened? You were doing so well."

"It was just one drink. I—" She stopped. Who was she kidding? If the bottle of vodka hadn't smashed on the floor, her one drink would have turned into a second, and then another, and another until the bottle was empty. "I'm sorry. I know I promised you I'd quit, but…" Again, her voice trailed off. "A…a letter came in the mail today." She licked her dry lips.

"What sort of letter?"

Athena's throat worked, and she struggled to swallow. "A registered letter, addressed to Margaret Anne O'Flynn."

Clara gasped.

"It's from a Vancouver lawyer." Athena inhaled a shaky breath. "Has…has anyone contacted you recently?"

"No, dear. No one at all. I would have told you." A pregnant pause, and then Clara asked the million-dollar question, "How did they find you?"

"I don't know, but they did. After all this time, they tracked me down." Tears stung her eyes.

Another long silence. The fridge motor hummed, a car's engine rumbled, the tires swishing on the pavement in front of the house. Somewhere down the block, a dog yapped.

"What…what did this lawyer want?" Clara's voice was rough, as if tears coated her throat.

"I don't know. The letter didn't specify." Athena tapped her fingers on the countertop. The staccato beat was strident in the silent kitchen, but her nerves were strung tight, and she couldn't stop. "The lawyer wants to meet with Margaret O'Flynn regarding an important personal matter. Apparently, it's urgent."

"Oh, my dear. I'm so sorry. I know you didn't want this." Clara's voice broke, and she sniffled. "What are you going to do?"

"I don't know."

"I understand how you must feel, but have you considered this meeting could involve information about your parents? Maybe this lawyer knows something about what happened."

Athena stopped tapping and squeezed her hand into a tight fist. "Or maybe it's a ruse to lure me into the open. Maybe the nightmare's starting all over again."

"You have a tough decision to make. If you ignore the letter, you'll always wonder. Or—"

"I know." Athena heaved a sigh. "I…I should meet with this lawyer and find out what she wants. I mean, what could it hurt? Right?" Her laugh was brittle.

"Promise me one thing." Clara cleared her throat. "Promise you won't have another drink. No matter what this lawyer wants, or what you decide to do about the request, promise me you'll stay sober."

Even though the hunger for a drink and the sweet oblivion alcohol promised raged through her like a wildfire, Athena promised. And she meant every word. She wouldn't drink, not anymore. Not today, and God willing, not tomorrow.

"I'm so proud of you, dear. Your parents would be too."

Tears filmed her eyes. "Thanks, Aunt Clara." She ended the connection and tossed the cell phone on the counter. Her aunt's unfailing confidence in Athena's ability to stop drinking was misplaced but gratifying. Someone believed in her.

Tearing off more paper towels, she squatted and mopped up the spilled liquor. She dumped the sodden paper towels into the garbage can and strode to the closet and retrieved a broom. Sweeping the broken glass into a dustpan, she discarded the mess into the garbage. Washing her hands in the sink, she dried them on a towel. Her chores completed for the day, she wandered into the living room. Clara was right. Athena had a decision to make—ignore the letter or meet with the lawyer and find out what the hell she wanted.

Otis was stretched out on his bed in the corner by the gas fireplace. He opened his liquid brown eyes as she passed, and his tail thumped the floor in greeting. In another second, his eyelids drooped closed again, and a loud snore rumbled.

Her gaze fell on the envelope lying under the coffee table, and a chill rattled through her. What was she afraid of? She wasn't a frightened, traumatized child. The past couldn't harm her. Not anymore. Inhaling a deep breath, she picked up the envelope and tugged the letter free. Sinking onto the couch, she smoothed the paper on her lap.

The letter was typed on official letterhead paper from a Jennifer Smythe at Smythe & Sons, Attorneys at Law, situated at 365 Palmer Avenue in the heart of downtown Vancouver. She scanned the salutation.

Dear Margaret Anne O'Flynn.

She flinched at the long-unused name. Twenty-three years had passed since anyone had called her Maggie O'Flynn. After her parents disappeared without a trace from Shelter Island, the press's relentless fascination with the tragic story had elevated a horrendous time into pure torture.

Reporters had camped on Clara's front lawn, their cameras pointed at every window. They dug through the trash, called the house phone at all hours of the day and night begging for interviews, and followed Athena and her aunt everywhere, blasting them with questions they couldn't answer.

Going to school was impossible, so Clara had homeschooled her. Isolated and stuck inside, the months after the tragedy were the most frightening and loneliest of Athena's life. The constant spotlight added to her heartbreak.

When the media attention became too much, Clara sold her house. They packed up their belongings and moved across the country, staying in one city after another for a month or so before moving on and ending up in Calgary where no one recognized Athena as that "poor, pitiful child whose parents deserted her."

The person she was then, Margaret Anne O'Flynn, needed the space to rest, and even, maybe, to be forgotten. A few months later, Clara helped Maggie change her name. Maggie enjoyed the Greek mythology stories her father had read to her before bed. Her favorite goddess amidst the pantheon of Greek deities was Athena, the goddess of wisdom, courage, and warfare.

She loved the strong and powerful name. Athena symbolized everything she wasn't, everything she hoped one day she'd become. And so, she'd shed her old name like a second skin. Maggie O'Flynn disappeared, and Athena Reynolds was born. Years later, she made the name change legal.

But now this Vancouver lawyer had tracked her down and wished to speak with her as soon as possible on *an extremely important and time-sensitive matter*. The letter ended with a plea for Athena to call and arrange a meeting as soon as possible. The paper crackled as she crumpled it in her fist.

How had the lawyer tracked her down? The question rang through her aching brain in an endless refrain. Few people who knew her as Athena Reynolds were aware of her birth name. After she'd changed her name, and with the many moves around the country, the media lost track of her whereabouts. Neither she, nor Clara, had been contacted by a reporter in years.

But someone had tracked her down. Someone knew her true identity.

Was Clara right? Could the lawyer have information about Athena's missing parents? If so, that was the ultimate bait guaranteed to draw her out of hiding. She licked her dry lips. What if the lawyer was working for Angus Crawford? The pounding in her head intensified to a deafening booming, and the overwhelming, bone-deep ache for a drink raged through her like a Category Four hurricane. She tossed the ball of paper across the room where it landed on Otis's front paws.

He raised his head and sniffed at the paper ball. His ears pricked, and questions shone in his expressive eyes.

"Sorry, boy. Poor shot."

He yawned, exposing sharp, white canines, laid his head back on his paws, and closed his eyes.

She sank back on the couch, drawing her knees to her chest and hugging a blue velvet throw pillow. Closing her eyes, she inhaled a shaky breath through her nose and released the air from her mouth, focusing on the slow rise and fall of her abdomen. The furious pounding in her heart eased, and a heavy exhaustion settled over her. She drifted off to sleep.

Chapter 4

Tears streamed down her cheeks. Terror iced her heart as she raced from room to room, calling their names. A fresh onslaught of fear staggered her at the ominous emptiness surrounding her. "Mom! Dad! Where are you? Please don't leave me." But her pleas were too late. They were gone.

A shape materialized out of the gloom...tall, lean, dark...infinitely terrifying.

She whimpered, pivoted, and fled out of the house, stumbling over hidden roots and rocks, crashing into trees, fighting through the clinging prickles of wild raspberry bushes.

She ran until her chest heaved and her lungs burned as if they were on fire. Her heart pounded with such ferocity she feared it would burst from her chest. Too exhausted to run farther, she sank to the cold, damp sand, curled into a ball, and closed her eyes.

Her pursuer's labored breathing pierced the late-night air. "Maggie!"

Risking a peek, she opened her eyes and shuddered.

He loomed over her. "Why are you running from me, Margaret? I'm here to help." His glower fixed on her; his gaunt face twisted into a parody of a smile. His thin lips shifted upward, teeth gleaming in the glow of the flashlight he carried.

She scuttled behind a washed-up log, her small hands scrabbling in the soft sand, tangling in the crackling strands of dried seaweed and broken shells.

His fingers wrapped around her shoulders, his nails digging into her tender skin as he dragged her from her hiding place.

She opened her mouth to scream, but her throat was too tight, and no sounds emerged.

She lurched up, heart pounding, adrenaline coursing. Her body vibrated with the primal instinct to fight or flee. In the next breath, she realized where she was—home, safe—and she sagged back on the couch. The remnants of the nightmare dissipated like gossamer wisps. Panic drained out of her, and she clutched the pillow to her chest.

Nails scrabbled across the bare floor, and Otis galloped across the room.

He launched himself at her, landing with a thump that shook the couch and knocked out her breath. Plopping his big body on top of her, he licked her face, washing away her tears.

She patted his head and velvety soft ears. "I'm okay, boy." Oh man, she loved this dog. He had a sixth sense where she was concerned and knew when she was upset and needed comfort. She wiped the perspiration dampening her brow and wrinkled her nose. The sour smell of fear and dog slobber hung in the air. Giving Otis a final pat, she heaved him aside and crawled off the couch and headed to the bathroom for a shower.

She tugged her shirt over her head and shoved her leggings off her hips. Next came her bra and panties. Stepping into the shower, she turned the water up as hot as she could stand. As the cleansing spray washed over her, the sharpness of the all-too-familiar dream faded.

When the social workers sent Athena to live with her aunt, disturbing dreams plagued her, and nearly every night she'd awakened in tears. Clara held her for hours until Athena calmed enough to go back to sleep. Over the years, as the rawness of her loss faded, so too had the nightmares. But along with the cessation of the frightening dreams came a far worse fate—she couldn't remember what her parents looked like or the sound of their voices.

Clara had an old photo album that had been rescued from the family's small home on Shelter Island. Pictures of Athena's mom and dad were glued to every page.

When Athena studied the photographs, she felt as if she were looking at strangers. She knew the couple were her parents, but only because Clara told her.

It was only in her dreams that her mother and father came to life, but that too faded with the passage of years. What hadn't diminished, what lurked in the dark corners of her brain, was the terror of that night, the sense of inexplicable loss, and her fear she'd been abandoned. No amount of therapy, or the pharmaceutical cocktails prescribed by a series of well-meaning therapists, nor the passage of time, helped. For a while, alcohol deadened her pain, but that too failed when her drinking careened out of control.

The letter from the Vancouver lawyer resurrected the old fears, and with it, the soul-destroying pain and sorrow. Her memories of that awful night so long ago were confusing, but her helpless terror when she saw Angus Crawford looming over her remained all too vivid.

He'd found her in her parents' house and chased her to the beach. She hadn't wanted to go with him, and she'd fought him, kicking and screaming, but he'd overpowered her and carried her to his cottage on the far side of the island. He'd taken her inside and set her on his couch where she'd huddled under a thick quilt, shivering and sobbing, clutching the soft folds until hours later when the police arrived.

And then her nightmare deepened.

Her parents had vanished. They weren't on the island. The only item missing was the small skiff her father used for fishing and setting crab traps. Search parties scoured the island for days and searched the surrounding ocean inlets and small, rocky islands, covering every inch of the rugged terrain, but no one found any signs of the missing couple, their boat, or clues as to what happened.

Weeks later, when the police investigators packed up and left, Clara offered a sizable reward for information concerning the events of that terrible day, but no one came forward. Anna and William O'Flynn disappeared without a trace, leaving their only child behind.

The media had a heyday with the sensational story. Angus Crawford, the wealthy, elusive owner of Shelter Island and the couple's landlord, was a prominent businessman in the city. He was often featured in the celebrity pages of magazines and newspapers, always with a beautiful, much younger, woman on his arm. His notoriety added fuel to the fire. He never gave interviews, despite repeated requests. His stoic silence increased the frenzy, as reporters vied to win a coveted interview. Any scandal involving the dashing, wealthy bachelor was news. Big news.

With no viable leads to follow, and after months of investigation, the police reached the conclusion that her parents, for unknown reasons, had sailed away on the missing skiff and were lost at sea in the cold, rough waters off the Pacific Northwest coast. But that didn't explain why they'd left their only daughter behind, or why they hadn't taken any of their possessions. The meager savings in their bank account remained untouched.

Rumors ran rampant...the couple was involved in drug smuggling and had met a bad end, they owed money to unsavory characters, they'd set out on an afternoon sail and were washed overboard and lost at sea... A local psychic even suggested they'd been abducted by aliens.

A year later, Clara hired an expert in locating missing persons, hoping he'd uncover a clue the police had missed.

Nothing turned up.

To this day, the disappearance of Anna and William O'Flynn remained a mystery. In the years since, the tragic story was featured on countless true crime television shows and podcasts. Every year on the anniversary of their disappearance, the media rehashed the incident and wondered what part, if any, Angus Crawford played in the mystery.

Athena had her own ideas about what occurred. Nothing short of death would have convinced her parents to desert their twelve-year-old daughter. Angus Crawford was on Shelter Island that fateful day. She and her father had watched from a rock bluff as Angus sailed into the bay on his luxury sailboat, lowered a small dinghy into the ocean swells, and rowed to shore.

Her father had walked down to the beach to greet him.

The man tied Athena's stomach in knots, so she'd run into the forest and scampered home. Later that afternoon, she was reading under her favorite tree in the front yard, and her mother and Angus Crawford began arguing. She couldn't hear what they said, but the fury in his voice after her mother ordered him to leave chilled Athena to the bone.

When her parents went missing later that day, she knew Angus Crawford was responsible. As a twelve-year-old child, she was sure he was guilty. Twenty-three years later, she was just as certain. She twisted the tap and increased the hot water pelting her body.

She'd tried to convince the police of Crawford's guilt, but the detective in charge of the case had smiled pityingly, mouthed meaningless platitudes, and ignored her suspicions. No one listened to her. She was just a kid.

No one believed the wealthy, powerful man was involved in anything so evil as the malicious disappearance of two people.

Angus Crawford played his role of concerned landlord well. He'd joined the search parties as they scoured the tiny island for clues, and he surprised everyone by offering to take Athena in as his ward. The media had gone crazy over that fascinating twist.

A shudder of revulsion washed over her. Fortunately, Clara Reynolds, her mother's estranged sister, had shown up before Crawford's claim was taken seriously, and Athena was whisked away to live with her aunt.

At first, she and Clara lived in Vancouver, but the media started hanging out on the street in front of the house, and the phone never stopped ringing from reporters begging for interviews with *poor, abandoned Maggie O'Flynn.* They'd packed up their belongings and moved.

Their stay in the prairie city of Regina was only a year because an intrepid reporter tracked them down. Then they lived in the Canadian capital, Ottawa, for six months before someone recognized Athena as Margaret O'Flynn, and once again they were forced to flee. Returning to the west, they settled in the bustling, modern cow town of Calgary, Alberta. Athena changed her name, and they left Angus Crawford and the media hounds behind.

Athena was on constant alert. She checked over her shoulder for watching eyes and viewed new acquaintances with a heavy dose of suspicion. But as the years passed, and the story slipped from the headlines, she grew complacent. Her tragic past was buried. She was Athena Reynolds. No one was aware of her real identity. At least, she'd thought that was the case, until the letter from the Vancouver lawyer arrived and proved her wrong.

The water had turned lukewarm before she twisted off the tap and stepped out of the shower and toweled dry. She shrugged into her terrycloth robe and scrubbed her short, red hair, leaving the damp strands standing in bright tufts. The craving for a drink was so strong her mouth watered. She closed her eyes and gripped the porcelain sink and hung on, digging deep for strength.

Come on. Just one little drink. What would one

drink hurt?

She bit hard on her bottom lip until she tasted blood, blocking out the insidious voice. She'd promised Clara she wouldn't drink. She'd already broken one promise she made to the dear old woman; she wouldn't break her word again no matter how strong her thirst.

Chapter 5

Coffee!

The single word blazed through her like it was illuminated by a thousand-watt spotlight. Coffee—strong and dark, mixed with two heaping tablespoons of sugar—gallons of sweetened coffee. She tightened the sash on her robe and headed to the kitchen. Flicking on the lights, she bustled about the small room, grinding coffee beans and filling the pot with water from the tap. She set the glass pot on the coffee machine and punched the Start button.

The gurgle and hiss of the coffee maker promised relief from her craving, and the kitchen filled with the rich, earthy scent of dark roast coffee. Her hand trembled as she poured the steaming drink into a mug. She shuffled over to the table and settled on a chair. Spooning sugar into her cup, she stirred the sweet mixture. Her first sip scalded her tongue. She winced but risked another mouthful. In seconds, the caffeine-and-sugar bomb eased the sharp edge of her craving.

She peered through the window over the sink. Red-and-orange streaks from the rising sun bathed the distant, snow-covered mountains in a pink glow. Her nerves jittered from the coffee, her eyes gritty from lack of sleep.

Otis hadn't shifted from his bed in the corner. He lay curled in a ball, his nose buried under his tail as if he were an Alaskan sled dog living in a frozen world of snow and ice and not a pampered pet lying on a padded dog bed in a warm, centrally heated house.

She poured another cup. Sometime during the long night, she'd reached a decision. No more hiding. Better to face the truth than cower in fear that her past had returned. At the start of business hours in Vancouver, she'd contact the legal firm. Talking to the lawyer who'd sent the letter was the only way she'd find out what the woman wanted.

Her gut reaction was to throw the letter in the trash, but she doubted that would be the end of it. She knew lawyers. Heck, she was one. They were a feisty, persistent bunch. The Vancouver lawyer would contact her again and again, until she received a response. Curiosity or masochism, Athena had to know what the lawyer wanted. She just prayed she wasn't making a terrible mistake.

Otis growled low and deep in his throat.

She jerked and knocked over her cup. Damn!

Hot coffee spilled across the table and dripped on the floor.

Another vibrating snarl sounded from deep within Otis's chest. He perched on his haunches and stared at the back door; the hairs on the back of his neck rose, becoming a darker stripe down his spine.

"What is it, boy?" She shoved back her chair, crossed to the window, and peered into the backyard.

Typical for the sprawling city in the shadow of the Rocky Mountains, the weather had changed over the past few minutes. The sun had vanished behind heavy, dark rain clouds that hovered low over the valley. A spring prairie storm was on the way. Streaks of rain already spotted the window glass, and a light drizzle spattered the back porch. The gloomy morning light didn't penetrate the shadows lurking under the budding lilac trees against the back fence.

Otis growled again low, deep, and menacing.

Her stomach knotted. "What's wrong, boy?" She peered outside again, but nothing stirred.

A second later, a small, dark shape slipped from behind the garden shed and streaked across the lawn to the cedar-planked fence. The black cat scampered up and over the fence and leaped into the neighbor's yard.

The tightness in her belly eased, and she let out a breath. "It's just Charlie, Otis."

For all his size and bluster, Otis was terrified of cats, especially Charlie, who'd swiped Otis's nose with a sharp claw upon their first meeting a year ago.

She rubbed his smooth head, but his hackles remained erect, his gaze fixed on the door.

Her unease returned. Maybe the cat wasn't the reason he was nervous. She shook her head. What else could it be? No one was lurking in the backyard. She'd checked. Otis was just a big baby. Unlocking the back door, she nudged it open. "Do you want out? It's okay. The big, mean cat's gone. You're safe."

He didn't budge and stared out the door, his tail between his legs, growling.

She shoved his rump toward the open door. "Go on. Go pee." Muscling his resisting body until he was on the back porch, she stayed in the doorway, watching as he raced, barking furiously, toward the back fence.

After a few minutes of sniffing the ground under the lilac bushes, his barking stopped, and he loped across the lawn, pausing at each tree trunk and bush.

When he raised his leg and peed on her favorite rosebush, she stepped back into the warm kitchen and closed the door. All was safe. She locked the back door but unlatched the doggie door so Otis could get back in when he was finished patrolling the back yard.

She checked her watch. Time for the phone call. No point putting it off any longer. Ripping off several sheets of paper towel, she wiped the sticky spilled coffee from the table and floor. She eyed the coffee maker, but she'd had enough coffee. Her gut burned from caffeine overload, and her muscles jittered, her nerves on edge.

Scooping her cell phone from the counter, she strode into the living room and picked up the crumpled paper ball from the floor beside Otis's bed. Her hand shook as she punched in the phone number of the offices of Smythe & Sons.

The line rang once, twice, three times, four…

Hang up. You don't need messy complications in your life. You have enough on your plate.

Five rings.

"Smythe & Sons, Attorneys at Law. How may I help you?"

"I…er…hello. I received a registered letter from your office, and—" Her foot tapped the floor in a rapid tattoo.

"Your name please?" The woman's voice was pleasant, but all business.

"Ath…er, I mean Margaret Anne O'Flynn." The name tasted wrong and unfamiliar on her tongue. Her heart raced, and moisture beaded under her arms.

The distant clicking of computer keys filtered down the line. "Oh yes, Ms. O'Flynn. Thank you for calling." More tapping. "Ms. Smythe is able to see you this morning if that works."

That soon? "I'm in Calgary."

"Oh, that's right. I've been directed to tell you that Smythe & Sons will pay your transportation to Vancouver and your accommodation expenses while you're in town."

Athena pulled the phone away from her ear and stared at it as if she could see the woman on the other end of the line. The legal firm was willing to pay her expenses? She clenched and unclenched her hand, her fingernails digging into her palm. They were serious about the meeting. Why? What did they want?

"Ms. O'Flynn? Are you still there?" The assistant's tinny voice drifted from the phone.

Athena held the phone up to her ear. "Yes. I'm here."

"Good. How about tomorrow? Could you be here by then?"

"I…I don't know." Athena rubbed the tightness in the back of her neck.

"Our firm prides itself on our integrity, Ms. O'Flynn. I promise you everything that transpires here will be held in the strictest confidence. We wouldn't ask you to travel all this way if the appointment wasn't important."

Static crackled in Athena's ear. "Okay. I'll be there tomorrow." Yikes! What was she thinking? Tomorrow?

"That's great. I know Ms. Smythe is anxious to meet with you."

Anxious. The word drilled through her. "Really? Why is that?"

"I'm afraid I'm not at liberty to say. She'll explain

all the details when she sees you." Distant, muted voices and the jarring peal of a ringing phone sounded in the background. "I'll put you down for right after lunch. Say one o'clock?"

Athena chewed on her wounded bottom lip, already regretting agreeing to the meeting. "I guess I'll see you tomorrow."

"I look forward to meeting you. Have a lovely day." The line disconnected.

Have a lovely day.

Was the woman kidding? Athena's entire world was falling apart. No damn way this day was going to get better. Tomorrow would be even more challenging. Her breath hitched in her throat.

Tomorrow.

She checked her watch.

Twenty-eight hours.

She'd get to the bottom of this nightmare in twenty-eight short hours. Rubbing her arms in an effort to warm her chilled skin, she swallowed back the unsettling certainty she'd stepped onto a precipice and was teetering on the edge of a bottomless pit. Something warm and wet lapped her hand.

Otis sat on the floor at her feet. His long, pink tongue snaked out, and he licked her hand again.

She knelt and wrapped her arms around his large, hairy body. "Oh, Otis, I don't know what I'd do without you." Ever since she'd found him wandering the alley behind her house, his hair matted and covered in burrs, his ribs poking through his dull coat, they'd been inseparable.

Over the past two-and-a-half years, the dejected, abused little puppy had grown into a large, gangly, hairy, slobbery creature who resembled no recognizable dog breed. He was there when she needed him, offering a warm body to cuddle, a loving lick, or an interested, non-judgmental listener. His gaze followed her every word as if he understood what she was saying.

"It's just the two of us, eh, boy?"

He cocked his head to one side, and his furry tail thumped the floor. Flopping on his side, he rolled onto his back, legs spread, waiting for her to scratch his belly.

Her fingers trailed through his thick coat, some of the tension easing. "You're such a big baby." He certainly had her well trained. She grimaced. At least one of them was.

Chapter 6

Athena climbed out of the taxi and wove through the sidewalk teeming with pedestrians, cyclists, and street vendors. Pulling out the wrinkled envelope, she checked the address. The offices of Smythe & Sons should be somewhere on the block.

Modern office buildings, covered with gleaming glass and metal, towered high overhead. Cherry trees, their branches thick with fragrant pink blossoms, lined the street. Fallen petals drifted like snow in the gutters. A large, circular fountain with a bronze dolphin rising out of the water in the center, spewing an endless stream of water from its gaping mouth, dominated the middle of a small square.

People in business-casual attire sat on the smooth cement edges of the fountain, eating bag lunches and texting on cell phones. Other men and women, with take-out paper cups clutched in their hands, strode down the wide sidewalk enjoying the warm spring sunshine.

She blinked in the glare. Too bad she hadn't brought her sunglasses. Intending to stay just for the day, she'd packed light for the trip but had stuffed a pair of leggings, fresh underwear, a T-shirt, and a pair of sneakers into her oversize purse in case the meeting ended early. Maybe she'd have a chance to go for a run before she caught her return flight. After dropping a dejected Otis at his favorite kennel and promising him she'd be back that evening, she'd hopped into a ride share and headed to the airport and boarded her plane to Vancouver.

Being in the coastal city was unsettling. How many years had it been since she was last there? Not enough time had passed for her to forget. She swallowed and focused on her surroundings. Jostling past a trio of giggling young women, Athena coughed at the cloud of smoke from their cigarettes. She studied the front of a massive gray stone-and-smoked-glass building. The address matched that on the letterhead. Nice digs. The monthly rent for an office in the high-end building would be more than the yearly mortgage payments on her house. Smythe & Sons Attorneys at Law were doing well, very well indeed.

Inhaling a deep breath, she thrust her shoulders back and marched up to the wide, double-glass doors, but paused before grasping the ornate, brass door handle. The back of her neck tingled with the visceral awareness that someone was watching her. She whirled around and studied the crowded square. No one seemed to be paying her attention, but she couldn't shake off the certainty she was being watched. A flicker of movement caught her eye.

A tall, heavyset man with a bushy orange beard, wearing a red ball cap with some sort of black design inscribed on the crown, dark sunglasses, and a long-lensed camera slung around his neck, turned and strode away, vanishing amidst the crowd.

Her gut knotted with the certainty she'd seen him before. Where? At the busy airport when she landed? Maybe. Was he following her? She scanned the milling crowd but couldn't spot the man with the red hat.

She turned back to the glass door. Her nerves were on edge about the upcoming stressful meeting, and she was imagining things. No one was following her. Why would they? No one knew her true identity. Except, the lawyer knew, didn't she? Her firm had managed to track Athena down.

She pushed the door open and stepped inside, then shivered at the chill of the blast of air-conditioned air. Bright afternoon sunlight streamed through the windows and gleamed on the tiled floors. People, probably employees from the offices in the tower, milled about the cavernous lobby as they returned to their jobs after the lunch break. The noise of their conversations and bursts of laughter was deafening.

Dodging fashionably dressed office workers, she made her way across the lobby to a bank of elevators against the far wall. Focused on their cell phones, the other passengers didn't look up as she stepped into the waiting elevator. She squeezed past four men and three women and fitted into a small space at the rear.

"Hold the elevator, please," a man shouted from the crowded lobby.

Without looking up from his phone, the young millennial standing at the front of the lift, held his hand in the opening, blocking the doors from closing.

The harried passenger squeezed into the already packed car. "Thanks." He was taller than the other passengers, and his suit-clad broad shoulders crowded the tiny space.

She wedged her back against the cool, burnished metal wall. The air was thick with the cloying scents of expensive perfumes, aftershave lotions, hair styling products, and stale cigarette smoke. Her stomach roiled, and she plugged her nose and breathed through her mouth.

The elevator rose quickly and silently. In seconds, it slowed to a stop, and the door slid open. Two people fought to the front and stepped off, and the door swished closed, and the elevator continued its smooth ascent.

She peered over the shoulder of the man in front of her at the illuminated floor indicator. Next stop was the fifteenth floor. Her floor. She licked her dry lips.

The elevator slid to a halt, and the door whooshed open.

The tall, broad-shouldered man who'd rushed to catch the elevator and a heavy-set, middle-aged woman disembarked.

Treading on toes and murmuring apologies, Athena shouldered through the press of bodies and stepped off the lift.

The woman who'd exited the elevator entered an office across the hall.

The tall, well-built man, black leather briefcase in hand, strode down a corridor with a long-legged, confident stride.

Athena puckered her brow. There was something about the set of his tall, lean body and shiny cap of dark curls that was familiar. Impossible. She didn't know anyone in Vancouver. The last time she was in the city she was a child. Her nerves had her on edge. No wonder. Being there, meeting with the lawyer, was a big risk. An all-too-familiar thirst shadowed over her like the silent, but deadly approach of a ravenous shark. She'd give anything for a stiff drink.

Anything.

A gleaming brass sign on the cream-colored wall across from the elevator indicated the offices of Smythe & Sons were down the hall.

She tightened her hold on her purse and headed down the wide corridor. Thick carpeting muted the clatter of her heels.

Expensive-looking paintings lined the cream-colored walls on one side. Immense banks of floor-to-ceiling windows on the other wall offered stunning views of the city, the glistening Pacific Ocean, and the Coastal Mountains beyond.

The tall man from the elevator halted before a frosted glass door and wheeled around. His eyes widened. A heartbeat later, a wide grin wreathed his handsome face. "Why, hello again."

She stuttered to a stop. "You!"

His grin widened, and the devastating dimple in his right cheek popped out. "Hello, Athena." His golden-brown eyes sparkled with appreciative warmth as his gaze swept her body.

Heat seared her cheeks. The last time she'd seen him was in the park near her house in Calgary. "What…what are you doing here?" A chill rippled up her spine, and she narrowed her eyes. Why *was* he there? He'd mentioned he lived in Vancouver, but what were the odds he'd show up in that building at the same time as her appointment? Astronomical. Was he a reporter? Was word out the infamous Margaret O'Flynn from Shelter Island was in town? "Are you following me?"

He chuckled. "I could ask you the same question." He advanced, stopping inches from her.

The subtle scent of his spicy aftershave surrounded her, and the heat from his body sizzled the air.

She opened her mouth to say something... anything...but the words stuck in her throat. He leaned closer, and she gaped, caught under the immobilizing power of his golden gaze.

His warm fingers grazed her cheek as he brushed a lock of her hair behind her ear. "Nice to meet you again. When you ran away from me in the park, I thought that was the last I'd see of you."

"I...I didn't run away. I...I had—"

One dark eyebrow arched.

She gulped. "I had things to do."

"Really? Huh." The dimple danced, and he cocked his head, making no secret he was fighting back laughter. "How's Otis?"

He remembered her *dog's* name? "Good. He's really good." She swallowed. "Did the bike rental company charge you for the damaged rim?"

"I told them the brakes were loose, and that's why I crashed." He chuckled. "They were too worried I'd sue to charge me."

Unable to resist, she returned his smile with one of her own. "You didn't mention that Otis caused the crash?"

"That's our little secret." He grinned and released his dimple like a deadly weapon.

The heat in her face revved to a five-alarm blaze. Before her brain could function again, the thud of heavy footsteps filled the corridor.

A middle-aged man with gray, thinning hair and a sizable paunch marched down the hall. He gripped a metal briefcase in one hand and held a cell phone pressed to his ear with his other hand. His voice was loud and impatient as he talked on the phone, oblivious to the two people blocking the hall.

She stumbled back a step.

The hunk from the park grasped her arm and steadied her.

His touch burned through the light fabric of her coat, and the skin on her arm tingled.

As if he too felt the searing heat, he released her and stepped back.

She resisted the urge to rub her arm, or to remove her coat and see if the skin was blistered.

Without acknowledging their existence, the older man marched past, snapping orders into his cell phone. He paused before a door farther down the long corridor and rapped. The door opened, and he greeted someone and stepped inside, closing the door behind him.

Recalling why she was there, she glanced at her watch. "I…I'm sorry, but I'm late for an appointment." She stepped around the all-too-handsome man and edged to the door. "Nice running into you again."

"Russ."

Her hand on the door handle, she paused and glanced back. "What?"

"My name's Russ, in case you forgot."

Forgot? She hadn't forgotten a single thing about him. Every detail of their encounter in the park was embedded in her brain. "I remember."

He nodded, a smug expression on his rugged face. "Allow me." He lifted her hand from the door handle and pushed open the door. With a theatrical gesture, he motioned for her to enter the room beyond.

She bit her lip to halt the giggle threatening to

escape. "Thank you." She swept through the door into the offices of Smythe & Sons and crossed the tastefully appointed waiting room to a desk where an older, gray-haired woman worked on a computer.

The woman glanced up with a welcoming smile. "Hello."

"I have a one o'clock appointment with Ms. Smythe."

The secretary's smile widened. "Oh, yes, Ms. O'Flynn. Ms. Smythe is expecting you."

A sharp inhalation of air filled the room.

Athena spun around.

Russ's gaze riveted on her, but this time the expression in their honey depths wasn't male appreciation, but suspicion.

Startled, she asked, "Is something wrong?"

"You tell me." His face was impassive, but blatant animosity shone from his hooded eyes.

He definitely disapproved of her. Talk about a three sixty.

Before she could demand an explanation, the receptionist called, "Ms. Smythe will see you now, Ms. O'Flynn."

Eager to escape the inexplicably angry Russ, Athena followed the woman across the small waiting area and through a door into a spacious office. The door closed behind her on silent hinges.

Chapter 7

A plump, matronly woman sat behind a large oak partners desk that dominated the room. She rose and walked around the desk and extended her hand. "Ms. O'Flynn, I'm Jennifer Smythe." A warm smile wreathed her face. "Nice to finally meet you."

She was at least six inches shorter than Athena, and every time she shifted, her chin-length, glossy chestnut curls bounced around her chubby cheeks. She resembled a suburban soccer mom more than a hard-edged, cutthroat city lawyer, but her clear brown eyes behind thick glasses shone with an alertness hinting at a keen intelligence.

Athena shook the woman's hand. "Hello, Ms. Smythe."

"Please call me Jennifer."

The office was tastefully decorated, with a stunning panoramic view visible through the floor-to-ceiling windows that took up most of one wall. The distant mountains gleamed with a fresh mantle of snow. Ships chugged across the glistening waters of English Bay, streams of dark smoke trailing from their tall stacks.

Athena's workspace at Schuster & Corbin had a single, narrow window providing a view of the foothills and distant mountains if she stood on her chair and peered between two neighboring buildings. "Nice view.

I don't know how you get any work done. I'd spend all day looking out the window." Her face heated. She was babbling, a trait that showed up when she was nervous. "From your firm's name, I assume this is a family business. Do your sons work with you?"

Jennifer's smile was warm. "You'd think that, wouldn't you?" Laughter bubbled in her voice. "Smythe & Sons is a small concession to the vagaries of modern business. Clients feel more confident when they think men are running the show." She chuckled. "There actually are sons involved...I have two boys of my own, but they're thirteen and ten. They're smart, but they haven't passed the Bar yet."

In spite of her wariness, Athena found herself liking the woman. Her warm, easygoing charm was hard to resist.

"Please sit down." Jennifer gestured toward a comfortable-looking leather chair situated in front of the lawyer's desk. Returning to her own chair behind the massive desk, she rested her clasped hands on the gleaming desktop. "Thank you for coming." She pierced Athena with a sharp look. "My secretary told me you were reluctant to meet with me. Would you mind telling me why that is?"

Athena smoothed her damp palms on her skirt, but she remained silent. Until she knew for certain what was going on, she was hesitant to reveal too much.

"That's okay. You don't have to answer that." Jennifer nodded. "I'll tell you what I know, and we'll go from there. You legally changed your name, and you moved around a lot." Her eyes narrowed. "The private investigator I hired is one of the best. He had a hard time tracking you down."

Athena squeezed her hands until her fingers ached, hiding their shaking. The craving for a shot of vodka roared through her like a ravenous bear demanding to be fed. *Leave. Now. Get up and walk out. Run to the nearest bar and order a double, maybe even two.*

She blocked out the insistent voice in her brain. If she walked out, she'd always wonder what the lawyer wanted. Digging deep for strength, fighting to think through her insatiable thirst for alcohol, she schooled her face into a neutral expression and made a point of studying her watch. "Why am I here? I'm on a tight timeline. I have to be back in Calgary tonight."

"Of course." Jennifer nodded, and her curls danced. "I understand your reticence, but both I and my client are grateful you came here today." Her easygoing friendliness vanished, replaced by an all-business demeanor. She tugged open her desk drawer, slid out a thick file folder, and set the file on her desk. "Before we begin, I'll require proof of your identity…a driver's license, birth certificate, passport…anything like that."

Swallowing over the rising lump in her throat, Athena groped in her purse and tugged out her wallet. Slipping her driver's license from the leather slot, she handed the identification card to the other woman.

The lawyer studied the license. "Your legal name is now Athena Reynolds?"

Athena nodded.

"But your birth name was Margaret Anne O'Flynn?"

Again, Athena nodded, like a bobble-head doll. Admitting the truth went against everything she'd believed all these years, but what was the point of hiding her identity? The lawyer knew who she was.

"What year were you born?"

The questions, requesting minor and unthreatening details, flowed one after the other, and Athena relaxed. Maybe the meeting wouldn't be so awful, but she still hadn't learned why the lawyer had sent her the letter.

"How long did you live on Shelter Island?"

Athena jerked alert. "How...?" She coughed and tried again. "How did you—" Of course. The lawyer had searched the news databases and found the old stories. She knew everything.

Jennifer Smythe met her startled look with a knowing one of her own. "That's one of the reasons I asked you to come here today."

The walls of the large office closed in around Athena. She struggled to swallow, her throat rough as if filled with sand. Man, she needed a drink. Real bad. Really, really bad. "This...this was a mistake." She shot to her feet.

Jennifer stood. "Margaret...Athena, wait, please. Give me a chance to explain."

Athena blocked out the woman's pleas. There had to be a bar close by, somewhere dark and quiet where no one knew who she was, and she could lose herself in the bottom of a bottle. She lunged across the room, flung open the door, and walked into a wall of solid male flesh.

"Athena, or should I call you Margaret?" Russ's voice rumbled in the smooth, velvety tones he'd used earlier, but underlying anger sharpened the words, so they cut like a knife. "Where are you going?" Gone was his bone-melting engaging grin, replaced by a cold sneer. "Are you taking your loot and running, *Maggie*?"

She was speechless at his unfounded animosity.

Her gaze locked with his, and she shivered at the iciness in their hazel depths.

"Mr. Crawford. I wasn't aware you'd arrived," sputtered an obviously flustered Jennifer Smythe. "I was just confirming a few details with Ms. Reynolds."

"Crawford? Your last name's *Crawford?*" Athena reeled. The lawyer's next words receded in a drone of meaningless sounds. Her breath rasped through a throat that threatened to close. The blood drained from her head, and the room spun in circles. Her legs wobbled, and she sagged.

Russ cursed and gripped her by the arms, holding her steady as he guided her across the room to a chair.

Her legs gave out, and she collapsed onto the padded chair, her mind whirling. The lawyer had called Russ *Mr. Crawford*. Was he connected to Angus Crawford? Of course, he was. One thing she'd learned over the years—there was no such thing as a coincidence. She gripped the sides of the chair and held on, fighting to breathe, two thoughts paramount—this meeting was a big mistake. She should have ignored that damn letter.

Her second thought—Oh man, she needed a drink.

Chapter 8

Russ studied the pale, trembling woman. His instinct was to offer her a cold glass of water, a handkerchief, his shoulder to cry on, anything to ease her distress. But then he remembered who she was, and instead of comforting her, he shoved his hands into his coat pockets and fought the urge to strangle her. He faced the hovering lawyer. "*She's* Margaret O'Flynn? You're sure of that? She's the woman we've been looking for?"

Jennifer nodded.

He scrubbed his hand over his whiskered chin. What were the odds? The most attractive woman he'd met in years was the one person he'd vowed to despise. Fate must be having hysterics.

When he first laid eyes on the owner of the big, shaggy, gray-haired dog that had run in front of his bike and caused his crash, he'd been instantly attracted. She was one good-looking woman. No question. Under the afternoon sun, streaks of gold shone in her short auburn hair. Add her luminous blue eyes framed by long dark eyelashes and a full, soft pink mouth unadorned by lipstick, and you had his full attention.

Her skin-tight black leggings did more to reveal than cover the long lines of her shapely legs. Her ample breasts swayed under her baggy T-shirt with its logo of the local Calgary hockey team printed on the front.

Aching to sweep her in his arms and run his fingers through those fiery curls, he'd fantasized about kissing her lips and finding out just how sweet they tasted. Instead, he'd stood, shuffling from one foot to the other, gaping like a gawky, acne-faced teenager meeting the queen of the high school prom. He swore he'd drooled.

To hide his embarrassment, he'd torn his hungry gaze from her and focused on her dog. He liked dogs. Good thing, because the damn beast slobbered, drizzling gobs of drool over him, and shed clouds of coarse gray hairs that floated in the air and stuck to his cycling shorts.

He'd intended to get her phone number and ask her out for dinner and drinks. He was in town on business and only had the one night free, but he had to see her again, had to explore the sparks shooting between them. But then his phone rang, and when he saw Jennifer Smythe was calling, reality intruded, and he forgot the drop-dead gorgeous redhead and focused on his lawyer.

When he hung up a few minutes later, both the red-haired beauty and her dog were gone. He'd hefted his damaged bike over his shoulder and limped after her. His hip throbbed from where he smashed into the hard ground, and the best he managed was a slow hobble. By the time he rounded the bend in the trail, she'd vanished. He hadn't thought he'd see her again, except in his dreams.

Until today.

When he heard the light footsteps approaching down the hall outside the offices of Smythe & Sons, he'd turned. And that's when Fate laughed. The woman of his dreams was approaching. He studied the trembling woman in the chair and grimaced. Woman of his dreams? His lip curled in a sneer. More likely, the woman of his nightmares.

"I think it would be better if you left us alone."

Jennifer Smythe's soft voice broke through his whirling thoughts. "What?"

"Ms. Reynolds—"

He cut her off. "Ms. *O'Flynn,* you mean." The name left a foul taste in his mouth.

"Her legal name is Athena Reynolds, has been for years." Jennifer's brown eyes filled with sympathy. "She's distraught. I'm sure you can imagine how difficult this is. Let me explain to her what's at stake. I'll call you when I'm finished."

It was on the tip of his tongue to snap that Athena Reynolds wasn't the only one who found the situation challenging, but he bit back the words. Anger wouldn't get him what he wanted. His scrutiny strayed to the woman huddled in the chair, and an unwelcome spurt of pity softened the ragged edges of his fury.

As soon as the receptionist called her by name, and he realized who she was, every cell in his body alerted. She was the bitch who'd stolen his inheritance. He scowled, directing the full force of his disappointment and outrage on her.

As if she sensed his glower, she struggled to sit up straight. Her hand shook as she smoothed a shiny lock of auburn hair off her forehead. "Your...your last name is...is Crawford?"

Soft lips. Soft, kissable pink lips. In spite of everything, he still wanted to kiss her. What the hell was wrong with him? "Russell Crawford." He stepped closer. "And you're Margaret O'Flynn." The full scope of the irony settled in. "You're that girl, aren't you?

You're the girl from Shelter Island."

Her slight body seemed to fold in on itself, and she crossed her arms over her chest and shivered as if she were chilled. "How...how do you know who I am?"

Before he could answer, Jennifer cut in. "Mr. Crawford is my client. He hired me to find you." Her words hung in the room like specters.

"You...you were looking for me?" Athena's voice was a thin whisper. "Why?"

"You didn't make it easy. We were searching for Margaret O'Flynn. We didn't know you'd changed your name," Jennifer said. "Seems no one else did either."

His lip curled. "I should have known you were a phony. Who has a name like Athena?" She visibly flinched under the onslaught of his harsh words, and for a brief second, he regretted his outburst. But he was too worked up, and the angry words kept spilling. "What was wrong with Margaret? Too plain for you? Too pedestrian?" He pushed out a breath. "I'm surprised you didn't choose a name like Bambi or Tootsie. Those names would suit a gold digger like you better than Athena."

Her eyes widened, and twin red patches flared on her pale cheeks. "Who the hell are you? Why are you here?" She swung to the lawyer. "Why *is* he here?"

Jennifer patted Athena's shoulder and clucked her tongue. "I told you. He's my client. If you'll give me a minute, I'll explain everything." She faced Russ, sparks flashing in her eyes. "Give us some privacy, please."

He scowled. Fine, treat him like a schoolboy being sent out of the classroom for shooting spitballs at the cute girl. "Okay. I'll leave—" He glared at Athena...

Margaret…whatever the hell she called herself. "—but we're not done here." He nodded at Jennifer. "I'll be expecting your call."

Relief washed over her round face. "Thank you. I know how to reach you."

He marched across the room and out the open door into the outer office. Anger propelled him through the reception area and into the hallway. His boots pounded on the carpet as he stormed toward the elevator.

He was still seething when he burst out of the building onto the sunny street. Fishing in his pocket, he tugged out his sunglasses and slipped them on. He glanced up at the gleaming high-rise. What the hell had just happened? Who was that furious, bitter man who'd made such a damn fool of himself? He was usually even-tempered, and rarely angered, but Athena Reynolds, with her fresh-faced beauty, punched his buttons. Big time.

He scrubbed his fingers through his hair. Who could blame him for being furious? She'd used her feminine wiles and stolen his birthright. Damn her and damn Angus Crawford. Shouldering his way through the people crowding the sidewalk, he marched down the street to the parking garage.

Chapter 9

The lawyer's office felt like an airless vacuum after Russell Crawford stormed out. His anger had crackled like lightning, filling the air with the scent of ozone. Athena rubbed her damp palms on her skirt and fixed her gaze on Jennifer Smythe. "Okay, he's gone. Now tell me why I'm here and why that man hates me."

The lawyer strode to a teak table set against the far wall and hefted a metal carafe and poured water into a glass. She removed the lid on an insulated container and used a pair of metal tongs to lift out a couple of ice cubes and plunked them into the water. She handed the glass to Athena. "You look like you could use a drink."

Athena agreed. She definitely could do with a drink. Just not the water the lawyer was offering. "Thank you." Condensation filmed the cold glass, and the ice cubes clinked when she raised the glass to her lips and sipped, fueling her desperate need for a highball. The water soothed her parched throat, but not the ravenous beast lurking inside. She drained the glass and set it on the desk. "I really do have to get going. I left my dog in the kennel, and he won't be happy if I'm not back tonight."

Jennifer exhaled a deep breath. "How well do you know the Crawfords?"

"The Crawfords?" A bitter laugh escaped Athena's mouth. "I only know one Crawford—Angus

Crawford—and believe me, that's enough for a lifetime."

Jennifer eyed her, and Athena had the uneasy certainty the lawyer was trying to peer into the depths of her soul. She wouldn't want the woman to cross-examine her on the witness stand. Not if she was guilty of a crime. She'd spill everything she'd ever done wrong.

Jennifer marched around her desk and sank onto her chair. She studied Athena for another long moment. "As I said, Russell Crawford is my client."

"I...I don't understand. His last name is really Crawford? Is he related to Angus Crawford?" As soon as the question formed, she knew the answer. Of course, he was related to Angus. It was too much of a coincidence that a man named Crawford just happened to be visiting the same lawyer at the exact time as she was. And what about their *accidental* meeting in the park in Calgary? Was that staged? Was he the person who'd been following her these past months, whose eyes she felt on her back? She shivered. "I didn't know Angus Crawford had any children."

"Angus Crawford adopted him when Russell was fourteen." Jennifer's voice was calm and soothing as if she feared further upsetting Athena.

Athena's mouth opened and closed like a fish out of water. "He's Angus's son?" The handsome hunk was Angus Crawford's adopted son. "Really?" But that unfortunate filial relationship didn't explain Russ's animosity. There had to be more to the story.

"He was." The lawyer nodded, her glossy brown curls bouncing with each bob of her head.

Wait a minute. *Was*? The lawyer said Russell

Crawford *was* Angus Crawford's son. "What are you saying? Is…is Angus Crawford dead?"

"He passed away six months ago."

"He's really dead?" Could it be true? The man she blamed for murdering her parents, the boogeyman of her nightmares, was dead? Shock struck first, followed by a tidal wave of relief. Hallelujah! No longer did she have to fear she'd run into him on the street, or that he'd show up at her door. Angus Crawford was dead. There was a just God.

"I'm afraid he is. I'm sorry for your loss."

Athena snorted. "My *loss*?" She snickered, a brittle crack of sound. "I suppose it's too much to hope he died a slow, painful death."

"Mr. Crawford suffered a massive heart attack. I believe it was quick." Jennifer frowned and clasped her hands on her desk. "Would you like me to continue?"

Athena nodded, but for the life of her she couldn't imagine what the lawyer wanted with her. If the meeting was to tell her of Angus's demise, then the trip was worth it. But there was something in Jennifer's steady gaze that set her on edge with the certainty more shocking news was on the way. She clasped her hands on her lap and squeezed until her fingers ached. "Go ahead."

"As you can imagine, an estate the size of Angus Crawford's takes time to settle, especially in a case where there's…er…the potential for contention. There are also numerous legal procedures—"

Athena held up her hand. Corporate law was her specialty, but she knew enough about Estate law to know she wasn't going to like where this meeting was heading. "I've heard enough." She stood and gathered her purse. "I appreciate you contacting me to let me know of Angus Crawford's demise, but you could have phoned and saved me the trip."

"Wait. Please. I'm afraid I haven't been clear." Jennifer tugged on her earlobe. "Angus Crawford named you as a beneficiary in his last will and testament. He bequeathed you the majority of his estate."

Athena froze. "He left *me* his estate. His *entire* estate?"

"For the most part, yes." Jennifer cleared her throat. "Aside from a sizable bequest to his son, and a few relatively minor endowments to his long-time employees, and various charitable organizations, he left you everything."

Athena pressed her fingers to her temples and rubbed. Had she fallen into an alternate universe? None of what Jennifer Smythe said made sense. Why would Angus Crawford leave her anything? She hardly knew him. All these years she'd both feared and hated him, blamed him for her parents' disappearance. And now this?

"It's a substantial amount."

"How…how much?" The question slipped out. She didn't want to know, didn't want anything of Angus Crawford's.

The lawyer's eyes flickered as she named a vast sum of money.

Athena rocked back on her heels. "That much. Wow." She didn't know what else to say. Her head ached as she struggled to make sense of Jennifer Smythe's shocking revelation, but she couldn't wrap her brain around Angus Crawford, her sworn enemy, leaving her his fortune. She swallowed, her mouth arid dry. To hell with sobriety. If she'd ever needed a drink, she needed one now. The second she walked out of there she was hitting a bar.

"There's more." Jennifer tapped the papers on the desk in front of her. "He also left you his shares in his privately held company, Crawford Industries." She smiled. "Congratulations, Ms. Reynolds, you are now a very wealthy woman. Angus Crawford must have cared for you a great deal."

Nausea roiled in Athena's gut, and beads of perspiration popped out on her brow. She ignored her discomfort and zeroed her scrutiny in on the other woman. "That doesn't make sense. I didn't know him, not really. Why would he leave me so much?"

Jennifer shrugged, the movement sending her curls dancing about her plump face. "I'm not privy to that information. I wasn't the attorney who drew up the will. That's why I wasn't aware of your name change or your current home address. If Angus Crawford knew your current name, he chose to keep that fact a secret, or he was unaware of the change." A sympathetic look crossed her face. "The person to ask would be the executor of the estate."

"Executor?"

The woman nodded, and the coil of tight curls danced. "You met him today."

Athena stiffened. "Russ—I mean, that man who was in here—*he's* the executor of Angus Crawford's estate?"

Jennifer nodded, initiating another wave of bouncing curls. "Russell Crawford hired my firm's services to locate the main beneficiary of his father's estate—" She paused and stared pointedly at Athena. "—you."

A maelstrom of thoughts tumbled through her…Angus Crawford was dead…she was the main beneficiary of his will…the hot hunk from the park was Angus's son—adopted—but still his son. And he was the executor of Angus's will. Her headache ramped up.

"There's one more thing you should know."

Athena groaned inwardly. Judging by the grim expression on the lawyer's face, she wasn't going to like what she was about to hear. With a supreme effort, she pushed down the yawning ache to lose herself in a bottle and figure out why the hell her world had turned upside down and inside out. "What is it?"

"Angus Crawford willed Shelter Island to his son."

She sucked in a sharp breath. *Shelter Island*! How long had it been since she'd heard that name? Months? Years? And now this was the second time in the past hour that the island had been mentioned. She closed off a swirl of painful memories. The pieces clicked into place. "So that's why he was here today. He was claiming his rights to Shelter Island." If that was the case, Russ could have the island. It was all his. No problem. No problem at all.

For the first time since Athena met the lawyer, Jennifer looked uncomfortable. "Uh…ah…that's not why Russell was here."

Athena arched her eyebrows. "No?"

Jennifer shook her head. "He's disputing his father's will."

Athena ran her fingers through her hair, uncaring she was rumpling the carefully coifed style she'd spent a half-hour working on that morning. Her gaze skittered around the office. Surely a high-end law firm like Smythe & Sons would have a bar with bottles of pricey scotch and vodka for their well-heeled clients. She bit the inside of her cheek. The sharp pain overrode the yearning in her head, and she focused on why she was there. "What exactly is he disputing?"

"He's not happy with the will. He believes Angus Crawford was not of sound mind when he made his last will and testament, and that you exerted undue influence over a lonely old man."

Athena laughed a bitter, harsh sound that burned like acid in her throat. The man she detested more than any other person on Earth had left her his estate, and now his son was fighting her for it. *Well, he could have the whole damn thing.* "That's something he and I can agree on." She smoothed the wrinkles from her skirt. "Angus must have suffered from severe dementia when he considered leaving me part of his estate. I hardly knew him, and I certainly didn't like him." She lurched to her feet and jammed her hands on her hips. "Where can I find Russell Crawford?"

"I can arrange a meeting with him tomorrow if you'd like."

"Tell me where he is." Heat rose in her cheeks, but she ignored the avid curiosity shining in the other woman's eyes. She didn't owe her an explanation. "Look, Ms. Smythe…Jennifer, I flew out here and met with you in good faith. You owe me. I just want to talk to Russ. That's all, a simple conversation."

Jennifer wrung her pudgy hands, and her gaze shifted around the office.

The heavy silence stretched until Athena thought she'd scream.

Jennifer stopped fidgeting and met Athena's gaze. "I believe Russ said he was going sailing this afternoon."

"He has a boat?" Of course, he did. The man probably owned a sixty-foot luxury yacht manned by a crew of gorgeous, half-naked women. Why not? Angus Crawford had been rich. His son was probably swimming in money. "Where?"

"He keeps his boat at the Blue Vista Marina in White Rock."

"Thank you for telling me." Athena spun toward the door but paused on the threshold when the lawyer spoke.

"What are you going to do?" Jennifer patted her hand on the folder. "About the estate, I mean. What are your plans?"

"I'll let you know." She strode out of the office and down the hall to the elevator. With each step, her desire for alcohol faded, and her determination grew. She'd confront Russell Crawford and shove his father's estate in his handsome face. She wasn't a frightened twelve-year-old. Not anymore. She refused to be intimidated by anyone, especially a Crawford.

Chapter 10

Russ jammed his foot on the gas pedal, and the sleek red sports car surged ahead, blasting past the slower-moving traffic. Fire raged through his veins. He was driving too fast, but his anger was too hot, too visceral, and demanded release.

A bus pulled in front of him, and he cursed. Downshifting, he swerved, missing the bus's rear fender by inches. The top of the convertible was down, and the unseasonably warm spring wind tore at his hair, tugging it into a wild tangle. The powerful engine purred smoothly and ate up the pavement as he negotiated the early rush hour traffic.

"Damn it." The curse vanished in the swirl of air coursing through the car. Margaret O'Flynn—or Athena Reynolds—or whatever the hell her name was, wasn't the greedy, avaricious floozy he'd envisioned. He pounded his fist on the steering wheel. With her tousled mop of vibrant red curls, her creamy skin, the cute smattering of freckles across her pert nose, and fresh-faced beauty, she resembled a college coed—a very attractive coed.

A muscle in his jaw twitched, and he ground his teeth. When he met her in the park in Calgary, he hadn't known who she was. Her full, pouting mouth, arresting blue eyes, and soft, womanly curves had caught his attention.

And then some.

He'd grinned at her, even flirted a little. Her answering smile, filled with warmth, had him standing taller. He'd wanted to do whatever it took to spend more time with her. But now that he knew her true identity, he wouldn't be fooled. Sure, she was attractive, but she was a gold digger of the highest order. She'd used her youth and sex appeal and coerced his hard-edged, savvy father into leaving her his entire estate.

The terms of Angus's will hadn't made sense when Russ first learned of them. They made even less sense now he'd seen her. She wasn't the type of woman Angus usually favored. He should know. Ever since Russ's parents were killed in a car crash when he was thirteen, he'd lived with Angus until he'd moved out on his own at twenty.

During that time, a steady stream of women had passed through Angus's life. Some hung around for a few days, others for weeks, but no one lasted longer. There was always a new flavor of the month. The girlfriends varied in size and hair color, but they all had three things in common—youth, cover-girl beauty, and lush, over-inflated curves. Anyone could see what Angus got out of the relationships—a boost to his aging male ego.

The women had different agendas—their goal was to marry the very wealthy and elusive Angus Crawford, hopefully without signing a prenuptial agreement. Not one of the many women was successful, and the old man remained a bachelor until his death. Russ figured Angus had had his heart broken in his youth and pined for a lost love. Whatever the reason, he'd never married.

A blue van turned into the intersection ahead.

He slammed on the brakes, swerving around the offending vehicle. Once he broke through the snarl of city traffic and pulled onto the highway, he mashed the gas pedal to the floor. The powerful car surged ahead, the speedometer climbing, as he sped down the open road.

He stared ahead, ignoring the thick stands of western red cedar, Douglas fir, and Sitka spruce trees flashing by. The past six months had been tough. He'd loved Angus and grieved his passing. Though Angus was prickly and demanding and had high expectations for his adopted son, he was a good man. After Russ's parents died, the rich financier had taken the orphaned boy in and treated him like his own son. With Russ's consent, he'd adopted Russ a year later, making their relationship official.

Russ had trained to take Angus's place at the head of Crawford Industries when the time came. As Angus Crawford's only living relative, he assumed he was his sole heir. Hell, at Angus's suggestion, when the adoption took place, Russ had taken the old man's surname as his own. He'd legally become a Crawford.

The bubble burst a week after Angus's death when Russ was called into the lawyer's office for the reading of Angus's will. He gritted his jaw as he recalled his shock when the details of the will were revealed.

"Margaret O'Flynn?" He shot to his feet. "Who the hell is that? I've never heard of her." But he had, hadn't he? Somewhere in the back of his brain a memory struggled to break free.

"Calm down, Mr. Crawford. Getting angry won't

C.B. Clark

change anything."

He gaped incredulously at the pompous little man sitting behind the massive oak desk that dwarfed him. "Calm down?" He tightened his hands into fists at his sides. "You're asking me to calm down when everything I've worked for most of my life has just been snatched from me because of a horny old man's whim?"

"Now, it's not as bad as all that." The little man clucked. "Your father left you a sizable inheritance, as well as the property on Shelter Island."

Russ was nonplussed. Was the man being deliberately cruel, or was he that stupid? Did he honestly think Russ cared about Shelter Island? The island was a lump of useless rock in the middle of nowhere. Even worse, ever since the O'Flynns vanished without a trace, an aura of tragedy hung over the island like a bad smell. No one would buy the island.

Why would the old man have chosen to leave the majority of his assets to this woman? A stranger? A chill settled deep in his gut. "Wait a minute." He gripped the edge of his chair as if he were hanging on in the middle of high seas. "Margaret O'Flynn? Is that the same Maggie O'Flynn whose family used to live on Shelter Island?" He shook his head. No way. Impossible. But he still couldn't help asking, "Is she the girl whose parents vanished and left her behind?"

The lawyer shrugged. "I don't know. I suppose I could check."

Was it her? Even if she was that girl, that didn't explain why Angus left her his estate. He'd never mentioned Margaret O'Flynn. Hell, in all the years Russ had lived with Angus, he'd never talked about the

O'Flynns.

Maybe she wasn't the same woman. O'Flynn wasn't an uncommon surname, and thousands of women in the country were named Margaret. But if the girl from Shelter Island was the woman mentioned in Angus's will, what the hell had she done to convince Angus to leave her the majority of his assets? His upper lip curled. Was she that good in the sack?

The lawyer cleared his throat. "There's one more detail."

"What is it?" Russ tensed, every muscle turning rigid. The situation was already a disaster. It couldn't get any worse. Or could it?

"Mr. Crawford insisted on one condition in his will." The lawyer tightened his lips. "If Margaret Anne O'Flynn predeceased Angus Crawford, or she can't be located within one hundred and eighty days of the reading of the will, her portion of the estate reverts to you."

Six months.

His heart leaped, and he clutched at this thin strand of hope. Maybe this Margaret O'Flynn was long dead. People died all the time...accidents, sickness...whatever...they died. Not that he wished anyone dead, but in this case... "Have you tried to find her?"

The lawyer pursed his mouth. "I've had my people looking, but so far we haven't had any luck. I can tell you one thing—she doesn't live in Vancouver."

"What if you can't find her? I mean, what if the one hundred and eighty days pass, and you haven't located this woman?"

The lawyer shrugged. "I'm not sure. I've never

handled a will like this. I assume the contents of the estate, with all its benefits, would transfer to you."

He'd fired the pompous little man on the spot and hired the prestigious legal firm of Smythe & Sons to locate the unknown heir. Truth be known, he didn't want her found. No way. But he had to know for certain this mystery woman wouldn't appear out of the woodwork a few months down the line and try and claim the estate. A lawsuit like that would last for years. He could lose everything to lawyer fees.

He had to know for certain if Margaret Anne O'Flynn was alive. Jennifer Smythe had promised she'd find the woman, but as the days ticked by with no sign of the elusive heir, he'd begun to hope she'd never be found. But Jennifer Smythe lived up to her reputation. She was good at her job. Too damn good. She'd called last week and informed him she'd found the rightful heir. He grimaced. Two days remained before the one hundred and eighty days were up.

Two days!

His hopes crushed, he'd cut his trip to Calgary short and rushed to the lawyer's office, determined to confront the woman who'd stolen his birthright. A bitter laugh escaped his tightly compressed lips. And hadn't that been a kick in the nuts? Instead of the plastic-boobed, bleached-blonde bimbo he'd expected, she turned out to be the fresh-faced beauty from the Calgary park—the woman he hadn't been able to stop thinking about.

Go figure. Angus must be having one hell of a laugh.

Learning the truth of her identity had dumbfounded Russ. He'd been so flustered he hadn't denounced her for being an avaricious bitch. Oh no. He'd done something far worse. He'd flown off the handle and acted like a kid having a temper tantrum when he didn't get what he wanted.

From all appearances, she'd been as shocked as he was. Unless her stricken face and near-fainting spell was an act. He'd been determined to tell her just what he thought of her conniving; instead, worried she was going to pass out, he'd grabbed her arm and steadied her trembling body against his.

A mistake. A damn big one, piled on top of all his other mistakes.

He shouldn't have touched her, but hell, he couldn't let her pass out at his feet. The press of her soft breast against his arm, her scent—something flowery and feminine... He helped her to a chair, but he hadn't wanted to let her go. He ached to wrap his arms around her and press her sweet body against his.

That reaction pissed him off all the more, and he'd come out fighting. He raked his fingers through his hair. He wasn't proud of what he said, but he'd reacted from his gut and laid the blame for Angus's weakness for a pretty woman on her.

He'd calmed down. A bit. He had to think this through and figure out what he was going to do with the untenable mess of Angus's estate. One thing certain—he wouldn't let that woman's fragile beauty stop him from doing everything in his power to ensure she never got her greedy hands on a single penny. He didn't have loads of money to spend on lawyer fees, but he'd do this one thing, even if it left him broke and living on the street.

Angus hadn't been in his right mind when he made

his will. He'd always told Russ that he wanted him to run the company when Angus retired. Russ wanted that too. So why had Angus changed his will and left the business to a stranger, a girl whose family used to live on Shelter Island? Was that it? Was that the connection? Angus felt some sort of misguided guilt over what happened, and this was his way of making amends?

Spotting his turn ahead, he jammed on the brakes. The car skidded, the back end swerving until the tires gripped the asphalt, and he turned off the highway onto a narrow gravel road. A plume of dust followed as he steered the car along the lane. He swung into a small, gravel parking lot and pulled into a numbered stall. Turning off the engine, he closed his eyes, settled back in his seat, and allowed the silence to wash over him. He breathed, inhaling the familiar scents of fresh sea air and fish.

Seagulls squawked, the ocean swells washed against the oil-stained pylons, and the warm breeze teased his hair. The late afternoon sun was like a caress across his shoulders. The knot in the back of his neck eased, and he opened his eyes.

The sky was a clear robin's-egg blue. A bank of white, puffy clouds on the horizon reflected on the aquamarine waters of the small bay. A row of eight yachts, sailboats, and sleek motorboats were moored to the long wooden wharf. His was the only car in the parking lot. Not a surprise. The marina was busy on the weekends, but during the week, the small dock was quiet.

Perfect.

He wasn't in the mood for idle chitchat. Not today.

Not after meeting Margaret Anne O'Flynn. His sour mood returned, and he punched the button to activate the convertible roof. Once the hood was in place, he wrenched open the door and climbed out of the car. The little car shook when he slammed the door.

He stormed across the gravel parking lot and climbed the stairs to the wooden dock. His steps were steady as he marched along the swaying wharf past boats of every size and description. Nestled between a high-end, luxury cabin cruiser and a rundown fishing trawler was a white catamaran.

He studied her sleek lines and smiled with a familiar swell of pride. Thirty-four feet in length with a single, towering mast, the *Minerva* gleamed under the warm, spring sunshine. He'd bought her secondhand three years ago at a bankruptcy sale. She was in rough shape, and he'd spent every weekend sanding and staining her teak decks, painting the hull, installing new canvas sails, and refurbishing the interior.

Now she was a beauty, and he took her out at every available opportunity. Standing on the swaying deck, wind and salt spray in his face, the flap of the billowing sails overhead as the boat raced over the white-crested waves and cleaved a path through the wind-whipped water, instilled a sense of freedom and contentment. He left his worries behind and lived in the moment.

For the first time since he'd learned the shocking details of Angus's will and the existence of the infamous Margaret Anne O'Flynn, the gnawing unease in his gut subsided. He couldn't wait to board the vessel and sail her through the bay and onto the open ocean.

Chapter 11

Athena threaded the rental car through the throng of afternoon traffic as she headed out of the city. Keeping one eye on the surrounding cars, she read the directions she'd downloaded onto her cell phone.

Her plan was simple—confront Russell Crawford and inform him she had no intention of accepting any money, property, or business from Angus Crawford's estate. He could have the entire estate. Every last penny. Then she'd catch her flight to Calgary, retrieve Otis from the kennel, and continue on with her life, taking satisfaction in the fact Angus Crawford was dead.

She grimaced at the sudden squeal of brakes and irritated honking. Shooting an apologetic smile at the red-faced, glowering driver of a large silver SUV, she pulled over to the side of the road and allowed him to pass.

Another quick glance at the directions on her phone, and she pulled back into the flow of traffic heading out of the city. She passed the turnoff before she spotted the small, faded sign hidden by the leafy branches of a towering arbutus tree. Continuing down the road another two kilometers, she found a spot to turn around and headed back.

She swung off the highway onto the narrow lane. After a few kilometers, she rounded a curve in the road and was met with a beautiful vista of sparkling ocean gleaming like a sapphire under the afternoon sun. She rolled her window down and breathed in the fresh, salty air.

She pulled into a parking lot, empty except for a gleaming red sports car. Parking her car in a slot marked Visitor, she switched off the motor and reached in the back seat for her purse. Hauling the heavy bag onto her lap, she opened the zipper and fished for the clothes she'd packed in case she wanted to go for a run while she was in Vancouver. What she was about to do wasn't exercise, but she wanted to be comfortable for the upcoming confrontation.

She slipped off her heels and tossed them on the floor. Twisting and turning in the cramped space, her elbows and knees bumping the steering wheel and dash, she squeezed into the tight black leggings and tugged them up her legs and over her hips, then she shimmied out of her skirt and stuffed it in the bag.

Next, she unbuttoned her silk blouse, rolled it into a ball, and tossed it into the purse. Shrugging into a pink T-shirt, she smoothed the soft cotton over her stomach and hips and tugged on socks. She slid her feet into a pair of sneakers. Now she was ready to face anything Russell Crawford threw at her.

Opening the door, she climbed out of the rental sedan. A brilliant sun shone out of a clear, azure sky, cloaking her in welcome warmth.

Sea gulls swooped and dove in the surf, squawking as they searched for food amongst the clumps of seaweed snagged on the barnacle-encrusted rocks.

Memories of other shores and other times threatened to engulf her, but she shoved away the disturbing images. Inhaling a deep breath, she thrust her shoulders back and marched along the crushed seashell path to the wharf.

Confronting Russell Crawford was a frightening prospect. When he'd learned her true identity, his fury radiated off him in visible waves. Now that she knew the facts behind Angus Crawford's last will and testament, she couldn't blame him. Russ had pretty much been left out of his father's will. Of course, he was upset. Who wouldn't be?

Instead of following him to the marina, she should have called him and arranged to meet at a neutral location like a restaurant or a coffee shop. But when Jennifer Smythe informed her Russ was leaving for several days of sailing, she was left with little choice. She refused to wait until he returned from his trip. The sooner this matter was settled, the better. Besides, once he learned why she'd followed him, he'd be thrilled. She'd be his new best friend. Except he was a Crawford, so that wasn't about to happen.

Luxurious yachts, gleaming sailboats, and ritzy motorboats were moored along the old wharf. The boats were different sizes and designs, but they had one thing in common—they cost more than most people made in a decade. Their owners were probably wealthy businessmen from the nearby city, the boats their weekend toys.

Jennifer Smythe had told her Crawford's boat was called the *Minerva. Huh.* He'd named his boat after a Roman goddess. Her lip curled. And he thought *her* name was pretentious.

Passing a huge, motorized luxury yacht that had to be at least sixty feet in length, she paused and admired its sleek lines. A low whistle escaped her lips. With a teak cockpit, stainless steel bow protector, striped canvas main-deck sun awnings, and a row of below-deck portholes, the boat must have cost an easy million. Russell Crawford hung with the rich folk. Not a surprise.

Almost hidden in the shadow of the larger vessel, fiberglass hull gleaming, was the boat she sought. The *Minerva* wasn't in the same class as the other luxury watercraft in the small marina, but it was nice.

Very nice.

Russell Crawford wasn't hurting for cash. She frowned. So why was he so determined to possess Angus Crawford's money? The old saw must be true—a person could never be too rich. He was Angus Crawford's son. A simple case of nature versus nurture. Even though he was adopted, Angus's personality and values had rubbed off on Russ. On the deck, hunched over an open hatch, tools in hand, was the man she'd come to confront.

He worked shirtless in the unseasonably warm afternoon. The muscles on his back flexed under his smooth, bronzed skin. His cap of dark curls gleamed like a raven's wing in the sunlight. He stood and stretched, his long, powerful arms reaching high over his head.

Sweet Jesus!

The moisture in her mouth dried. She must have made a sound, probably a moan, because he lowered his arms and spun around.

His eyes widened, and their rich mahogany depths darkened. A furrow carved deep between his dark brows. "What the hell are you doing here?"

She stood rooted to the spot, pinned like a butterfly to a board, by his glare. Her vocal cords were frozen, and she couldn't speak. The screech of seabirds and the gentle lap of water against the boat's hull punctured the strained silence.

His gaze left her face, and he conducted a slow, lazy perusal of her from the tips of her sneakers to the top of her head, lingering on her breasts.

Her nipples puckered as if his hands caressed her rather than his gaze. She parted her mouth as her breathing quickened. A seagull swooped low, and its raucous call broke the spell holding her in its thrall. From his perch on the vessel's deck, Russ towered over her, and she craned her neck back. The setting sun was behind him and surrounded his body in an aura of dazzling light, making it impossible to see his expression. She finally found her voice. "We have to talk."

The silence thickened.

Why didn't he say something? Her nervousness vanished, and anger boiled to the surface. She'd driven through congested city traffic and over rough country roads to offer him everything he wanted, and the imperious, arrogant ass kept her standing beneath him like a peon awaiting the king's pleasure. "You have ten seconds to invite me aboard, or I'm leaving. And believe me, you will regret that."

One second, two seconds, three, four… The silent count continued. Five seconds…

Except for the tightening of his hands and the stiff set of his body, he didn't acknowledge her.

Six…Seven… Fury raged through her like molten lava. "Eight…" She continued the count aloud. She about-faced and stepped away from the sailboat. "Nine—"

"Welcome aboard the *Minerva*, Ms. O'Flynn."

She stopped and slowly turned. She still couldn't see his face, but the tone of his voice indicated he found the situation humorous. Let him laugh. She'd tell him what she'd come to say, and then she was leaving. She never had to see him again. Grabbing onto the ladder, she climbed aboard. The second her feet landed on the deck, she swung to face him, a slew of furious words on the tip of her tongue. The insults fizzled.

The play of muscles across the broad expanse of his bare chest beneath the smooth, tanned skin, lightly sprinkled with whorls of dark hair, was mesmerizing. She had the improbable urge to touch him, to feel his taut pecs, to run her hands over his washboard abs… She pressed her hand to her chest to still the fluttering. He was taller than even she remembered. In her sneakers, the top of her head reached his shoulders, and she had to tilt her head back to meet his gaze.

A smile transformed his handsome face from attractive to the visage of a Greek god.

She stumbled back.

A smug look of knowing amusement shone in his hazel eyes, making it more than evident he was aware of his effect on her. On all women, probably.

She cursed under her breath. This was a mistake. She shouldn't have come. Instead of changing her flight to a later one, she should have returned to Calgary like she'd planned and let the lawyers deal with the situation. But she'd wanted to see his face when she told him, wanted to make sure this chapter of her life was over once and for all.

She hadn't counted on his effect on her—he was too damn good-looking, and there was something about him that impacted her at a visceral level. Every instinct she possessed screamed warnings, but she stayed where she was, refusing to let his size or good looks intimidate her. She'd been around handsome men before, and she hadn't made a fool of herself. This time wouldn't be the exception.

He made no effort to hide his amusement. "How nice to see you again so soon, Ms. O'Flynn." His smile widened, though the light didn't reach his eyes. "Or do you prefer Reynolds? It's hard to keep up." He chuckled, the sound harsh. "Are you stalking me?"

She shuddered. A shark's feral grin wouldn't have been more intimidating. "You arrogant jerk." Her face flamed. This conversation wasn't going the way she'd envisioned. She'd pictured him filled with gratitude at her generous offer, tendering his effusive thanks. But not this. Not this icy disdain.

"Stop. Please. You'll turn my head with your sweet talk."

The gleam in his dark eyes made clear he enjoyed taunting her. Using what little control she had left, she struggled to rein in her temper. "You're just like Angus."

His face underwent a transformation. All traces of humor vanished, and cold hostility took over. "I hope so. Angus was a good man, one I admired."

Her lip curled in a sneer. "It wasn't a compliment." As soon as the words were out of her mouth, she regretted them. She didn't have to sink to his level. "I'm sorry. I don't even know you."

His eyes were hooded. "No, you don't."

"Look—" She swallowed. "—we got off on the wrong foot. Can we start again?"

"You're really something, lady, you know that?"

His bitterness surprised her. But should it have? He'd probably expected to inherit Angus's entire estate. The details of the will must have been a brutal shock. No wonder he considered her his enemy. She stood to gain a fortune while he was left with a mere pittance. She cooled her anger and fought to ignore his harsh words. She'd driven to the marina for a reason— closure. The sooner she finished this meeting, the sooner she could escape his unsettling presence and get on with her life. "You're probably wondering why I'm here."

His mouth tightened, and the ticking in his jaw ramped up.

Okay. So, he wasn't going to make this easy. "I convinced Jennifer Smythe to tell me where I could find you." She paused, but he remained stubbornly silent. "My reaction to meeting you this afternoon was a bit, er…"

"Melodramatic?" he supplied helpfully. "Over the top?"

Heat flooded her face, but she bit back her irritation. She was determined to follow through with her plan no matter how difficult this impossible man made the tense situation. "From what the lawyer told me, I understand that Angus Crawford left me the majority of his estate in his will."

His dark, intense focus remained on her face. "And you want to know what your inheritance is worth."

She blinked. "No, that's not why I'm here." Unable to remain still a second longer, she paced across the narrow deck, careful to avoid his glowering, half-naked form. "Look, Mr. Crawford…"

"Russell."

Startled, she looked up. "What?"

"My name's Russ."

"Okay, ah…Russ." She swept her fingers through her curls, turning her carefully styled hair into wild disarray. "The reason I'm here is to inform you I don't want Angus Crawford's estate. You can have his money and his company. It's all yours. Everything." She held her breath and waited, anticipating his profuse gratitude, maybe even tears of joy. When he remained still and silent, his scowl firmly in place, she did a slow burn. "Don't you understand? You won't have to contest the will. I don't want anything. Nothing. Nada. Zero."

He about-faced and crossed to the open hatch and slammed the lid closed with a loud bang. He glanced at her over his tanned shoulder. "What's the catch?"

"Catch? There is no catch."

He smirked. "Right, lady. Do you honestly expect me to believe you're willing to give up the rights to a fortune?"

"Yes." The last thing she wanted was anything from Angus Crawford. Whether he was alive or dead, she hated him. Deep in her gut she knew he was involved in her parents' disappearance. Accepting money from him, even though he was dead, would be like he was making her complicit in some way and buying her silence.

The creases at the corners of Russ's mouth deepened, and he laughed, a full-throated chuckle, made even worse because of the obvious phoniness.

She gripped the boat railing, her nails digging into the shiny metal. "Did you hear what I said? I don't want anything to do with your father's fortune. Nothing. Not. A. Damn. Penny."

His expression turned thoughtful. "You're serious, aren't you?"

She nodded.

"Why?"

"Why what?"

"Why would you give away a fortune?"

Frustration washed over her, and she struggled not to throw something. She grasped the railing tighter. "I've told you already. I don't want anything from Angus Crawford. How much clearer can I be?"

"You do know how much Angus was worth, don't you?" His eyes narrowed, and he studied her intently, as if he were trying to see into her soul.

Beads of perspiration popped out on her upper lip. "Jennifer Smythe told me."

He set his hands on his lean hips, and his steely glare lasered in on her. "Let's say I believe you. What do you want in return?"

She wanted to scream, to vent aloud her frustration at this stubborn, pigheaded man. How could he not comprehend what she was saying? "I told you. I don't want anything from you, except for you to take the damn inheritance."

"And I'm supposed to believe you?"

Enough. If he refused to accept the gift she offered, that was his problem. She'd donate the money to charity, give it to an animal shelter, or fund a school for girls in Africa, anything but keep the tainted money. "Fine." She spun toward the granny gate and stepped onto the aluminum ladder.

"Tell me one thing."

Despite her determination to walk away, she paused and shot him a glance. "What?"

"Why have you been in hiding?"

"Hiding? I wasn't hiding." Her mouth dried.

"Why did you change your name?"

She gripped the ladder, fearing her legs would give out. "That's—" She gulped. "—none of your business."

His expression was unreadable. "Did Jennifer Smythe tell you she had people looking for you?"

"So?" Where was he going with this third degree? It wasn't as if she'd committed a crime. She was trying to give him money, for God's sake. Lots of money.

"Did she also tell you that Angus's will stipulates that if you were dead, or you couldn't be found within six months of Angus's demise, the estate transferred to me?"

"Sorry to disappoint you." She climbed down the ladder. "As you see, I'm very much alive." Though the way her heart was pounding, she was at high risk for a massive coronary. Her feet landed on the dock. "And here I am. Look at that." She held her hands out to her sides, palms up. "Your lawyer found me."

He leaned over the railing. "Why did you change your name? Who are you hiding from?"

Her heart stuttered. She really was going to have a heart attack. "None of your damn business." She spun and strode down the dock, her sneakers thudding on the worn wooden planks.

Footsteps pounded behind her. "Athena… er…ah…Margaret, wait. Please."

Every instinct urged her to run to her car and

escape his probing questions, but she slowed to a stop and spun around, hands jammed on her hips. "What?"

He scrubbed his hands over his face. "Look, I apologize. I…I was…I guess I wasn't…" His throat worked. "I may have been a bit hasty. But you have to admit your offer is unusual, to say the least."

"I wouldn't have driven all the way out here if I wasn't serious."

"Look. This is a lot to take in." He smiled at her, and his face underwent a transformation. "Stay and we'll discuss your offer."

Her heart skipped a beat at the glow lighting his golden eyes, turning them a warm, taffy color. Her brain function slowed, her mouth hung open, and she gaped. She'd visited Florence and seen the statue of David carved in marble by Michelangelo. The statue, portraying the epitome of male beauty, had nothing on Russell Crawford. "You accept my offer?"

The dimple in his lean right cheek deepened as he grinned. His even white teeth stood out in marked contrast with his tanned skin. "I have to think about that, but in the meantime, why don't you come sailing?" His smile grew.

Butterflies fluttered in her stomach. "Wha…what? With you?"

"Yes, with me." He pointed at the clear blue sky and soft, puffy clouds. "Come on. It's a beautiful afternoon. There's no better place to spend a day like this than sailing on the ocean." His smile widened. "I'll have you back in a couple of hours. I promise."

His boyish enthusiasm caught her off guard. She looked at her watch. Her plane didn't leave until later that night. She studied the open sea. Frothy, white waves crested in the face of a slight breeze. Seagulls swooped and dove above the azure water. The sun shone warm on her back. She could almost feel the salt spray cooling her face and the wind tangling in her hair.

And just like that, her resistance faded. She loved sailing. As a child, she'd spent countless happy hours on the water with her parents on their small sailboat. Her father had taught her how to weigh anchor, rig the sails, and navigate the challenging waters off their tiny island. A familiar stab of pain rammed her like a punch to the gut. She'd lost so much, and it was all Angus Crawford's fault. She shoved aside the sad memories. Now wasn't the time to wallow in grief.

Warning bells clamored in her head, cautioning her against going anywhere with the all-too-attractive Russ. She didn't know him, didn't know if she could trust him. After all, he was Angus Crawford's son. She opened her mouth to refuse and tell him she was leaving, but the words that came out of her mouth shocked her. "Why not? I'd like that." She smiled at the widening of his eyes, proof he hadn't expected her to accept.

Well, he'd offered. She'd accepted. Done deal.

Her gut pinged. Done deal, indeed.

Chapter 12

The rope slipped the cleat for the third time, and he cursed under his breath. He'd done this task hundreds of times. He could do it blindfolded. Grinding his teeth, he forced himself to concentrate, but once again his gaze slid to his passenger.

She stood near the bow of the sleek craft, her long, shapely legs braced against the boat's rolling motion. The black pants were so tight they looked like they'd been painted on, and they revealed the taut muscles in her thighs and the curve of her sweet ass. Her hair, a bright, tangled riot of curls, danced about her face. The ocean breeze flattened her pink T-shirt to her body, revealing the soft mounds of her breasts.

He gulped and cursed again. Time to get his mind off her to-die-for curves and focus on more important matters. Like his future. Was she telling the truth? Who would give up a fortune? No one. No one with any sense at any rate, and she didn't strike him as stupid.

So…what was this about? What did she want from him? Because she sure as hell wanted something. No one gave away millions of dollars. Not unless they expected something in return, but for the life of him he couldn't think what that could be. It was early times yet. That was why he'd offered to take her for a sail. He wanted more time with her to figure out her motives, to suss her out and learn what she was really after. One thing was certain—she wanted something. He'd only to figure out what that was. In the meantime, he had to keep his hands off her and stop drooling like she was a prime cut of grade A beef, and he was a starving dog.

Why had she agreed to go sailing? He hadn't expected her to and was stunned when she'd said she would. The stiff set of her body had made clear she wanted to get away. But yet, there she was. On his boat. Sailing. With him.

The boat crested a wave and sank into the following furrow, and she staggered a few steps but braced her hands against the railing, holding steady. The rocking motion of the boat didn't seem to bother her. In fact, ever since they'd left the wharf, she'd had a smile on her face. No question, she was enjoying herself.

Maybe he'd misjudged her. Hard to reconcile her childlike enthusiasm and obvious joy of sailing with the conniving, devious bitch he'd thought her to be. Normally he was a good judge of character. In the world of business, that skill had stood him in good stead. Maggie O'Flynn, or Athena Reynolds, or whatever the hell she wanted to be called, was definitely an enigma.

As if sensing the weight of his scrutiny, she twisted around and grinned. The sun shone on her mass of red hair, turning it into molten gold glowing around her gamin-like face. Her eyes matched the azure blue of the afternoon sky. "This is great, isn't it?"

He swore his heart skipped a beat. As if under a spell, he stalked toward her, but then his brain kicked into gear, and instead of touching her, he jammed his hands into the front pockets of his pants and stared out at the sea, avoiding those tantalizing blue eyes.

"I'd forgotten how much I enjoy sailing." Her husky voice carried over the rush of wind.

He held his body stiff, determined not to look, not to lose what little was left of his cool. "Have you done a lot of sailing?"

"I used to sail with my parents, but that was years ago."

The pain in her voice slapped him, and he shot her a glance.

A cloud washed over her expressive face, and shadows dulled the vivid blue depths of her eyes.

Of course. Her parents were gone. They'd disappeared years ago from the island and left her behind. Why hadn't he kept his damn mouth shut? The hurt of her loss was still there. He was all too familiar with the pain of losing parents, but he knew what happened to his mother and father; she was left forever wondering.

The sudden urge to offer comfort and ease her grief overwhelmed him, but he thrust the impulse aside. He refused to let sympathy for her affect his judgment. She wasn't an innocent, abandoned child anymore. She was all grown up and devious enough to convince Angus to write her into his will as the main beneficiary. No, she was no saint. That was for damn sure. "How well did you know my father?"

The color left her face. "Ang…Angus Crawford?"

He fixed her with a steely regard, searching for signs of deception.

"I didn't. Not really."

His gaze sharpened. "Then you understand why I'm curious as to why he left you an estate worth millions."

"I have no idea." A tiny frown line formed between her eyebrows. "Does it matter?"

"Yes, I think it does." *Does it matter?* How could she ask that? He'd lost everything to an old man's whim.

"Angus owned the island where I lived as a child. He knew my parents." She shrugged. "Maybe…maybe that had something to do with his decision."

He scrubbed the palms of his hands over his whiskered cheeks. "I remember. You and your family lived on Shelter Island. Your parents—" The stricken look on her face froze his words. Angus had refused to discuss the tragedy that occurred on the island he owned, but the story of the young girl whose parents disappeared from Shelter Island had inundated the news headlines.

Shadows clouded her blue eyes. Her face was pale, and she looked as if a breeze would blow her over.

Another unexpected wave of compassion washed over him. The police hadn't discovered what happened to her parents. They vanished without a trace. "Look, I'm sorry. I didn't mean to—"

"Don't worry about it. It was a long time ago." Her eyes flattened. "That's the reason I changed my name. I don't want anyone's pity."

Her words said one thing, but the anguish on her stricken face made clear what he'd said was anything but okay. "I'm sorry." Damn. Were those the only words he knew?

He licked his dry lips and attempted a change of topic, anything to erase the raw pain on her face. "I saw you once, you know. Years ago, on Shelter Island. Do you remember?" Angus had taken him to the island for a weekend of male bonding. They'd fished for salmon, dug on the beach for butter clams, and caught crabs on the incoming tide. The next day, Angus was busy with paperwork, so Russ had gone exploring. He'd found a small, sandy, crescent-shaped beach and was searching for shells and glass bottles from faraway lands when he spotted movement amongst the rocks.

A girl, skinny and gangly, all legs and arms, head topped by a mass of fiery red hair reaching the small of her back, clambered over the rocks above the small beach.

He hadn't known anyone else was on the island, and he waved and called out.

For a second, their gazes locked, but then she wheeled around and scampered across the rocks and vanished into the forest.

He'd asked Angus who she was and was told the northern part of the small island was leased to a family. The girl Russ had seen was their daughter. Russ was intrigued. His favorite movie at the time was *Swiss Family Robinson*, a story about a family who were shipwrecked on an isolated island. He'd wondered what the redheaded girl's life was like growing up on the rugged island with only her parents for companionship. But he was a kid himself and distracted by his all-too-fresh grief over the loss of his parents, and so he didn't ask any more questions.

Shortly after that trip, Angus asked if Russ wanted to live with him on a fulltime basis in his sprawling house in West Vancouver. Russ liked Angus, and he'd agreed. It wasn't like a slew of relatives were lining up to take him in. He was fourteen and alone. His choices were either move in with Angus or enter the foster care system.

Living with Angus had been okay, but Angus never took Russ to Shelter Island again. Russ had asked many times if he could visit the island, but Angus always had an excuse—he was too busy to get away, the weather forecast called for a storm, the sailboat was in for repairs... Russ had his own problems dealing with grief and starting a new school, and he didn't push. Before long, memories of the island and the skinny girl with the long red hair faded.

Until the story of her missing parents hit the news. It was a tragedy that caught the nation's attention. The couple had a young daughter who'd been left behind.

He couldn't stop thinking about the girl he'd seen. He'd been fascinated by the tragedy. Something about her inexplicable loss resonated. He'd read every newspaper article he could get his hands on, watched the TV news shows, even asked Angus if he knew anything regarding the missing couple. Angus refused to talk about the O'Flynns and made it clear he didn't want Russ pursuing the matter.

That hadn't stopped him, of course. Angus's reticence added fuel to Russ's adolescent curiosity, and he'd continued his clandestine research. But eventually, the news story dropped from the headlines, and other events—making the cut for the basketball team, the cute girl from his French class whom he wanted to ask to the dance—caught his attention and, other than a secret trip there in his senior year with a bunch of buddies, he forgot about Shelter Island and its tragedy.

Now, after all those years, the details of the incident were fuzzy. According to the official reports, after the O'Flynns disappeared, the police scoured the island. The couple's small boat was also missing, so the authorities sent divers into the stormy seas, checked nearby islands for wreckage, and pleaded for anyone with information on the couple's disappearance to come forward. There'd even been a substantial reward posted, but no witness came forward. No evidence of foul play was ever found, and as far as he knew, the case remained unsolved.

He studied the woman in front of him. The waif he'd spotted on the headland so many years ago had grown up. The skinny, awkward child was long gone. She'd grown into a beautiful woman with mouthwatering curves and clear, almost translucent skin.

"I remember seeing you." She threaded her long, slim fingers through her red curls. "I wondered who you were. We didn't get many visitors."

"My parents—" He swallowed. "—my parents, well, something happened to them, and Angus took me in." *Something* happened to his parents? Really? Was that all it was? A vision of the car crash that ended his parents' lives flashed before him, but he squashed the painful memory.

Her gaze softened. "I guess we have something in common after all."

Her silent understanding hurt more than if she'd been openly curious about what happened to his parents. *Stop!* The command blazed through his brain. This wasn't a therapy session. He didn't need or want her sympathy.

He'd invited her to sail with him for a reason. He wanted time alone with her so he could dig for answers.

Now was as good a time as any. "Why would Angus leave you his estate? Your family leased the land on Shelter Island, but you were just tenants." He'd already asked, but she hadn't given him an answer, not one that made sense. "What did you do to convince him? Did you sleep with him?" Of course, she had. She was too pretty. Angus would have been all over her. He wouldn't have cared about her tragic past. Or maybe that was the wedge she used to get into his good graces. His lip curled. "You must be pretty damn good in the sack." The cruel words hovered in the air between them like birds of prey on the attack.

She stumbled back a step. "You tell me. Leaving me his money was probably his sick idea of a joke." She glared. "Do you want to know the truth?" She didn't wait for him to answer. "I hated him. I'm glad he's dead." She enunciated each word as if it were chipped from ice.

A heavy silence thickened the air as he digested her heated words. Her attitude didn't make sense. If she hated Angus so much, why would he leave her his fortune? A chill rippled along his spine as the truth dawned on him. "He did something to you, harmed you in some way, didn't he?"

Her eyes blazed, but her lower lip trembled as if she fought back tears. "He destroyed my life."

"You'd better explain."

Her face was devoid of color, her eyes haunted. "He murdered my parents." She sank onto a padded bench and averted her face, attempting to hide her tears.

What the hell was she talking about? Angus wasn't a killer. He rubbed the tightness in the back of his neck. His father hadn't been perfect. Not by any means. He was a hard-nosed businessman who'd been demanding of those around him. He worked hard his entire life to achieve success, and he'd been respected in the business community. He raised Russell with a stern hand, but underlying the rigidity, Angus had possessed a deep sense of honesty and integrity. No way would he have deliberately harmed anyone, let alone this woman's parents. "I don't believe you."

Tears shimmered in her blue eyes, but her mouth curled in a sneer. "You're just like the police investigators. They didn't believe me either." She swiped the back of her hand over her damp eyes. "But I know what I know. Angus Crawford murdered my parents."

He rocked back on his heels, stunned by her venom. Was she insane? Was that what this was about? Had she lost her hold on reality? Or was this a scheme to trick him? She was holding all the cards. Angus had left her pretty well everything. That didn't make sense either. Was it guilt? Is that why Angus left her so much? Had he somehow harmed her parents and was trying to make up for his crime? Was Angus's gesture of generosity his version of repentance?

He dug the pads of his fingers into his throbbing temples. "If the police didn't believe Angus was involved in your parents' disappearance, why are you so convinced he's guilty? What exactly do you think he did?"

She shot to her feet. "You won't believe anything I say, so why should I bother?"

She was right. He didn't believe, not for a hot minute, that Angus murdered anyone. But her tone spoke volumes. *She* believed Angus was guilty. The raw pain in her compelling eyes struck him like a slap to the back of the head. Was it possible she was telling the truth? Was Angus responsible for what happened to her parents?

Nah. No way. She was delusional. Either that or her following him from the lawyer's office and showing up on the dock was part of a crazy scam. What she hoped to gain from her baseless accusations was beyond his understanding. He dragged his gaze from her pale face. One way or another, he'd find out what she was up to. Damn straight. He'd find out the truth, and then he'd toss her sweet ass off his boat.

Chapter 13

Athena dug her fingers into the bench seat's canvas-covered cushion and held tight as the boat rode the waves. Russ's probing into the painful past had ripped off a scab and resurrected the old hurt and anguish. He didn't believe her claims. She wasn't surprised. No one believed her—not the police, not the private investigator her aunt had hired, not even Aunt Clara.

She'd agreed to go sailing with Russ so she could convince him to accept her offer and maybe find out why Angus had left her so much. Her plan had flopped. Russ hadn't given her a chance to explain. That look in his eyes said he didn't believe her. What was wrong with him? She was offering him a fortune. Why wouldn't he take the damn money and be happy? Why all the questions?

A wave smashed the side of the sailboat, and a spray of icy seawater cascaded over the deck. The *Minerva* rose high in the air and plunged with a resounding thump into a deep trough.

Thrown off-balance, she lost her grip and fell, landing with a painful thud on the unforgiving deck. Before she could scramble up, Russ grasped her by the arms and hauled her to her feet.

"Are you all right?"

She stared into his golden eyes. Her skin tingled

where his large, warm hands held her. "Ye…yes, I'm fine." She tugged her arms free and stumbled back a step. "Thank you."

A frown furrowed his brow. "The weather's turned, and we're in for a bit of a blow. We should head back."

She scanned the sky. "Look at those dark clouds." Absorbed in her thoughts, she'd failed to notice the approaching storm. "They look pretty menacing."

Loud slapping split the air as the mainsail halyard broke loose.

"Do you need help?" she shouted over the rising wind. At his hesitation, she planted her hands on her hips. "I haven't sailed for years, but if you tell me what needs doing, I'll do it. It's like riding a bike, right?"

He hefted open the lid under the bench seat and held out a vibrant yellow lifejacket. "Put this on. You can take the wheel while I adjust the sails."

She struggled into the musty-smelling life preserver, adjusted the straps, and zipped up the front closure.

He slipped into a matching lifejacket. Clasping her hand in a firm grip, he supported her as they staggered across the heaving deck toward the cockpit.

The wind howled, and salt spray blinded her as waves pounded the small vessel. She stumbled again, and he steadied her, pressing her close, shielding her with his body from the worst of the storm. Heat from his hands seeped into her chilled skin, but all too soon they lurched into the cockpit, and he relinquished his hold. The walls of the small enclosure blocked the gale-force winds and kept out the worst of the raging storm. She wiped her streaming face with the back of her hand.

He guided her to the wheel. "Hold on tight, and keep the bow pointed into the wind."

The boat bucked and swayed like a wild animal fighting to break free. The wind shrieked as it blasted the small sailboat.

Two-meter-high waves crashed over the bow, drenching her with icy spray and mixing with the freezing rain pelting down from the sodden sky. She fought to keep her balance and hold on to the resisting wheel.

Russ, hair dripping, water streaming down his face, his clothes drenched, scrambled with sure-footed grace across the rocking deck, battening hatches, trimming the sails, and tightening ropes.

The boat plummeted into a cavernous trough, and the wheel jerked from her hands. She yelped as she tumbled to the deck and smashed into a metal storage box. Fighting for breath, she sprawled on the heaving deck until her lungs expanded, and she inhaled fresh sea air. Lurching to her knees and then her feet, she grabbed the wheel and hung on.

The wheel spun wildly, and the boat altered course, running crosswind. Waves struck the hull broadside, threatening to capsize the small vessel.

Her muscles cramped as she yanked and wrenched the wheel, but it wouldn't budge. Saltwater sprayed her face and dripped from her hair, mixing with her sweat and rain, blinding her. She shoved again, grunting with the effort. The wheel gave an inch and then another. Slowly, but inexorably, the boat swung around until the bow faced the oncoming waves.

Thanking whatever gods were watching over her, she tightened her grip and fought the resisting wheel, straining to keep the vessel on course. The sea and rain drenched her, plastering her hair to her head and soaking her clothes. Goose bumps prickled her skin. Her hands cramped, and pain shot up her arms, but she clung to the wheel, refusing to let go.

Russ materialized out of the storm and seized the wheel.

Gratefully, she released her grip and rubbed her aching hands.

Placing his mouth close to her ear, he shouted, "We can't make it back to the marina. Not in this storm. Let's try for a nearby island and wait it out there."

The brush of his warm breath across her face and neck, and the heat from his body, drew her like a moth to a flame. She inched closer until her shoulder and hip bumped his. Clinging to the side of the cockpit, she leaned into him, reveling in his warmth.

The wind raged, rain poured down in buckets, and waves crashed over the gunnels, threatening to swamp the sturdy boat.

Russ's knuckles were white, and his face grim, as he braced his body against the wild rocking and steered the boat into the face of the storm.

A dark smudge appeared on the horizon, barely visible through the fog and driving rain. The vessel dropped into a trough and careened up the other side. The smudge grew larger, revealing a rocky shoreline and thick forest of tall coniferous trees.

He guided the *Minerva* into a small, protected bay. The storm continued to rage, but inside the safety of the cove, the waters were relatively calm. "You okay?" He waited for her nod before he flicked a switch, and the engine rumbled to life. He grasped her hand and led her to the throttle. "You're doing great. We're almost there. Follow my directions while we get anchored. Can you do that?"

She was soaked through, and her teeth chattered, but she nodded.

"Good girl." He patted her hand. "Hold onto the throttle and be ready to reverse the engine when I tell you." Moving with lithe, athletic grace, he lowered the furl of the mainsail, scampered forward, and let down the jib sail. Moving to the bow, he hefted the anchor and dropped the rope over the side. "Okay, Athena. Reverse her at idle speed."

She'd done this task a dozen times when she was a child, and the familiar motions returned.

The engine rumbled, spewing blue clouds of diesel into the air.

She pulled the throttle toward her, inch by inexorable inch.

He played out the braided nylon rope and cinched it to a cleat. The boat straightened, tugging on the rope, and he set the anchor. "That's good, but keep it coming." He tied the anchor rope around a bow cleat and gave the rope a tug. "Okay. Now we have to snub the anchor. Reverse hard until the rope straightens out. Then kill the engine."

The second the anchor rope tightened and the anchor dug into the sea bottom, she shifted the throttle into neutral and switched off the engine.

After the loud rumble of the inboard diesel engine, silence descended, broken by the crash of waves rolling onto the distant shore and the raucous cries of seagulls swooping and diving in the low tide. Freezing rain poured down, and the wind drove in gusts out of the northeast. Protected in the little bay, the boat rocked gently at its mooring.

Teeth chattering, she wiped her wet face. "That was some sailing."

"You're a great first mate. I couldn't have done it without your help."

"Aye, aye, Captain." She saluted and chuckled.

His warm laughter washed over her like liquid honey.

Their gazes locked, and something intangible sparked.

The slight widening of his eyes indicated he too felt the connection.

Heat rose along her neck and settled on her cheeks. Her heart raced so loud the pounding overpowered the roar of waves crashing on the distant, rocky shore. She tore her gaze from his and peered through the rain at the rugged bay's shoreline.

Jagged fingers of black volcanic rock jutted into the sea. The small crescent of pebbled beach was littered with graying, washed-up logs and mounds of tangled seaweed. A tree-covered ridge on one end and a headland of large boulders on the other sheltered the beach. The foamy crests of crashing waves surged over the barnacle-covered rocks.

A trill of unease washed over her. "Where are we?"

His gaze bore into hers. "I thought you might recognize the place. We're just off the shores of Shelter Island."

"What?" The strength fled her knees, and the world spun. A wave of blackness engulfed her, and she grabbed onto the wheel, but it slipped from her fingers, and she fell.

Shelter Island.

The name howled through her brain, echoing in a haunting refrain.

Shelter Island.

The one place she swore she'd never visit again.

"Athena! What's wrong?"

His voice grew fainter as she slipped into oblivion.

Chapter 14

Warm. So wonderfully warm. She snuggled under the blankets.

Blankets?

Her eyes shot open. She was lying on a bed. Faint gray light streamed through a small, circular porthole. She was on a boat. The gentle rocking motions and steady patter of rain on the deck above were soothing. She stretched, and her thigh grazed something solid and warm. She sucked in a breath and turned her head.

Russ sprawled on the bed beside her, the blankets draped low over his flat stomach.

She shoved back the bedding and surged to her feet. "What…what are *you* doing in my bed?"

The bed springs squeaked as he opened his eyes and pushed up on a pillow. The corners of his mouth twitched. "Well, technically this is *my* bed. And it's called a berth…you know…because we're on a boat."

His warm drawl liquefied her muscles, and her legs wobbled as she struggled to remain standing. "But…but what…"

He leaned over and switched on a small lamp built into the wall. A pool of light illuminated the berth in a soft glow, revealing his tanned, muscular chest with a sprinkling of dark hair. A lock of his hair had fallen across his broad forehead.

Sweet Jesus!

"Wha...what? Why...?" She waved her hand at the berth with the rumpled blankets. "How did we...?" Damn. Her brain wasn't functioning. How on God's green earth did she end up in bed with *him*?

His mouth quirked in a crooked grin, and the devastating dimple in his right cheek danced. "Relax. Nothing happened. At least, not what you're thinking." He threaded his long fingers through his tousled hair. "You fainted, and I carried you below. I was worried you were suffering from hypothermia, so I put you in bed and climbed in beside you." He grinned, his eyes darkening to a rich mahogany. "There's nothing like another body to warm a person. At least, that's what all the first aid manuals say."

She opened her mouth to protest, but the glint of humor in his hazel eyes stopped her. His disheveled appearance only added to his earthy, male attractiveness. She fought to keep her gaze fixed on his face so she wouldn't drool over the expanse of bronzed muscles gleaming in the cozy light.

A cold gust of wind blew down the ladder through the open hatch, and she shivered. For the first time she realized she was wearing a large white T-shirt. Nothing else. Just the T-shirt and her panties. Her heart stuttered. "You...you removed my clothes?"

"I had to. They were soaked through, and you were freezing." His grin widened. "Don't worry. I didn't peek." He held two fingers up to his head and saluted. "Scout's honor."

"*You* were a Boy Scout?"

He chuckled. "I know, right? Hard to believe." He thrust out his chest. "Eagle Scout." Once again, he made the iconic salute.

Eagle Scout. Of course, he was. He seemed like the overachiever type. No doubt he was also president of his student council, class valedictorian, and king of the prom.

"Are you feeling better?"

The concern in his husky voice drew her out of her jaded thoughts. She sank onto the mattress and dragged the sheet over her legs. "What happened?"

"You don't remember?"

She shook her head. Visions of the storm, the pounding rain, the bone-shaking cold, the wildly rocking boat, and fighting to hold onto the wheel rose before her, none of which explained her present circumstances.

"The storm came out of nowhere." He rubbed the back of his neck. "I don't know what happened. I checked the weather forecast before we sailed, and the weatherman was calling for clear skies and light winds." He grimaced. "Thanks to your help, we made it to this bay. We'd just lowered the anchor when you passed out." He blew out a breath. "I was worried about you. Your clothes were soaked, and you were shivering."

A chill swept her, and she wrapped her arms across her chest. "Where are we?"

"What's wrong? Are you cold?" His deep voice was filled with concern. "There are more blankets in the cupboard." He sat up and grasped the sheet as if he were going to toss it off and climb out of the bed.

"No...no...I...I don't need a blanket. I'm not cold." Her voice was a thin squeak. Dear Lord. Was he naked under the sheet?

The corners of his eyes crinkled. "Okay. If you're

sure, but I don't mind getting you one. Just say the word."

"I'm fine."

He lay back against the pillows.

"Where are we?" she asked the question again. Her heart hammered. Somehow, she knew she wasn't going to like the answer.

"We're anchored in a bay off a small island."

"What island?" But she knew. Oh, she knew. The room swayed, and she grabbed onto the mattress, holding tight, determined not to black out again. "What. Island. Is. This?" She bit off each word.

"Shelter Island. The island you used to live on. The island I now own, thanks to the terms of my father's will."

And just like that, the moment of shared intimacy ended.

She sucked in a ragged breath.

His brow furrowed. "I'm so sorry, but we didn't have a choice. We had to find a protected bay, and Shelter Island was the closest landing." He blew out a breath. "I had no idea being here would upset you so much. As soon as the wind dies, we'll set sail. I promise."

She fought to swallow over the lump in her throat. What happened on Shelter Island had happened a lifetime ago. Russ wasn't Angus Crawford. He wasn't responsible for the tragedy. He'd been a kid when the nightmare occurred. Besides, she wasn't *on* the island. They were moored offshore. Clutching the sheet, she tugged, ripping it off the bed and wrapping it around her waist.

"Hey." He lay on the mattress clad only in his

underwear—a very small pair of underwear—that exposed his strong thighs and the full glory of his chest.

She gaped for a heart-stopping moment but then recalled where they were and what was at stake, and she rose and peered out the small porthole. Through the streaks of rain on the thick glass, the all-too-familiar silhouette of rocky shores and heavily treed hills was visible. Her stomach rolled.

****

He slid across the mattress and climbed out of the berth. Gripping her chin with gentle fingers, he tilted her head, so she was forced to meet his gaze. His heart ached at the wounded vulnerability shining in the blue depths of her eyes.

The urge to slay dragons, to fight the bad guy, to stop the racing train…anything to protect her, raged through him like a living force. "Please don't cry." He wiped a tear from her soft cheek with the pad of his thumb. "We'll leave as soon as the storm dies. You don't have to step foot on the island. You don't even have to look at the place. Stay below deck, and I'll tend to everything."

The tip of her pink tongue darted out, and she licked her lips. "I…I guess I should explain."

He shook his head. "You don't have to tell me anything. It's none of my business."

"I want to." She sniffled and used the edge of the sheet to wipe her damp face. "You should know the truth about what happened. It'll help you understand why I don't want anything from Angus Crawford—not his money, not his business, nothing."

An overwhelming urge to kiss her rushed through him, but he tightened his hands into fists and held them at his sides. He wasn't an animal. He didn't act on every base impulse. Sure, he wanted to rub his mouth against hers and discover how sweet her lips tasted. But he wouldn't. Not now. Not when naked anguish blazed from her blue eyes. Not when she was ripped raw from memories of her painful loss. He tore his gaze from her enticing mouth and focused on her words.

"I spent the first twelve years of my life on Shelter Island." A soft smile lit her face, lending her pale skin a pearly luminescence. She described her childhood explorations of the isolated island's rugged shores, and her joy at finding treasures like Japanese glass fishing floats and bottles washed up on shore. "It sounds corny, but we had an idyllic life. Mom made crafts from shells and driftwood, and Dad painted seascapes. They sold their artwork at farmers' markets on the mainland. I took correspondence courses. We lived on fish, oysters, clams, and crabs, with wild berries, and produce from Mom's garden. We didn't need much. Just being together was enough."

"You weren't lonely?"

"Lonely? Why would I be lonely? I had everything I wanted. I had my parents, and I had the island. That's all I needed." A sob hiccupped in her throat. "We were happy."

"You must have had visitors." He pictured her as he'd seen her that long-ago day. At her first sight of him, she'd run away like a timid island deer.

"Hardly anyone. A man brought our monthly supplies on his boat, and my parents had a few friends who came to visit every couple of months, but most of the time we were alone. Just the three of us."

"The island's pretty, that's for sure." He'd visited

Shelter Island a few times over the years, and he understood why she had such fond memories. Before their passing, his parents had been good friends with Angus. Angus had invited the family twice for a weekend of fishing, fun, and sailing.

Russ's third visit to the isolated island was shortly after his parents' accident. Even with the tragedy looming over him, his time on the island was magical. He and Angus had sailed for hours in Angus's catamaran. They'd caught halibut, salmon, prawns, and crab for their dinners. In the evenings, Angus taught him how to play chess.

Russ knew about the family who resided on the other side of the island, but other than his fleeting encounter with the skinny, red-haired girl, he'd never bumped into them. "You didn't see my father?"

Her mouth tightened. "Hardly ever. His cottage was on the far side, and as far as I know, he didn't visit the island very often, and when he did, he didn't come to our side." She slipped a stray curl behind her ear. "Mom and Dad met with him, of course. They had to give him the rent money." She rubbed her arms. "To be honest, I was afraid of him. If I knew he was coming to visit, I hid in the forest until he left." Her hands twisted the cotton sheet, tying it in knots.

He narrowed his eyes. She wasn't telling him everything. So far, she hadn't said anything that explained why Angus had left her the bulk of his estate. It would have made more sense if he'd left her the island, but he'd willed Shelter Island to Russ. And that didn't make any sense at all. "It sounds like you enjoyed living on the island."

"I did...until..." The color drained from her face,

accentuating the dark circles under her eyes.

He studied her tear-ravaged face, and something shifted deep in his chest. His every instinct urged him to take her in his arms and soothe her anguish. But she looked so brittle, he was afraid if he touched her, she'd break. "What happened? Please, tell me."

"Angus did something terrible to my parents. I don't know what, but one morning they were going about the normal everyday chores, and by the afternoon they'd vanished without a trace. I *know* Angus Crawford was responsible. It had to be him. He was the only other person on the island."

He blinked at the acid lacing her voice. She'd uttered the same accusation earlier, but he'd ignored her comments as dramatics, a bid to trick him in whatever game she was playing. But now he wasn't so sure. The anguish shining in the troubled depths of her eyes, her trembling body, all seemed authentic. Either that or she was a damn fine actress. He scrubbed the bristles on his unshaven cheeks. "You still haven't explained what Angus supposedly did to your parents."

"He killed them." Her eyes burned like hollow beacons as she glared, resembling the avenging goddess she'd named herself after. "Isn't that enough?"

"You really think Angus murdered your parents?" Even as he asked the question, his heart protested. Angus wouldn't have hurt anyone. No way.

"You don't believe me." Her accusation hung in the air.

"I don't know what to believe. Angus Crawford was a decent man. He was good to me. He wouldn't have harmed anyone, especially your parents. They were his tenants. Why would he hurt them?"

She shook her head, and her unruly red curls swirled about her face like dancing flames. "You're just like all the others." Tears shone in her eyes. "The police, the private detectives...no one believed me. I told them what I suspected, but no one listened. Even Aunt Clara wasn't convinced."

"Well then, convince me. I'm listening. Tell me what awful thing you believe Angus did to your parents."

She met his gaze, her eyes bleak. "That's just it. I don't know." She clutched a pillow to her chest, drew in a deep breath, and recited the details of that horrible day. Her voice held little emotion, as if the events hadn't destroyed her life.

Her tragic tale of a young girl's pain and loneliness tore at him, all the more because of the ring of truth infusing each word. Whatever had happened that day, she believed her version of the events.

When she finished, she stood and stumbled to the porthole and stared outside. The thin, almost-transparent, oversize white T-shirt revealed the enticing mounds of her lush breasts and her long, shapely legs.

He gulped. *Don't look.* The command thundered through him. But he looked. Damn right he did. Not something an Eagle Scout would do.

Definitely not.

Chapter 15

She stared through the porthole's thick glass and studied the waves crashing on the gravel beach and the familiar rocky headland. How many times had she climbed over those rocks searching for treasures that had washed ashore on the wild west coast surf?

Russ cleared his throat. "You really believe that Angus was involved in your parents' disappearance?"

"I can't prove it, but I know he did something to them, something bad."

He sat on the edge of the bed, his hair mussed from sleep, clad in a pair of navy briefs that only added to his sexiness. "Does anyone else believe your version of the events?" Doubt clouded his golden eyes.

She wasn't surprised. Why would he believe the adoptive father he'd loved, a man who took him in after Russ's parents died, was a cold-blooded murderer? Somehow, she found the courage to meet his gaze. "If it's any consolation, no one else believes me either."

A swirl of emotion blazed in the depths of his eyes. He stood and enfolded her in his arms, gathering her against him.

His unspoken compassion broke the dam, and tears flooded her eyes, slipped down her cheeks, and dampened his bare chest. She inhaled his male scent and burrowed closer to his comforting warmth. The steady beat of his heart beneath her ear was calming.

As if reluctant to release her, he tightened his embrace, but then he heaved a deep breath and dropped his arms and stepped back. Grabbing his wrinkled shirt from the floor, he tugged the T-shirt over his head and shoved his legs into his jeans and yanked them over his hips.

A sense of loss weighed her down, and she sagged on the bed.

"I'm sorry we anchored here. I can see that the island brings back a lot of upsetting memories, but we needed a safe bay to ride out the storm." He scrubbed the dark stubble on his jaw, and the rasp of whiskers filled the small space. "As soon as the storm dies down, we'll sail back to the mainland like I promised."

Relief coursed through her at the thought of escaping the painful ghosts of the past haunting Shelter Island's mist-shrouded shores. "Thank you for understanding."

"No problem. I always look after my crew." He smiled, releasing that devastating dimple.

Her heart fluttered. *His crew*. When had that happened? When had she gone from being his sworn enemy to a member of his crew? More to the point— why did she like the sound of it so much?

"In the meantime, why not try and get some rest?" He gestured at the rumpled double berth. "I'll check the weather forecast." He headed up the ladder and disappeared through the hatch.

She was exhausted, and her head throbbed. For years, she'd struggled to shut away the painful past, but today she'd ripped off the scab and discovered the pain was as fresh as twenty-three years ago.

Slumping back on the bed, she closed her eyes. The

gentle rocking of the boat, the steady patter of rain against the porthole window, the fresh rain-scented air drifting from the open hatch was soothing, and she dozed off only to awaken, her pulse pounding, the old, familiar terror raging.

She jerked up. Pink wisps of dawn's early light seeped through the porthole. Somehow, she'd slept through the night. The bed beside her was empty with no indication Russ had slept beside her. Relief, mixed with a tinge of regret, washed over her.

In the past few days her world had been rocked to the core. Angus Crawford was dead. That knowledge should have been a relief and ended her nightmares once and for all. But for some inexplicable reason, he'd left her his fortune, and the old terrors had returned full force as if he haunted her from his grave. She shuddered and tugged the blankets to her chin. And now, mere meters of ocean separated her from Shelter Island, the one place populated by the ghosts of the past.

Add in the unexpected complication of her increasing attraction to Russ, and she was in a real mess. She'd expected to detest him like she hated Angus, but Russ was kind and compassionate. To say nothing of his rugged good looks and body like a Greek god. She shouldn't be thinking of him in any aspect other than the necessary ordeal of settling Angus Crawford's will, but there was her dilemma. Her brain told her one thing, but her body had entirely different ideas.

Oh man. Did it ever.

Tossing back the covers, she swung her legs off the bed and stood. Her clothes, wrinkled but dry, hung from a wooden rail at the foot of the berth. She slipped out of the oversize T-shirt and grabbed her leggings and wriggled into them, tugging them over her hips. Shrugging her bra and shirt on, she crossed the cabin to the head.

The tiny washroom was compact with no wasted space. She used the toilet, and then washed her face and hands in the miniscule metal sink. Peering in the mirror, she bit back a groan. She hardly recognized the woman looking back. Her face was pale, and dark circles underscored her puffy eyes. Even worse, her hair was a disaster. The short red strands were flattened from gale-force winds, salt spray, rain, and tossing and turning on the pillow. She cupped her fingers under the tap and splashed water on her hair, attempting to tame the unruly locks.

She grimaced. Hopeless.

Opening the door, she left the head and strode to the ladder. She'd reached a decision. If she had any hope of vanquishing the specters of the past, she had to face the nightmare head-on, even if the thought of doing so made her head ache and her heart pound. She climbed through the hatch and stepped onto the deck.

"There you are." Russ smiled, white teeth flashing in his tanned face. "How are you feeling?"

"I'm okay." She flushed at the blatant untruth. Her stomach churned, and her head throbbed. "How about you? Did you get any sleep?"

He pointed toward the stern of the small boat. "I stretched out on the bench for a couple of hours."

"Oh. That's good." What more could she say? Tell him she wished he'd snuggled in the berth beside her? This *thing*—attraction? lust?—between them was wrong on so many levels. For starters, he was Angus Crawford's adopted son. Add in his resentment of her for being the main beneficiary of Angus's estate, and the circumstances spelled trouble.

Trouble? More like a complete disaster.

If that weren't enough, she wasn't into one-night stands. And she certainly wasn't interested in a fling, no matter how attractive he was. They lived in different provinces, hundreds of kilometers apart. The only possible outcome was a broken heart, and she was too smart for that. Damn right, she was. She ignored the tiny voice laughing inside her head.

"The storm's pretty much blown itself out." He rubbed his hands. "We can heave anchor whenever you're ready."

Light rain pattered the deck.

She studied the menacing clouds. "Are you sure?"

He nodded. "I checked the weather report, and things are looking good. Barometer's rising. We should have a smooth sail home."

"I...I—" Her voice broke. "—I've changed my mind. I want to visit the island." She inhaled a shaky breath. Every cell in her body protested her decision, but she held firm to her resolve. "Maybe if I see my old home again, I'll be able to move on."

His eyes narrowed. "Are you sure?"

"No, but this is something I think I have to do. I should have visited the island long before this." For years she'd avoided returning to Shelter Island. She'd fought against the suggestion when both her therapist and Aunt Clara broached the idea. But maybe, now Angus was gone, seeing the old homestead, as painful as that would be, would give her closure.

Maybe.

Chapter 16

An hour later, they stood on the rocky shores of Shelter Island. Surf foamed around Athena's sneaker-clad feet, washing ashore broken pieces of clamshells, sea glass, and smooth pebbles with every surge. Long, ropy strings of bull kelp and eelgrass littered the beach. Red and purple sea urchins and anemones clung to the rocks in the clear tidal pools. Tiny sand crabs scurried for cover under driftwood and rocks, as squawking gulls swooped and dove, hoping for an easy supper.

She led the way as they climbed the slippery wet rocks to the headland. The rain had stopped, but water dripped from the branches of the trees towering overhead. She inhaled the familiar smells of fresh sea air, cedar, and rich, wet earth. "Nothing's changed. Everything looks the same as I remember." A slew of memories assailed her, and the lump in her throat made swallowing difficult. The island looked the same, but a lot had changed. She didn't live on the island anymore, and her parents were gone, vanished from these very shores.

"Your old house is north of here, isn't it?"

She nodded. "Our place was about a kilometer over that hill, on a rise overlooking a small bay. There should be a path here somewhere that follows the ridge. We used the trail when we hiked to this beach to harvest oysters." She searched under the soaring red cedar, Sitka spruce, and hemlock trees for signs of the old trail.

Hidden in the shadows under the leafy fronds of western sword ferns, Salal, and the tangled mats of huckleberry bushes was a slight indentation in the hard-packed earth. "There's the trail." She scuffed her feet through the soft sand, hesitating. Did she really want to continue the trip down memory lane?

As if sensing her indecision, Russ moved beside her. "We can go back to the boat. Just say the word, and we're outta here."

"I'd like nothing better than to take you up on your offer, but I have to do this. I should have come here years ago." She stiffened her spine, set her jaw, and started along the path.

Brambles tore at her leggings as she scrambled over gnarled tree roots and the massive, moss-covered trunks of fallen trees blocking the path. Every step carried the weight of an old memory. The trail wound past an outcropping of smooth, moss-covered basalt rocks that she used to imagine was a castle. She'd stood on top and scoured the sea, searching for attacking pirates.

She paused by an ancient Sitka spruce. The massive tree stretched into the heavens. Its trunk was more than a meter thick, the bark rough and cracked with deep crevasses. The branches, as thick as her thighs, were coated with draping fronds of gray, feathery moss. Her father had told her the tree was over five hundred years old.

She ran her hands over the indentations scored into the thick bark. *Maggie*, encased in a small heart, was still visible. She'd been six when her father had used his hunting knife and carved her name into the tree. Fearing he was hurting the tree, her tears had flowed, and she'd tried to stop him when the tree sap bubbled to the surface of the fresh wound.

He'd taken her in his strong arms and assured her the tree would be fine, and the wounds would heal, but her name would remain carved in the bark forever. She closed her eyes and, for the briefest heartbeat, inhaled a whiff of the sweet-cherry pipe tobacco her father smoked. Tears stung her eyes.

"You okay?" Russ's deep voice broke through the haze of memories.

She patted the carving. "Being here is—" She shrugged, unable to express with words her mixed emotions.

He rested his warm, broad hand on her shoulder. "I can't imagine how difficult this is."

Fighting the desperate urge to lose herself in his warm embrace, she shrugged off his hand and swung away from the tree. Setting one foot in front of the other, she continued along the trail. If she wanted peace, if she wanted to stop drinking, she had to see this through. But, oh man, was it difficult.

The closer they came to the small clearing where her family home had stood, the heavier her steps. Twenty-three years had passed. The west coast's punishing winds and rains were hard on manmade structures. Would the house still be standing?

Dark, frightening memories of that last night threatened to overwhelm her, and her pace slowed, each step like slogging through thick, viscous mud. She paused at the final fringe of trees, struggling to gather the courage to enter the clearing.

Russ draped his arm around her shoulders and pulled her close, offering her silent support.

The desire for a drink roared through her, almost driving her to her knees. If it hadn't been for Russ's supporting arms, she'd have fallen. It would be so easy to turn back to the boat and sail away from the island, to never face the nightmare of her past. So easy.

But could she live with herself if she took the coward's way out? She'd wasted too many years living in fear, buried in the past. Squaring her shoulders, she stepped out of the dense forest.

Thick, waist-high mats of blackberry and wild raspberry bushes choked the clearing. Wild sea grass and orange-and-purple wildflowers swayed like waves in the ocean breeze. A huge Douglas fir had blown down. The thick trunk lay across the crushed remains of the shed where her father had kept his tools. Beyond the shed, on a slight rise, was the house.

Her breath caught in her throat. The rancher was smaller than she remembered. Moss covered the cedar-shake roof, and white paint flaked from the walls, revealing the faded gray of weathered wood. The glass in one window was shattered, and a tattered, faded curtain fluttered in the breeze as if the building had declared a truce against the unrelenting attack of the elements.

Her father had built the house with his own hands. Every spring he applied a fresh coat of white paint to the outside walls in a futile attempt to stave off the damaging assaults of the damp salt air and fierce nor'easters.

The wooden garden boxes, where her mother had grown vegetables and strawberries, had rotted, spilling rich black dirt onto the weed-choked ground. The old hen house had collapsed in a jumble of rotting wood and chicken wire.

"Your parents picked an ideal location. You can see all over the bay from here." Russ shoved aside a fallen branch and stepped over a rusted shovel lying half-submerged in the ground.

She smiled through her tears. "Mom loved looking out the kitchen window when she was cooking or doing dishes. She said this spot was her little piece of paradise."

"The roof is still standing, and the place looks safe. Do you want to go inside?"

Did she want to enter the house? She swallowed.

She did.

And she didn't.

The last time she was inside the house, the nightmare of her missing parents had spiraled into a terrible reality. But she was there to face her demons. She sucked in a shaky breath. "Let's check it out." Placing one unsteady foot in front of the other, she waded through the brambles to the front of the house.

The wooden porch steps sagged, a large, ragged hole where the bottom step had once stood.

"Careful." Russ grasped her arm and helped her over the gap and up the rickety steps to the small covered porch.

The wood planking groaned and creaked under her weight. Curls of faded red paint peeled off the weather-stained, wooden front door. She thrust off an image of her mother singing her favorite old-time rock and roll songs as she wielded a paintbrush and painted the door a vibrant crimson. Athena had helped by swiping her own brush across the smooth surface, dripping more paint on the porch than the door.

"That might be a problem."

She wiped her damp face with her sleeve and shot Russ a glance. "What are you talking about?"

He pointed at a shiny new padlock hanging on a thick chain between the doorframe and the tarnished door handle. "Looks like someone doesn't want people going inside."

"The door's locked?" She blinked. They couldn't go inside the house. A spurt of relief washed over her. But she'd come all this way. "Why would it be locked?"

He shrugged. "The lawyer told me Angus had a guy look after his cottage. Maybe he watched this house as well." He tugged at the chain. "The caretaker still lives on the island. The estate's paying him now."

"Why would the caretaker lock this door? I can't imagine there's anything of value in the house. Not after all these years."

His brow furrowed. "Your parents' disappearance was all over the news. People are still curious about what happened." He nodded at the padlock. "The lock's probably to stop nosey people from snooping."

She tugged on the door handle, rattling the chain. Now that she'd come this far, she refused to be turned away. "Isn't there something you can do, some way we can get inside?"

"You really want in there, don't you?"

"That's why we're here."

"Okay." He leaped off the porch and, shoving brambles aside, he strode across the clearing and disappeared behind the collapsed shed. He returned seconds later with a rusty shovel.

"What are you going to do with that?"

"Smash the chain."

She pressed her hands to her cheeks. "That's breaking and entering."

"Are you forgetting the terms of Angus's will? I own this island. I assume that means all the buildings, including this one." He lifted the shovel over his shoulder and swung, grunting with the effort. The blade struck the chain with a loud metallic thunk.

The links broke apart, the padlock fell to the porch with a clatter, and the chain dangled.

He kicked the lock aside and grasped the door handle and yanked. The door wrenched open with a loud, protesting squeal of long-unoiled hinges. He grinned and gestured. "After you, m'lady."

His attempt at levity fell flat. Her knees wobbled as she stared into the dark musty interior, preparing herself. After all these years, mice, birds, rats, and raccoons would have moved into the deserted house and left their mark. Inhaling a deep breath, she stepped over the warped threshold.

Pale afternoon sunlight streamed in through the kitchen and living room windows. The worn linoleum floor gleamed as if recently mopped, and the kitchen counter shone. The large oval maple table where the family ate their meals sat in the middle of the room with four matching wooden chairs placed around it. There wasn't a speck of dust or rodent droppings anywhere. Other than a pervasive musty smell, the house was exactly as she remembered.

A flood of memories washed over her as she crossed to the living room. The braided rug, its vivid reds and greens long faded, lay before the plaid-covered, cushioned recliner that was her father's favorite place to read on stormy days. Her mother's embroidered knitting basket, filled with colorful balls of wool, was on the floor beside the wooden rocking chair just as it had always been.

The floor creaked as she shuffled down the dark, narrow hall and paused before her parents' bedroom door. Turning the handle, she forced open the warped door. Just like the rest of the house, the room was clean and tidy. The bed where she'd spent countless hours cuddling with her parents, secure in their love, while her father read her stories of the ancient Greek and Roman gods and their exotic adventures, was made up, the pillows covered in clean pillowcases. The quilt her mother had spent hundreds of hours making in the evenings by the crackling fire was folded neatly on top. The closet door was ajar, revealing a neat row of clothes hanging from rusted, metal hangers. A sob hiccupped in her throat.

"What is it? What's wrong?"

Russ's broad shoulder brushed hers, and the instant jolt of awareness snapped her out of her shock. "This room, the house—" She pointed at the tidy bed. "—nothing's changed. It looked exactly like this the last time I was in here." She swallowed back tears through the tightness in her throat. "How is that possible after all these years?"

He shrugged. "Someone looks after the house, probably the caretaker."

His words hung in the air like smoke. Why had Angus Crawford instructed his caretaker to install the padlock on the front door and keep the house clean?

Why hadn't he let the elements run their course and the house slowly collapse? Had he cared for the long-gone occupants? Was that it?

"This must bring back a lot of painful memories." Russ's voice was a soft husk.

"There's sadness, for sure, but we were happy here." She studied the familiar room. Her father's deep laughter echoed from the shadows. She closed her eyes and saw her mother's warm, loving smile, and her sparkling blue eyes... The image switched to the night she found the house empty and cold, and her terror, knowing something was terribly wrong, that her life had altered forever— She shut down the onslaught of bittersweet memories, spun around, and ran out of the room as if she were being chased by the ghosts of the past.

"Where are you going?" Russ called. "Wait."

Closing her ears to his pleas, tears blinding her eyes, she charged out of the house and stumbled down the creaking steps.

Chapter 17

Russ's heart ached as he watched her escape through the front door. No wonder she was upset. Every inch of the old house must possess poignant memories. Tragedy hung in the air, and the rooms echoed with a cold emptiness. No one had lived in the house for a very long time, yet the place was spotless, untouched since the day the couple vanished. It was as if he were standing in a museum. Or—he shivered—the house was waiting for the occupants to return.

After his mother and father, returning from a holiday in the States, were killed in a car accident when he was fourteen, the pain and anger at their sudden demise had almost destroyed him. Athena's pain had to be a thousand times worse. She'd left her home one morning to play in the forest and returned hours later to a scene of inexplicable loss. The not-knowing ate at her soul and was infinitely worse than the most awful truth.

He retraced his steps down the hall and eyed the other closed door. Unable to rein in his curiosity, he twisted the door handle and, pressing his shoulder against the warped wood, shoved. The door opened with a protesting screech.

A fresh, cool breeze blew through a broken window, mixing with the musty smell of the long-unused room. Faded pink frilly curtains fluttered in the window. The narrow bed was covered with a pink blanket dotted with rainbows and winged, multi-colored ponies. A doll, missing one button-bright eye, rested on a pillow. Except for the broken window, the room was as tidy as all the others.

A loose floorboard squeaked under his weight as he crossed to a wooden bookcase set against the far wall. A collection of rocks, seashells, and small pieces of driftwood lined the top shelf.

The bottom two shelves were jammed with dozens of books of all shapes and sizes, their corners curling from the damp. A stack of dog-eared comic books was piled on the floor beside the bookcase. Board games and puzzles, the boxes covered with patches of mildew, teetered in a crooked stack on the shelf.

A hardcover picture book, the pages yellowed with age, lay open on a pine desk. He flipped to the cover. *A Child's Guide to Greek Mythology*. He riffled through the book. Each page revealed a different Greek god or goddess followed by a brief description. The corner of one page was dog-eared. A drawing of Athena, the goddess of war, wearing a tall crown and carrying a spear in one hand and a shield in the other, filled the page. The head of the Gorgon, Medusa, with writhing snakes for hair, lay at the goddess's feet.

The gruesome drawing would have fascinated a precocious twelve-year old, and it explained the source of Athena's name. She'd been an unusual child; no doubt a product of her unique upbringing on this remote, rugged island. Isolated from her peers, with only adults for company, she'd retreated into books and the heroic stories of the ancient Greek gods.

His mouth twisted in a smile. He'd also been fascinated with the ancient Greek and Roman civilizations. As a boy, he'd read both the *Iliad* and the *Odyssey* by Homer, and he'd devoured books on Greek and Roman history. He'd even named his boat *Minerva* after the Roman goddess of wisdom. Wasn't Athena the Greek counterpart of Minerva? He read the description in the book. Minerva and Athena were the same goddess. One was Roman, and the other Greek. How weird was that?

A love of Greek mythology wasn't the only thing he and Athena had in common. They'd lost their parents at a young age, and they both had connections to Angus Crawford and Shelter Island. If he didn't know better, he'd think a greater power was behind their meeting—some force in the universe that wanted them to be together.

What the hell? He threaded his fingers through his hair. This old house with all its ghosts was getting to him. Athena Reynolds was a beautiful woman. It was only natural he was attracted to her. And then there was her tragic past. He felt sorry for her. Who wouldn't? But that's all it was. There was nothing else between them. Nothing at all. Nor would there ever be.

He strode out of the room and headed back to the living room. What happened here twenty-three years ago? Had the O'Flynns chosen to leave their young daughter behind and start a new life somewhere else like the police thought? Moving to the brick fireplace, he picked up a small clay ornament on the shelf above the fireplace. The crude sculpture of what was maybe supposed to be a clown had obviously been made by a child. The figurine held a place of honor on the mantel. The people who lived in this well-loved home would never have deserted their child.

Not unless they didn't have a choice.

Could Athena be right? Had someone harmed the couple? Angus? He shook his head. No way. He didn't believe his father was involved. But was there someone else?

A large, framed oil painting hanging on the wall by the couch caught his eye, and he moved closer. With bold strokes and a keen eye, the artist had recreated the stunning view from the front window of the little house. The colors were subdued and had faded over time, but the seascape pulsed with life. W. O'Flynn was scrawled across the lower right corner. William O'Flynn. Athena's father had painted the picture.

Yet another trait he and Athena had in common. He'd always wanted to be an artist. He'd taken a few art classes in college but quit after Angus made his opinion clear. Pursuing art was a waste of time. The hard-nosed tycoon refused to pay the expensive tuition. They'd argued for weeks, but in the end, Russ quit the art courses and registered in business school. Five years later, he'd graduated with an MBA.

Angus was pleased. Russ—not so much.

His adoptive father's reluctance to talk about the island now struck Russ as a red flag. Were Athena's suspicions correct? Was Angus somehow involved in her parents' disappearance? Russ had lived with Angus for years, but he was beginning to think he hadn't known him at all. At the time, Russ wasn't surprised by the man's actions. Angus liked his privacy, and he'd refused to give a statement to the press after the O'Flynns' disappearance, even though reporters followed him everywhere he went, shouting questions.

He rubbed the tight knot of muscle in the back of

his neck. So many unexplained mysteries, and so few answers. Nor was there likely to be any resolution now Angus was gone. His tread was heavy as he plodded out of the house.

****

Russ found her down by the beach, standing on the soft, golden sand at the water's edge, staring into the distance. Her arms were crossed over her chest as if she was chilled, and a pall of sorrow stained her tear-ravaged face. Her anguish struck him like a knife to the chest. "Athena." His voice was a hoarse croak. "Athena…" Words failed him. What could he say to reassure her and take away her pain? He couldn't bring her parents back. He couldn't return to her the life she'd so suddenly lost. "I'm sorry."

He cursed under his breath. Could he be any lamer? All the apologies in the world wouldn't help. Only time would heal her wounds. Without stopping to think about the consequences, he wrapped his arms around her and drew her slim, unresisting body close.

Seagulls swooped and dove into the incoming surf, their raucous cries slicing the air like the excited chatter of children. The setting sun vanished behind a bank of menacing, dark clouds. A cold wind gusted, raising tiny swirls of sand and flattening the sea grass. The air was heavy with the tang of fish, salt, and impending rain.

She burrowed into his embrace.

He breathed in her scent—wild roses, spring rain, woman. Her silky red curls tickled his neck, the strands catching in his whiskers. He caressed the length of her back, gliding his hands over the delicate grooves of her spine. Giving in to temptation, he tangled his fingers in the bright halo of curls framing her pale face. Her hair, just as soft as he'd imagined, slipped through his fingers. His breathing quickened, and his blood heated. He tightened his embrace, drawing her closer.

She lifted her head. Her mouth parted, and the dainty tip of her pink tongue emerged as she moistened her lower lip.

His heart rate zoomed into the stratosphere at the same time warning bells clanged in his head. He should release her and run as quickly as he could back to the *Minerva*. But he was just a man, and she was one hell of an attractive woman. He'd wanted this ever since her beast of a dog forced their introduction in that park in Calgary. Groaning, he lowered his head and covered her lips with his.

What began as a gentle tasting deepened as the heat within him burst into flames. He traced the contours of her warm inviting mouth with his tongue, urging her to open.

She mewed and allowed him to plunder her moist heat. Her hands gripped the back of his neck and tangled in his hair.

He deepened the kiss until they were both breathing hard. Smoothing his hands over the rounded firmness of her hips and the impossible narrowness of her waist, he groaned. His heart threatened to beat out of his chest.

Oh man. He wanted her. Bad.

And she wanted him. He wasn't the only one in a state of heat. But this was wrong in all sorts of ways. She was vulnerable. Hell, she'd just seen her childhood home where unimaginable tragedy had struck. She wanted comfort, companionship, a compassionate friend.

He wanted something else entirely.

He should step away, but the sensations rocketing through him were too hot, his need for her too intense. The passion rioting through him made thinking difficult. But the part of his character that ruled his life, the piece that made him the man he was, a man he was proud of, prevented him from acting upon his passion. Gritting his teeth until they ached, he dropped his arms and lurched back.

Her shiny curls were tousled from his fingers, her cheeks flushed, and her lips moist and swollen.

He drew in a ragged breath. Being noble sucked. His body throbbed with burning desire, but he'd done the right thing, the decent thing. Why the hell did acting like an honorable man hurt so damn much?

She held her body stiff and rigid like stone, avoiding his gaze. "I'd like to leave. Please take me back to Vancouver." Turning toward the bank of trees, she strode across the overgrown clearing and into the shadows of the forest.

"Athena, wait."

She ignored his call and kept walking.

Cold emptiness filled him as he trailed after her. He'd give her time to think, to consider everything that had happened. And then they'd talk. Somehow. he had to explain why he couldn't keep his hands off of her. He grimaced. How the hell would he do that when he didn't understand himself?

Chapter 18

She hurried along the overgrown trail, stumbling over roots and half-buried rocks. Tears filled her eyes and streamed down her cheeks, blinding her. She tripped, staggered a few steps, and fell. Her left knee landed on an exposed root, and she let out a yelp. Using her sleeve, she wiped her streaming eyes and scrambled to her feet. Mud caked the knees of her black leggings. Her knee throbbed. She tested her weight on her injured leg and winced.

Hobbling down the path, she soldiered through the pain. A vision of clinging to Russ, thrilling at his touch and welcoming his kisses, flashed before her. She stumbled over a rock and would have fallen again if she hadn't grabbed onto a low-hanging branch.

What was wrong with her? How could she react so strongly to a man she'd met only yesterday? Worse, a man so closely connected to Angus Crawford. Her traitorous body tingled where he'd touched her as if his warm, callused hands had branded her.

She hadn't wanted him to stop. Far from it. She'd ached to dissolve in his arms, to get lost in his caresses, anything to take the edge off her anguish. But the escape from her torment would be temporary. The second the euphoria was over, regrets would return full force. She'd hate herself. Him too, probably, though he wasn't to blame.

Revisiting her old home, that was unchanged after twenty-three years, her family's possessions in the places they'd been left that day, was even harder than she'd expected. The familiar rooms rehashed painful memories and opened old wounds until the walls of the house closed around her and she couldn't breathe. Like a coward, she'd run, fleeing the heartbreak, escaping to the fresh air.

Visiting the island was a mistake. She limped around a fallen tree branch and clambered over a large boulder. Where was the damn trail? She was determined to leave the island, even if she had to swim all the way to Vancouver, but she hadn't paid attention to where she was going. And now she didn't know where she was. She should have reached the beach where they'd left the dinghy by now.

The trees towering over her swayed, creaking and groaning in the face of a rising wind. Dark, ominous clouds filled the sky, and the air was heavy with impending rain. Another gale was on the way. The storm would make it impossible for the *Minerva* to sail back to Vancouver.

"Athena!" Russ's voice echoed through the forest, rising above the screech of wind. He loped along the path, his long legs eating up the distance between them. "Where are you going? You're on the wrong trail." His words puffed out between gasps of air. "This isn't the way to the bay."

She glanced at the unfamiliar surroundings. "I…I didn't realize."

"Another storm's blowing in." He looked up at the patch of sky visible through the thick canopy. A furrow creased between his dark eyebrows. "We're a long way from the bay where we left the dinghy. I don't think we'll make it back to the *Minerva* before the storm hits."

As if to confirm his prediction, the wind rose to a shriek, the heavy, dark clouds burst, and a torrent of rain pelted them. "Come on." He grabbed her hand and tugged her behind him as he trudged down the path.

Limping along the uneven trail, struggling to keep up with his long-legged stride, she bit back a moan, as with each step, her weight landed on her injured knee.

He stopped and peered at her through the driving rain. "What's wrong?" His brow furrowed. "Are you hurt?"

"My knee. I—"

He released her hand, crouched on the mud, and rolled her legging over her knee. Even in the muted light, the discoloration and swelling of her knee was obvious. "Why didn't you tell me?"

Rain streamed in her eyes and plastered her hair to her head. "I...I—"

"Never mind." He stood and, in a single fluid motion, lifted her in his arms.

"What...what are you doing?" She shoved against the wall of his chest. "Put me down."

"You can't walk." He trudged along the narrow, muddy path, carrying her as if she weighed nothing. "Let me help you."

She stopped struggling. He was right. She couldn't walk very fast, and the storm was getting worse. Already her clothes were soaked through, and goose bumps riddled the exposed skin on her arms. Numb from the penetrating cold, she snuggled closer to his warmth.

Rain poured down, and the wind raged as he followed a worn trail through the old-growth forest. He broke through the trees and stopped at the edge of a large, manicured, emerald-green lawn. Lowering her to the grass, he kept his arm around her waist and held her steady.

She wiped the rain from her face, and her blood chilled.

A wide, winding path of crushed oyster shells led to a huge ranch-style house. Set on a grassy hump that overlooked the bay, the graceful lines of the cedar-and-stone cottage with large, gleaming windows fit the rugged landscape like a hand in a glove. A covered deck wrapped around the front of the house flanked by wide, stone steps at either end. A white garden swing sat on the deck, rocking in the wind.

"This is Angus Crawford's cottage." Panic thickened her voice as a blast of memories of the last time she'd been there struck.

"We need shelter from the storm. This is the closest building." He wiped the rain streaming into his eyes with his sleeve.

"But—"

"I didn't think you'd want to go back to your old house. Was I wrong?"

She shivered and shook her head. Her stomach heaved at the thought of those cold, empty rooms.

He tugged her hand. "Come on. Let's get out of this storm."

She pulled back, refusing to budge.

"What is it? What's wrong?" Russ's shirt was plastered to his chest. Rainwater dripped off his dark hair.

Shivers wracked her body.

Whitecaps crested on the choppy water visible through the trees, and large booming breakers crashed onto the rocky shore as if reclaiming the land. Rain poured down, and the wind howled with increasing fury.

Her heart sank. The waves would capsize the small rubber dinghy, so unless they swam to the *Minerva,* they were stuck on the island. If they stayed out in the raging storm they'd freeze.

"Come on. Let's get inside." Russ tugged on her arm, urging her forward.

"I...I..." She bit hard on her bottom lip. What was she afraid of? She wasn't a frightened twelve-year-old child, and he wasn't Angus Crawford.

The warm light of compassion shone in his hazel eyes, turning them liquid gold. "There's nothing to be afraid of. I'm here, Athena, and I'll be with you every step of the way."

His words washed over her like a soothing balm, and the fight drained out of her. "I'm sorry. It's just..." How could she explain her long-held terror of his adoptive father? A frigid blast of air whipped her sodden hair about her face, and icy water dripped down the back of her neck. Her teeth chattered, and shivers wracked her bones. "We'd better get out of this rain."

"Attagirl." Clasping her hand, he helped her across the lawn and up the steps to the covered porch. He reached above the doorframe to a narrow ledge and removed a key. Unlocking the carved wooden door, he turned the handle and opened the door.

She clutched his arm, stopping him. "How did you know where the key was?"

"What?" His brow furrowed.

"I thought the last time you were on the island was years ago. How did you know the key was above the door?"

A sheepish look crossed his handsome face. "I was here a few weeks ago."

"What? You came to the island?"

"After I learned the details of Angus's will, I wanted to check out the island and see what I'd inherited. I hadn't seen the place in years. The lawyer told me where the key to the cottage was hidden. I spent the weekend exploring the island, but I didn't have time to check out the northern part where your old house is." He ran his palm over his hair, slicking the dark, wet curls back from his forehead. "Now, do you have any more questions, or can we go inside and get out of the rain?"

She released her grip on his arm.

He stepped into the house. "Come on."

Inhaling several deep breaths, she inched closer to the open door. *She could do this.* The mantra ran through her head in an endless refrain. *She could do this.* Sucking in a deep breath, she limped through the door and into the house.

The door slammed closed behind her, and she jumped.

"Easy. It's just the wind." He prowled around the large room, opening the heavy drapes, letting in the dim light of the dreary day.

Shivering, she wrapped her arms across her chest. Rainwater dripped from her clothes and puddled at her feet onto the gleaming oak floor. The sweet scents of lemon furniture polish and dried roses permeated the air. Antique tables, their glossy surfaces gleaming, a plush oversized leather couch, and two matching reclining chairs filled the expansive room.

A river-stone fireplace, fronted by a gleaming brass screen, dominated one wall. The spacious hearth was filled with a pile of neatly stacked kindling. A bundle of split firewood, encased in a stylish canvas bin, was set beside the fireplace. Watercolor paintings featuring vibrant seascapes covered the cream-colored walls.

Russ rubbed his hands together as if trying to warm them. "When Angus passed away, I asked the lawyer to keep the caretaker on. It didn't seem right to let the place fall apart."

"The caretaker must look after my old house too."

"We'll have to ask him. I'm sure he'll come by when he sees we're here." He shivered. "I'd better get a fire going before we freeze to death. Why don't you check the bedrooms and see if you can find some dry clothes?" He removed an antique enamel tin from the mantel and tugged a long wooden matchstick free. Crouching before the stack of kindling, he struck the match against the stone hearth and ignited the wood. Flames flickered, promising warmth. He rubbed his hands together in front of the fire. "There's a generator in a shed out back. I'll see if I can start it, and you'll be able to have a hot shower."

In spite of her bone-deep chill and her sodden clothing, she stayed where she was. Angus Crawford's larger-than-life presence was everywhere, from the original artwork lining the walls to the expensive antique furnishings. The thought of searching the cottage for dry clothing made her stomach heave. A bout of shivering released her from her paralysis.

Angus was dead. Freezing to death because she was afraid of a ghost was ridiculous. She limped down the dark hall.

The first door she opened revealed a spacious room filled with a massive, king-size bed covered by a thick burgundy bedspread and matching pillow shams. A hint of cigar smoke and men's spicy cologne scented the air. Several pieces of heavy, dark mahogany furniture shone in the pale light glimmering through the sheer drapes covering the floor-to-ceiling window.

Her breath caught in her throat.

Angus Crawford's bedroom.

Who else but the owner of the cottage would have such a large master suite? She backed out of the room as if poison filled the air and slammed the door. Leaning against the cold wood surface, she struggled to steady her breathing. In spite of the chill of her soaked clothing, perspiration beaded her forehead.

Shaking off the paralyzing fear, she inched along the wide hallway to the next closed door. She clasped the doorknob and opened the door. The room was dark, with not even a hint of light. Edging into the room, she felt along the wall for a light switch. She breathed a sigh of relief when the overhead light flickered on, dispelling the shadows. Russ must have started the generator. If she found some dry clothes, she could locate the bathroom and have a shower. The thought of hot water cascading over her chilled body lent her the courage to step into the room.

A queen-size bed covered with a thick navy quilt and four overstuffed pillows was set beneath a large window. Heavy brown drapes covered the window, shutting out any outside light. A golden pine dresser and matching armoire filled the small room. Unlike the first bedroom she'd stepped into, this room had an impersonal feel and was most likely intended for guests. She grimaced. She couldn't imagine dour-faced Angus Crawford entertaining visitors.

Crossing to the dresser, she slid open a drawer. Folded cotton T-shirts and sweaters filled the drawer. She chose a navy-blue, long-sleeved shirt and held it up. The shirt was a man's large, but the fabric was soft and dry and better than her wet shirt.

The second drawer contained a collection of casual pants. She pulled out a pair of gray sweatpants and prayed the clothes hadn't belonged to Angus Crawford. The image of that elegantly dressed man wearing sweatpants and a T-shirt was ludicrous. He must have kept the clothes in the spare bedroom for guests.

Borrowed clothes in hand, she searched for the bathroom. Like the rest of the cottage, the bathroom was luxurious and contained a jetted bathtub large enough for four people, and a tiled walk-in shower they could all rinse off in after their soak in the tub.

Struggling out of her wet clothing, she wrung her leggings and T-shirt out over the sink and hung them on a towel rack to dry. She twisted on the taps, and in seconds, the room filled with billowing clouds of steam.

Grabbing a bottle of body wash from the glass shelf over the sink, she stepped into the spacious shower and under the warm spray. The hot water streamed over her chilled skin, easing the stiffness in her sore knee. She squirted a handful of soap into her palm, and the soothing scent of lavender filled the stall. She closed her eyes, shut down her mind, and relaxed for the first time since she'd arrived on the island.

The water was cooling when she turned off the tap and stepped out of the shower. Shivering in the chilly room, she grabbed a thick, white cotton towel from a pile on a shelf and dried her body. She tugged the T-shirt over her head and pulled on the sweatpants. The waist gaped, and the fleece pants dragged on the floor and bagged around the legs. The T-shirt hung past her knees. She looked like a child playing dress up in her father's clothes. But they were warm, and that's what mattered.

She wiped the fogged mirror with a corner of the towel and studied her reflection. Her towel-dried auburn hair stood out in wild spikes from her pale face. Shadows were etched beneath her eyes, and an angry-looking scratch from a too-close encounter with a blackberry bramble marred her right cheek. Good thing she didn't care what sort of impression she made. Yeah, good thing she wasn't attracted to Russ.

Liar!

She ignored the snarky inner voice and smoothed the palm of her hand over her hair and pinched her cheeks to add color to her face. Clutching the loose waistband, she opened the bathroom door. Scented steam billowed into the hall as she retraced her steps to the living room.

Chapter 19

The large room had undergone a transformation in her absence. Warm pools of golden light from two antique brass table lamps glowed, and a cheerful fire crackled in the fireplace. A ceramic mug with steam rising from it was set on an end table beside a brown leather recliner. Russ was nowhere in sight.

Settling on the recliner, she curled her legs under her and lifted the steaming cup. The drink smelled yummy—sweet with a hint of cinnamon and velvety rich chocolate. Tiny white marshmallows melted on the surface. She smiled, remembering the countless times her mother had made her hot chocolate sprinkled with a handful of marshmallows as an extra treat.

She blew on the hot liquid and sipped. The cocoa slid down her throat like silk. Tendrils of warmth trickled through her body. She drank again, and a bone-deep lethargy settled over her, and she slumped back on the butter-soft leather and closed her eyes.

"How's the hot chocolate?"

Her eyelids popped open, and her heart skipped a beat.

Russ stood with his back to the fire. His hair was damp, and the dark curls gleamed like ebony under the room's soft lighting. Unlike her, he hadn't had any trouble finding clothes that fit him. His faded blue jeans outlined the powerful muscles of his thighs, and the white, short-sleeved T-shirt clung to his chest, revealing his firm pecs and flat stomach.

The moisture in her mouth evaporated. She fumbled for her cup and gulped the dregs. "The drink's delicious. Thank you. What did you put in the cocoa?"

He grinned. "Something my grandmother used to add to my hot chocolate." His smile widened, and his dimple made an appearance. "It's a family secret."

She sucked in a breath. "You didn't put any alcohol in the drink, did you?"

"No, why? Is that a problem?"

Is that a problem? Yes. No question. "I...I don't drink." She cleared her throat. "I mean...er...I don't drink alcohol." She swallowed. "I...I have a drinking problem." The second the words left her mouth she wanted to snatch them back. The confession hung in the air like a specter, her deepest, darkest secret out in the open. Only Aunt Clara, her boss at work, and the anonymous strangers at her AA meetings were aware of the depth of her struggles. And now she'd told him, a man she hardly knew. A man she wasn't sure she could trust.

He nodded. "Okay."

Okay? That was it? That was his response? She'd bared her soul, and all he had to say was *okay*? "It's not like I—" She stopped. He didn't want to hear all the sordid details of how her recreational drinking after work and binge drinking on weekends had slowly developed into a dependence on alcohol, one that ruled her life for the past three years. No one wanted to listen to her air her dirty laundry.

The silence between them lengthened. The fire crackled and popped, rain pelted the windows, sounding like tiny nails scratching the glass, the wind gusted, and the house creaked.

He cleared his throat. "I see you found something to wear." His gaze raked her from head to toe, and the corners of his mouth twitched as if he were fighting a smile.

She set the empty mug on the table and adjusted the cuffs of her sweatpants where she'd rolled up the legs so they wouldn't drag on the floor. "They're a little big."

He chuckled, his hazel eyes twinkling. "A little?" He swaggered closer and tugged on the baggy gray pants where they dwarfed her slim legs. "Two of you could fit in those pants."

To her surprise, she found herself returning his smile. Their gazes met. Her smile faded, and the air between them sizzled. Her breathing quickened.

His irises deepened to the color of warm molasses. His pupils dilated and reflected the flames of the fire.

The lights flickered, faded to dark, and then flared back on, breaking the spell.

He jerked his gaze away. "Let's hope the generator lasts. It doesn't look like the storm's going to let up any time soon." His voice was a rough husk. "We're going to have to spend the night."

"We're staying here tonight?" She fiddled with the soft cotton of her shirt.

His dark eyebrows arched. "Is that a problem?"

She was spending another night alone with *him*? Just the two of them? She swallowed. Lord help her. He was too damn attractive, and she didn't trust herself. When he smiled at her with those golden eyes, her brain shut down, and her usual restraint and common sense melted away. Look what happened on the beach. One kiss, and she'd made a fool of herself. "We...I...I can't stay here."

"Why not? The generator's running, and we have lots of diesel, so we'll have lights and warmth. I found some food in the pantry, so as long as you'll eat canned stew or chicken noodle soup, we won't starve. And there are plenty of bedrooms. We won't have to share, unless..." His eyebrows arched, his meaning clear.

The heat searing her face ramped up to a four-alarm blaze. He was teasing, trying to ease her discomfort, but he was way off base. She wasn't worried about her maidenly virtue, No. That wasn't the reason for her nervousness. She *wanted* to spend the night with him. *That* was the problem.

"What's wrong then?" He jerked his thumb at the dark, rain-spattered window. "The gale's dangerous. You must remember what these spring storms on the coast are like."

As if proving his point, a loud, ear-splitting crack resounded through the window, followed by a thudding boom that shook the house as a tree gave up its battle in the face of the fierce wind and crashed to the ground.

She shuddered. He was right. With the storm raging, they wouldn't be safe outside. The house was warm and cozy. Only a fool would attempt to leave. She was stuck in Angus Crawford's cottage with Angus's all-too-attractive son. Lord help her. "Okay." Her lips were stiff and wooden as she forced out the single word.

"How about I make us another cup of cocoa? And then we'll see about scraping together some dinner." Without waiting for her reply, he grabbed her empty cup and headed out of the room.

The room felt empty and devoid of energy after he left. She stared into the dancing flames. Staying the night was a mistake. She'd known him two days—a short forty-eight hours—but already she couldn't stop thinking about him. Every nerve in her body tingled with an almost visceral awareness when he was near, and all she could think of was kissing him.

But she couldn't go there. Not again. She'd made one mistake; she wouldn't repeat it. No more kissing Russ, no more falling into his arms, no more lusting after him. That foolishness was done. He seemed like a decent man, but she'd been left a fortune and the business he wanted, while he got a small rocky island in the middle of nowhere. That disparity had to rankle.

The lawyer had told her Russ was contesting the will. Was seducing her his way of convincing her to hand over Angus's estate without the hassle and expense of going to court? If so, he didn't have to bother. She'd followed him to the marina with the sole purpose of informing him she didn't want Angus's estate. The money, the business, everything was his. But instead of leaping at her generous offer, he'd taken her sailing. She threaded her fingers through her damp hair. His reaction didn't make sense. Unless he had an ulterior motive.

His footsteps sounded in the hall, and she sat up, preparing to ask some hard questions. She was a lawyer. A damn good one. She knew how to grill a witness.

Chapter 20

He strode into the room and almost stumbled under the power of her luminous sea-blue eyes. The firelight played over the soft planes of her heart-shaped face and burnished her red-gold hair. His hands shook, and a dollop of hot liquid slopped out of one of the cups and splashed on the floor. *Oh man!* He sucked in a steadying breath.

"Russ?"

He discarded his fantasy of taking her in his arms and kissing her senseless and managed to stumble the last few steps to her chair without making a complete fool of himself. "Careful, it's hot." Her fingers skimmed his when he handed her a cup, and his skin burned at her touch.

He backed away from her all-too-tempting presence and sank onto the couch, keeping a safe distance so he didn't do something idiotic. Setting his mug on the side table before he spilled the hot drink all over his lap, he focused on slowing his racing heart. What was it about her that made him act like a geeky adolescent?

Shaking his head in disgust, he asked the question guaranteed to cool his ardor, "What are your plans?" With those four words, he forgot her soft lips and focused on his anger at Angus's betrayal.

"My plans?"

"You're a wealthy woman now. What are you going to do with your inheritance?"

She pursed her soft lips and blew on her steaming drink.

His heart skipped a beat. Okay, so he was still entranced. The thought of the millions of dollars and the company he'd lost hadn't cooled his passion. Maybe a cold shower would do the trick, or a swim in the bay. The frigid waters of the North Pacific Ocean would shake some sense into him. Either that or kill him.

"I've already told you. I didn't want anything to do with Angus Crawford's money. That's why I followed you to the marina. I was planning to turn everything over to you."

"And now?" He held his breath.

"I don't know. I mean, I still don't want anything from that man, but I'd like to find out why he left me his fortune; why he left me anything at all. I was the daughter of his tenants. I didn't even know him. Not really." Her eyes narrowed, and her penetrating gaze pinned him to the couch. "Do you know why he made his will the way he did?"

"No idea." He struggled to keep the hurt out of his voice. "He led me to believe I'd inherit his money and his business. After my parents died, he took me in. After a year, he offered to make our relationship official and adopted me. I was the closest thing he had to a relative."

"No wonder you're upset." She sat forward, and her breasts swayed under the thin cotton of her blue shirt. "Angus betrayed you."

The realization she wasn't wearing a bra smacked

him like a blow to the solar plexus. Anger fought with desire. The last thing he wanted was her pity. "It was his money. He could do what he wanted with his assets. I'll get over it." He swallowed back the bitter taste of the lie.

"He left you Shelter Island."

"Yeah. Shelter Island, this cottage, and some shares in the company. Lucky me." He shot to his feet and stomped across the room to the window and stared out at the raging storm.

Dark, low-hanging clouds scudded across the sky. The wind howled like a wild beast as the gale blasted the trees. Branches swayed, creaking and snapping. The lawn was littered with fallen limbs and leaves. The waves pounded the shore with a resounding roar.

"He was wrong." Her soft voice reached him over the storm's fury. "You were his son. He should have left you the bulk of his estate. He shouldn't have left me anything."

He turned from the window. "We'll never know what was going through his mind when he made out his will." Suddenly, he was exhausted. The emotional turmoil of the past days overwhelmed him, and it was all he could do to stumble to the couch and sag onto the cushions. He leaned his head back and closed his eyes.

"Jennifer Smythe told me you're contesting the will."

Her voice, all velvet and cream, broke through his exhaustion. He opened his eyes and pinned her with a sharp look. "She told you that?"

"I won't fight you. The estate's yours. All of it."

"You made that offer before." He tightened his jaw. "Are you telling me you were serious?"

She nodded.

He studied her. Suspicion and confusion edged into his lust. Was she for real? He opened his mouth to say something, anything, but the words stuck in his throat. What could he say when she was offering him everything he wanted, everything he'd dreamed of? He rubbed his eyes. Don't be a fool. She was up to something. He couldn't for the life of him figure out what that was, but no question—he couldn't trust her.

The storm raged, but the house was warm and cozy. The only sounds in the large room were the cheerful crackling of the fire and the creaking of the house as the gale force wind buffeted the sturdy walls.

"What will you do with the island?" Her soft voice punctured the tension.

He exhaled. "Sell it, I guess."

"What if I were to offer you a deal?"

"What sort of deal?" He sat up, all tiredness forgotten.

She sipped hot chocolate. "I'll give you my share of Angus Crawford's estate, everything free and clear." The pink tip of her tongue slipped out, and she licked the chocolate from her lips.

He struggled to focus on what she was saying instead of getting lost in thoughts of kissing the chocolate off her mouth. "What do you want in return? How much money?"

"Don't you get it?" She plunked down her cup with a clatter and jumped to her feet. "I don't want anything to do with Angus Crawford's money. His estate is yours. All of it. Every damn penny."

Now she had his full attention. "Why would you do that?" Yes. Why would she give up a thriving business and a fortune worth millions? A thousand conflicting thoughts raged through him. He'd spent his life training so one day he could take over Angus's business. Hell, he'd even gotten that MBA just to make his adoptive father happy. He'd worked hard to help Angus build the company to the success it was today.

At Angus's suggestion, he'd agreed to change his name so the company would remain in the hands of a Crawford after Angus passed. Was it any wonder Russ was shocked when the will was read, and he learned everything he'd worked for had been left to a stranger? Now that stranger was offering him a reprieve. He sat forward. "You're serious, aren't you?"

"You bet I am. That's why I followed you to the marina. I needed to talk to you face-to-face, so you'd know I was serious." She clasped her hands. "What do you think? Will you accept my offer?"

"I'd be a fool not to." Hope flared, but he tamped down his eagerness. Angus had cautioned him that when something sounded too good to be true, it *was* too good to be true. "You do realize what you'd be giving up?"

"I do. Jennifer Smythe explained the full extent of the inheritance."

Maybe she was serious. Maybe she felt guilty for inheriting so much wealth from someone she purported to hate. Yeah, and maybe pigs could fly. He didn't know what her game was, but she was playing him. No one—absolutely no one—gave up a fortune. Two could play her game. He plastered a shit-eating grin on his face. "Then what else can I say? I accept. Thank you."

"There is one condition."

And there it was. He'd known the deal was too

good to be true. There had to be a catch. "What's that?"

A furrow formed between her brows. "I'll sign over my share of Angus Crawford's estate if you'll help me find out what happened to my parents."

He blinked. He'd expected her to demand any number of conditions—his first-born child, the skin off his back, his left nut—but not this. "Why do you think I can help? I'm not a detective."

"You have access to Angus's house, his office, his personal papers, this island. You can search places I can't. You knew him better than anyone."

He studied her, trying to see through her guileless gaze to her real reason for offering such a one-sided arrangement. "What if I can't find what you're looking for? Will that void the deal?"

"The police didn't find answers, nor did the private investigator my aunt hired." Tears welled in her eyes. "No one found out anything; yet my parents vanished without a trace." She wiped the back of her hand over her eyes. "Someone kidnapped my mother and father, or murdered them, I don't know, but something bad happened. I want to—" She licked her bottom lip. "—I *have* to find out what happened."

"I'm not a trained investigator. Why do you think I'd have any better luck solving the mystery of their disappearance?" He shook his head. "It's been twenty-three years. Any evidence would have long since been destroyed." He hated to dash her hopes, but what she was asking was impossible. Whatever occurred on the island that long-ago day would forever remain a mystery. He couldn't accept her offer and not uphold his end of the bargain.

He wanted to. Damn straight he did. But he

wouldn't.

"The police didn't know Angus, not like you did. You lived with him." The pulse in her throat fluttered like a hummingbird's delicate wings. "You're my last hope. If you search Angus's papers, check his filing cabinets at his office and his home, maybe you'll find something that'll prove he was responsible for what happened to my parents."

What she was asking was impossible. He'd loved Angus. There was no way in hell his father harmed her parents.

The ridiculous pants bagged around her ankles and pooled at her feet. The tips of her bare toes peeked out. She steepled her hands in a pleading gesture. "Will you help me, Russ? Can I count on you?"

He couldn't tear his gaze from the earnest appeal in her sapphire eyes, and he struggled to swallow over the stone stuck in his throat. God help him. He wanted to say yes, but he seriously doubted he could help. "Okay. You have a deal." He caught his breath. What the hell? Had he just agreed to help her solve a twenty-three-year-old mystery? What was he—one of the Hardy boys? Was he that entranced by her bedroom eyes?

Oh man. He was in some deep shit.

"I knew I could count on you." Her cheeks flushed. The soft mounds of her breasts swayed against the thin material of the T-shirt.

He struggled to breathe, shoved his libido down, and focused on her astounding offer. "I'll do what I can to help you find what happened to your parents, but I refuse to accept Angus's money or his company." He scrubbed his hand over his whiskers. Had he lost his frigging mind? She'd offered him everything he ever wanted, and he turned her down?

A look of bewilderment crossed her pretty face. "I told you I don't want Angus Crawford's money. Or his business."

"You shouldn't make such a big decision until you've talked to a lawyer." He was giving up his chance of retaining Angus's company, but it was the right thing to do.

"I am a lawyer."

He blinked. "Are you? I didn't know."

She nodded.

"Still, you should discuss this with an estate lawyer. Aside from the funds Angus left you, his business is worth a hell of a lot. Only then will you understand the full scope of what you'd be giving up."

"Okay." She nodded again. "I'll talk to the lawyers, and then I'll give you back your company. Either that or I'll sell the company and donate the money to charity."

He rolled his eyes at her stubborn persistence. Was she for real? Was she willing to give him everything she'd inherited if he helped her with her hopeless quest?

Her chin jutted out, and her mouth set in a firm line. "You don't sound like you want the money. Why is that?"

He shrugged. For the life of him he couldn't figure his reasons out either. He should accept her proposition and run like hell before she came to her senses. She'd offered him the world he dreamed of, the one he'd been led to believe was his right, and he'd turned her down.

Chapter 21

Athena shuffled along the dark hallway and into the living room. Faint traces of light filtered around the edges of the curtains covering the two large picture windows. Had the storm passed? Would they be able to leave in the morning?

A part of her wished that after Russ had shown her to a spare room and helped her make up the bed, he'd stayed with her. But like a gentleman, or an Eagle Scout, he'd said good night and left to sleep in Angus's old room.

She'd crawled into the comfortable bed and slipped under the covers. Alone. A thousand thoughts, mainly about Russ, whirled through her mind. From the moment she saw him in Beaton Park, he'd caught her attention. He was one fine-looking hunk of a man. Over six feet of lean, sculpted muscle, dark, curly hair, mesmerizing hazel eyes, and when he smiled... She blew out a breath.

She crossed to the window and swept the heavy drapes aside. The cold light from a full moon shone through scattered clouds. The wind still raged, but its force had weakened. Broken branches littered the manicured lawn, and puddles glimmered in low-lying dips on the shell path. A shadow detached from the gloom under the trees, and a figure—a person? a large animal?—darted across the lawn, disappearing behind the thick trunk of a cedar tree.

A frisson of unease trickled along her spine. She pressed closer to the window, her breath fogging the glass.

The trees swayed, their branches waving in the wind, and dark shadows shifted within the thick undergrowth.

What had she seen? A deer? The island used to have lots of deer. Her mother was in a constant battle to keep the ravenous beasts away from her vegetable garden. She stared at the dark patches under the towering trees. All was still, but the unsettling sensation someone—or something—was out there in the dark watching, set her on edge.

She shivered and snapped the curtains closed. She was imagining boogeymen where none existed. No wonder, with all that had happened these past stressful days. She was exhausted and emotionally drained. A drink would help. The second the craving sneaked into her brain, she couldn't stop thinking about alcohol. Had Angus been a drinker? Maybe there was a bottle stored somewhere in the cottage. Only one way to find out.

The house loomed around her, cold and silent, and she shivered, wishing she'd worn the heavy sweatpants instead of just the voluminous cotton T-shirt. The cottage gave her the creeps. She didn't like being alone in the dark at the best of times, but she'd walk through the very gates of Hell and face Cerberus, the three-headed dog who kept in the damned, if it meant she could have a drink. Just one sip of rye, rum, vodka…anything. Lord knew, she wasn't fussy.

Where would a man like Angus keep his liquor? Not in the living room. She'd have noticed last night.

The kitchen? Or would he have a room dedicated to storing his fancy liquor collection? Some wealthy people did that. Her mouth watered at the thought.

The hallway was dark, but she didn't turn on the lights. A floorboard creaked beneath her bare feet, and she froze. The last thing she needed was to wake up Russ. She didn't want him to witness her desperation. Or maybe being with Russ was just what she needed. His sexy presence would switch her single-minded drive for a drink to something else—like kissing him.

Except for her rapid breathing, the cottage was silent and still. Placing one careful foot in front of the other, she shuffled down the dark hall. There. Just ahead. A closed door. Another bathroom? A study? Studies often had liquor cabinets. Her hand shook as she turned the knob.

The door opened on silent hinges onto a dark room. Feeling along the smooth wall, she found a light switch. Blinding light filled the room, revealing a gleaming teak desk and a large leather chair. Seascapes lined the white walls. A teak credenza, the type of cabinet where people kept their liquor bottles, was against the far wall, a neat stack of highball and wine glasses set on the top.

Yes!

She crouched before the cabinet and swung open the door. A large cardboard box filled the dark space. She tugged it out and set the heavy box on the floor. Lifting the lid, she peered inside. Instead of a row of gleaming liquor bottles, the box was filled with stacks of photographs.

Disappointed, she hefted the box to lift it back into the cabinet but stopped and set the box down with a thump. She picked up a photograph, her breath whooshed out as if she'd been punched, and she fell back on her butt. The picture slipped from her fingers and fluttered to the floor, landing faceup.

The photograph was black and white, three inches by five inches. A young girl, her hair bound in tight braids, sat on a weathered log in the candid photo. A collection of seashells lay on the sand in front of the girl. A look of happiness shone on her heart-shaped, freckled face.

The room swirled and tilted, and Athena closed her eyes. When she opened them again, the face in the photo hadn't changed. *She* was the girl in the photograph.

A bone-numbing chill settled over her, and she lifted out another photograph. And another, and another until the floor was littered with pictures. The photos, taken over a number of years as the child aged from a young toddler to a girl on the edge of adolescence, had a single subject—her. No one else was in the photos. Just her. She swallowed, but her throat had gone to sand.

The pictures looked as if they'd been taken from a distance, as if the photographer had used a telephoto lens. Her open expression and relaxed posture made clear she was unaware her picture was being taken. Another shiver rippled through her, and she rubbed the goose bumps on her arms.

Who had taken the photographs? Her parents had owned an old camera, and over the years they'd taken her picture at Christmas, birthdays, and picnics. She had an old photo album filled with photos of her and her family. But neither her mother nor her father had taken the pictures she'd found in this little room. She was certain of that.

Someone had spied on her, clicking pictures, as she played, unaware she was being watched. She shuddered, but no matter where she looked, she couldn't escape her own face. A cry slipped from between her lips and filled the room like the wail of a wounded dog.

"Athena? What the hell's going on?" Russ stood in the doorway. Deep lines furrowed his brow. He crossed the room in a single stride and crouched before her. "I heard you cry out."

A tear dripped off her chin and landed on the blue cotton of her shirt. She swiped the back of her hand over her face.

"Athena, answer me. Why are you crying?"

"I…I didn't mean to wake you. I…I…" She looked over his broad shoulder, and the nightmare reality of the photos struck her again. Fresh tears welled in her eyes. "Look…" She gestured at the piles of photos tossed across the floor. "The photographs…"

He picked up a picture, and then a second photo. After an eternity, he met her gaze. "What is all this?"

She shook her head. "I don't know."

"Is this you?" He gestured at a color photograph of a red-haired toddler playing in the surf.

She nodded.

He pointed at another picture. "You?"

Again, she nodded.

"All these pictures are of you?" A small pulse beat in his jaw. "Did your parents take them?"

"I…I don't think so." She stood and on shaky legs wobbled across the room and picked up an eight-by-ten photo and held it up. "My parents vanished when I was twelve." She jabbed the picture. "I remember this shirt. My aunt gave it to me for my *thirteenth* birthday."

The lines in his rugged face hardened. "Why are the photos in Angus's cottage? Why would he have them? I thought you said you hardly knew him."

Was that suspicion darkening his hazel eyes? "I...I didn't know him. I hardly ever saw him, and when he came around, I hid." She wrapped her arms tight over her chest. Memories of how uncomfortable Angus Crawford had made her feel chilled her. She hadn't encountered him often, and only in the company of one or both of her parents, but when she did, his cold, penetrating gaze studied her as if he were examining every detail. Even as a young child, his unwanted attention filled her with unease. "He scared me. He never smiled, and he always seemed angry."

"If that's the case, why would he have all these photos?"

Her head pounded. "He took them. He must have." She shuddered and wrapped her arms across her chest. "This was his cottage. He stored the pictures in the box in *his* den. Who else would have done it?"

Russ shoved a dark curl off his forehead. "I didn't even know he owned a camera. I haven't found one in the house." He prowled around the small room, stooping to pick up a photo, studying it, and then tossing it back on the floor. "You're the only subject in all these pictures." He scrubbed his hand over his face, the rasp of whiskers loud in the small room. "It's almost as if he stalked you."

Pressing the pads of her fingers to her temples, she rubbed, hoping to ease the shooting pain. "Look...look at this." She pointed at an eight-by-ten-inch color photograph. Her nine-year-old self grinned up at her from the floor. She held a red plastic pail in one hand and a small toy shovel in the other. A sandcastle was in the background. "How did Angus get this picture? I was afraid of him. I'd never have been so relaxed if he was around. He must have hidden in the forest and used a telephoto lens."

She indicated another photo. "And this one." The picture showed her as a young girl of fourteen or fifteen, all gangly legs and arms, sitting on a large rock. Her head was bent over a book, her red hair hanging over her face as she read. A field of brilliant yellow mustard plants was visible in the background. "This photo was taken when Aunt Clara and I lived in Regina. I'm sure of it."

She stumbled over to the box and, with a shaking hand, plucked out another picture. In the photo she grinned a gap-toothed grin and carried a doll in her thin arms. A chill rippled through her. "I remember that doll." She licked her lips. "Mom and Dad gave her to me for my seventh birthday." She blinked back tears. "I named her Patsy. I packed her everywhere." Her heart skipped a beat and flopped with a thud in her chest. "Why did Angus take these pictures? Why did he follow me? What did he want?"

Russ paced around the room, stopping every few seconds to inspect a photograph before moving on to another. "He wanted the photos for himself. Why else would he store them in that box and keep them in this room? This was his study. When he brought me to the island when I was a kid, I wasn't allowed in here, and he spent a lot of time in this room. He wanted these pictures somewhere he could look at them any time;

somewhere no one else would see them."

His words sent a spike of unease straight to her gut. All those times she'd thought she was alone, and Angus Crawford had been lurking nearby, spying on her, and taking his invasive photos.

Russ enfolded her in his arms and held her close. "This must be disturbing, but I promise you we'll get to the bottom of these pictures."

She burrowed into his embrace and gave in to the fear she'd been fighting to hold at bay. Her tears flowed, dampening his smooth, warm skin. Time stood still as she remained locked in his arms and breathed in his tangy male musk.

He cupped the back of her head with his palm, and his golden gaze fixed on her. "I can only imagine how you're feeling." He wiped a tear from her cheek with the pad of his thumb. "These photos are wrong in every way imaginable, but they were important to Angus." His jaw tightened. "I'll find out why he took them. I don't know how, but somehow I will." Determination blazed from his eyes.

Relief she wasn't in this nightmare alone washed over her. "Thank you."

"Don't thank me. Not yet, not until I figure this out."

"You will."

His gaze narrowed. "You're that certain?"

"I am." She nodded. "You'll find the answers to these photographs, and you'll find out what happened to my parents." She didn't know him well, but she knew one thing—he was a man of his word.

And he'd promised.

Chapter 22

"You've had a shock." Russ's voice was a deep, soothing rumble. "You're exhausted. Come on. I'll take you back to bed." He grasped Athena's hand and led her out of the room with its disturbing photos and into the dark hall.

A hundred thoughts fired at once. Her unease at being in Angus Crawford's cottage, the discovery of the shocking photos, Russ's nearness...all blended together in a continuous, confusing blur.

"Come on." He tugged her hand. "It's been a long night. We'll deal with the photographs in the morning after we've had some rest."

She stumbled after him down the dark hallway.

"Here we are." He released her hand and reached over her and flipped a switch on the wall. The ceiling light blazed, illuminating her bedroom. The sheets on the bed were twisted in a tangle. A pillow lay on the floor where she'd tossed it in her frustration at not being able to sleep. Her sweatpants were crumpled in a heap on a chair.

He picked up the pillow and set it on the bed and straightened the sheets. "Climb in." He nodded at the bed. "I'll cover you."

As if she were an obedient child, she shuffled to the bed and sat on the edge.

"Attagirl. Now lie down and relax."

She lay back and rested her head on the pillow.

He tugged up the covers, smoothing them under her chin. "I'll get you a glass of water, and then you should try and sleep." He strode out of the room.

Turning on her side, she drew her knees to her chest, as image after image of the disturbing photographs flashed through her mind like an old movie reel. She squeezed her eyes closed, but shutting her eyes didn't stop the images. The brush of a gentle hand on her shoulder startled her, and she sat up with a start.

For the first time she noticed what he was wearing…a pair of red-and-black striped, silk boxers.

Nothing else.

Even in her state of numbed shock, a part of her melted. His hair was disheveled, and his eyes heavy lidded from sleep. He was all virile male. Sweet mother of God. He was so close his enticing masculine scent filled the air. If she shifted her hand a couple of inches, she'd touch him, feel his heated skin. Another inch closer, and she could run her fingers through the silky dark hair covering his chest and arrowing in an intriguing vee down his flat abdomen, disappearing into the waistband of his boxers. His cute red-and-black striped underwear.

Oh man.

Russ handed her a glass. "Drink this. You'll feel better."

"Th…thanks." She grasped the glass with shaking hands and sipped. The cold water slid down her parched throat like silk, and she gulped again. Once the glass was empty, she handed it back.

Their fingers grazed, and their gazes met and held.

The scratching of rain pelting the window and the

creaks and groans of the gale-force wind gusting against the house were loud in the ensuing silence.

He tore his gaze from hers and backed up two steps as if he were afraid.

Of what? Her? Of the heated desire percolating through the room, thickening the air, making breathing impossible, let alone clear, rational thinking?

"Goodnight." He glanced at his watch. "Or I suppose I should say, good morning. It's almost dawn." He yawned. "I'm beat. I hope you're able to sleep." He turned to leave.

"Russ." She prayed he didn't hear the aching hunger in the thin husk of her voice.

He paused by the door. His dark brows arched. "What is it?"

"Please don't leave. I don't want to be alone." She bit hard on her tongue to prevent any more foolish words escaping.

A slew of emotions clouded his hazel eyes. His jaw worked, and his Adam's apple bobbed in his strong throat.

"Please." The damning word spilled out, drowning the inner voices warning her this was a mistake. One she'd regret. "I don't want to be alone. Not tonight."

Never taking his gaze from hers, he set the empty glass on the dresser and strolled to the bed. "Are you sure?" His voice was a throaty rasp, as if the sound came from deep in his chest.

She bit her bottom lip. *Was she sure*? Hell no. She was terrified. Of him. Of her strong feelings for him. Of where this—whatever *this* was—could lead. But she didn't want to be alone. Of that she *was* certain. "Yes. I'm sure."

He nodded, but still didn't budge.

Seconds turned into minutes, minutes into eons.

She held her breath.

He perched on the edge of the mattress, his body stiff and rigid. The veins in his arms bulged, his hands fisted at his sides.

A foot of empty bed separated their bodies, but the distance might as well have been a mile.

She drew in a shaky breath, and then another, and another.

Anticipation, expectation, doubt, and fear hung thick and heavy in the air.

Would he make a move?

Would she?

Should she?

****

This is a mistake!

The warning blazed through him like a lightning bolt. He wanted her all right. Damn straight he did. She drove him crazy with her beseeching blue bedroom eyes. He couldn't remember desiring a woman so much. Kissing her sweet lips on the beach, tasting her, breathing her in, had damn near brought him to his knees. And he wanted more.

The cells in his body had demanded he deepen the kiss and take what he so desperately wanted, but somehow, he'd dug deep and found the strength to release her and step away. The hardest thing he'd ever done.

Bar none.

Only a crazy man would have stopped kissing her. But he had. He'd lifted his mouth from hers and backed away, and nearly bitten his tongue off biting back a groan of regret. But that was his libido talking. Once he wasn't kissing her, and cool air settled between them, his brain started functioning. Taking her on the cold sand would have been wrong in so many ways. She was vulnerable and wanted comfort and reassurance, not raw primal sex.

Nothing had changed since that kiss on the beach. If anything, she was more vulnerable. Who wouldn't be after finding those photos? He clenched his hands to stop from reaching for her.

The bed shifted, and the mattress springs creaked. "Russ?"

Her soft voice washed over him like liquid honey, adding fuel to the fire burning deep in his gut. "What is it?"

The bed creaked again, and she sat up, leaning her back against the pillows. "Would...would you kiss me again?"

Heat streaked through his body like liquid fire. Had the world shifted on its axis? Had the heavens realigned? Had he heard her right? "What?"

"I...I asked you to kiss me."

The old saw was wrong. Lightning could strike twice in the same place. Miracles did happen. She wanted him to kiss her. Oh man. He was a fool if he gave in to his desires. He'd regret kissing her, but what red-blooded man could resist? Knowing what he was about to do was wrong, no matter which way he sliced it, he shifted closer and slipped his hand behind her neck. Lowering his head, he breathed in the sweet fragrance of her skin and claimed her mouth.

At the first brush of her lips, heat streaked through him like lightning. He sank into the kiss, teasing her mouth open with his tongue. His blood thickened and pooled low in his belly. His limbs grew heavy, and his breath rasped in and out. He drew her nearer until her breasts flattened against the hard wall of his chest. Alarm bells clamored through him in a frantic refrain. Kissing her, touching her, wanting her, was a mistake. But in that moment, he couldn't stop.

But then he did.

He broke off the kiss. Even more unbelievable, he spoke the words guaranteed to ruin any chance of kissing her again. "We need to stop before we do something we'll regret."

"You're right." She slid her soft fingers through his chest hair.

He sucked in a sharp breath and placed his hand over hers, halting her teasing touch. "I...I can't think when you touch me." *Think*? Oh, he was thinking all right, just not with his brain. He blew out a ragged breath. "I...I want to do the right thing, but I can't, not...not when you're so close."

"Just this once, don't be an Eagle Scout." She stroked his cheek. "I need you. I want to forget that room and those awful pictures." She kissed his chin, her mouth soft and warm against his skin. "Let's forget the world and what's right or wrong and just enjoy this moment."

His breath gusted out in a rush of air. Was she saying what he thought she was saying? He was ready. More than ready. But that annoying little voice in what was left of his functioning brain pinged an alarm, and he opened his damn mouth...again. "We're not doing this because you want to forget those photos. You don't need me for that. A sleeping pill would work just as well." He pulled back, putting space between them.

She studied him with wounded eyes.

Struggling to stick to his resolve, he rolled out of the bed and stood, keeping his back to her.

"Russ?"

He didn't want to look, tried his damnedest not to turn around, but he was flesh and blood and infinitely weak. So damn weak. He turned.

She met his gaze. "Make love with me."

The floor dropped out from beneath his bare feet. He sank back down on the bed and reached for her.

He was in deep, deep trouble.

Chapter 23

She wanted oblivion, but more than escape, she wanted him. Not just the primal relief sex offered, but *him,* Russell Crawford.

Once again, he pulled away from her embrace. "We shouldn't do this. Not now."

She bit back her frustration. "Why not?" Did she have to throw herself at him? Oh, wait—too late. She'd already begged him to make love. His reluctance was definitely not good for a girl's ego. Not good at all.

He threaded his fingers through his hair. "I don't have any protection."

She blinked. "You don't have anything?" She certainly didn't. The last time she'd had sex was so long ago, any condoms she'd bought would have long passed their expiration date.

He grimaced. "Not here. I have some on the boat, but not with me, and somehow, I doubt Angus kept any around."

His mention of Angus Crawford doused her passion like a blast of frigid water from a fire hose. She jolted free of his arms and sat up. "That's probably for the best." Even to her own ears, her voice sounded stiff.

"Look. I'm sorry, but this doesn't mean I don't want you." His eyes darkened. "You know that, right?"

She twisted her hands together in her lap. "You're right. We're adults. We don't want to do anything foolish."

"You little liar." He drew her closer, capturing her mouth with his.

A riot of sensations rocketed through her. *Damn, she wanted this man.*

He pulled back, his warm, chocolate-scented breath brushing her face. "Can we spend the night together?" He shook his head. "Not making love, though that would be awesome, but—" His throat worked. "—we could just hold each other. Would that be okay?"

She stared into his golden eyes, and her heart melted. He wanted to *cuddle*? With no possibility of sex? Wow! He really was an Eagle Scout. "I...I'd like that."

His smile widened, and the dimple in his lean cheek peeked out. "All right." He gathered her in his arms and pulled her close, tucking her head under his chin.

Strands of her hair caught in his whiskers, and the heat from his body engulfed her. She snuggled closer. Outside the window, the storm raged, but inside the dark, quiet room, wrapped in this man's arms, for the first time in years, she felt safe. "Mmmm. This is nice."

His chuckle rumbled deep in his chest. "Not too shabby." He planted a soft kiss on the top of her head. "Not too shabby at all."

"Thank you." Her voice was a whisper of sound.

"For what?"

"For this, for being here with me, for agreeing to help." She gulped. "Just thanks."

He smoothed the palm of his hand over her back. "So, tell me why you don't drink alcohol."

She stiffened. "You want to talk about that *now*?"

She didn't discuss her drinking issues. Not with anyone, not with her co-workers, not even with her closest friends. Even Aunt Clara had had to pry the truth out of her. How could she explain without coming across as pitiful?

He rubbed his callused fingers across her skin, his light sweeping strokes soothing. "Maybe you'd feel better if you did."

She chewed on her bottom lip and winced at the raw tenderness from his passionate kisses. What did she have to lose by revealing the truth? After he returned her to the mainland, and she signed over Angus Crawford's estate, she wouldn't see him again. They lived in different cities, hundreds of kilometers apart.

She inhaled a shaky breath. "I…I started drinking when I was thirteen, sneaking wine and hard liquor from my aunt's cupboard. I hung around outside liquor stores and convinced people to buy me booze so I could party with my older friends who drank." She grimaced. "Cliché, right? I guess I was trying to deaden the pain over the loss of my parents."

He tucked a curl behind her ear. "Did the alcohol work?"

She shook her head. "Not really, but I didn't stop. I was the life of the party. You know, the girl who could outdrink anyone. I was a champion. The boys thought I was pretty cool. So did I."

He continued his soothing caresses, holding her close, giving her the chance to spill her secrets.

"When I moved away from home to go to college and lived in a dorm, my drinking wasn't a problem. It was under control. At least I thought it was. I got drunk most nights, but I made it to my classes every morning.

I drank heavily all through law school. It's a miracle I passed." Now she'd begun, the hideous truth spilled out. "When the blackouts started, I'd wake up hungover, not knowing what I'd done the night before. Sometimes I wasn't even sure where I was." A sob hitched in her throat, but she swallowed it back.

"Soon I wasn't just drinking at night. I needed some hair of the dog in the morning and another shot of booze at lunch just so I could make it through the day. There were so many days when I lay in bed, and I didn't know if the sun was up or it was night, and the sky was dark. And I didn't care."

Tugging free of his embrace, she flopped onto her back and stared at the ceiling, willing away the burn of tears. "At first, I blamed everyone else." She swallowed. "You know, it's not my fault. Poor me. I need this drink because my parents abandoned me." Her mouth twisted. "I had a dozen excuses." The familiar sour taste of disgust filled her mouth. "Somehow I managed to get my degree, but the situation wasn't pretty."

The bed creaked as he shifted onto his elbow and stared down at her. "But you did it. You stopped drinking."

"Not at first, and not for a long time." She shrugged. "Not until Otis came into my life."

"Your dog?"

She nodded. "When I found him in that back alley, his fur was matted and dull, and his ribs were sticking out. He had a wound on his hindquarters as if someone had kicked him." She twisted the sheet into a knot. "He was so happy to see me, so loving, so trusting. He gave me a reason to stay sober and get up every day so I could feed him and take him for walks."

Russ chuckled. "He's quite a character, all right."

"But I still drank. Not all the time. I was trying to quit, but quitting wasn't easy." The sheet was in a knot. She forced her fingers to relax. If she kept ripping at the fancy material, she'd tear the high-thread-count silk. "My aunt encouraged me to go to AA, and my boss ordered me to get sober and stay that way." She met his gaze for the first time since she began her sordid tale. "You'd like Clara. She's a force of nature. Once she sets her mind on something, it happens. No choice about it."

He laid his hand on her hip.

She squirmed away. Might as well tell him all the details, the whole squalid saga. "I attended meetings, and they helped. Knowing I wasn't alone in my struggle was important. But I still drank." She heaved a breath. "Not like I used to. Not every day. I'd be sober for two days, sometimes even up to a week, but I always drank again.

"The longest I stayed sober was twenty-one days." She sniffled and wiped her damp eyes with a corner of the sheet.

"Twenty-one days is pretty good. That's three weeks. You should be proud of yourself." He caressed her arm.

She stiffened. She didn't deserve his compassion. "You don't understand. I broke that record the day I met you in the park." There. She'd told him. The truth was out in the world, warts and all.

"You were drunk?"

"No, but I did have a drink."

The bed bounced as he shifted closer. He smoothed

a lock of hair back from her damp face. "But you stopped. You only had the one drink."

"But I ruined my twenty-one days of sobriety."

He tilted her head so she faced him. "Thank you. I know telling me this wasn't easy."

She couldn't speak over the lump in her throat, so she nodded.

"I admire you."

She'd expected disgust, pity, any number of reactions, but not admiration. "Why?"

"You recognized you had a problem, and you're doing something about it. Not everyone does that."

"But—"

He placed a finger over her mouth, silencing her. "Getting sober is hard. I know people with drinking problems, close friends of mine. I've seen them struggle. You're trying. That's what counts."

She shivered at the rasp of his callused finger trailing across her cheek. "But—"

"Shhh." Again, he silenced her. "You're going to beat this. I know you will."

His faith in her warmed her soul, but it was misplaced. "I'm an alcoholic, Russ. It's not a disease you cure overnight. I'll always be an alcoholic, and I'll probably drink again. Falling off the wagon is inevitable."

He teased the skin on her neck with the pad of his thumb. "Now I understand why you're so determined to find the answers to what happened to your parents."

"I guess I'm hoping if I find out the truth, I'll have closure, and I won't have to deaden the pain with alcohol."

He nodded. "Okay. I'm in. I'll help you. No

promises that we'll find any answers, but I'll do my best."

"I didn't tell you of my drinking problem so you'd feel sorry for me." She didn't want his pity.

He grinned, and the dimple she found so irresistible popped out.

"Sorry is definitely not what I'm feeling." His eyes smoldered. "Athena Reynolds, you are one beautiful woman, inside and out. I want to kiss you more than I want my next breath. Is that okay?"

Okay? This was perfect. *He* was perfect. She smiled and nodded.

Chapter 24

Daylight seeped in through the gaps along the edges of the heavy curtains covering the window, and the dark bedroom was warm and cozy. The rain had stopped an hour before, and the gusts of wind buffeting the cottage had eased.

Athena slept on her side, her body molded to his. One arm was draped over his stomach, the other bent beneath her head. Her eyes were closed, and her long eyelashes swept her sleep-flushed cheeks. A gentle snore escaped her parted mouth.

Russ breathed in the smell of the lavender-scented body wash she'd used. Unable to stop himself, he traced his finger along the swell of her breast. Something fluttered low and deep in his chest, something he'd never experienced before. He tightened his embrace, never wanting to let her go. She felt right, smelled right, and fit his body like she was made for him.

When he met her in that park in Calgary, he'd found her attractive. Hell, yeah. But then he'd received the call from the lawyer informing him she'd tracked down the elusive Margaret O'Flynn. His plans for romance ended, and he'd hopped on the next plane for Vancouver.

How could he have known the woman in the park was the conniving, avaricious bitch who'd stolen his inheritance? His face heated as he recalled how he'd stormed out of the lawyer's office, determined to fight her for Angus's millions. But then she'd tracked him down. You could have knocked him over with a feather when he stood up from repairing the hatch cover and saw her standing on the wharf. He was even more shocked when she told him why she'd followed him.

Of course, he hadn't believed her. Only a fool would give up a fortune to a complete stranger, and she wasn't a fool. He'd known that five minutes after he met her. Intelligence shone from her clear blue eyes. She was up to something. He was certain of that. And so, he'd invited her for a sail, hoping to get to the bottom of the mystery.

He hadn't counted on the physical attraction between them and the ensuing complications, but he should have seen it coming. She was a beautiful woman. He was a healthy, virile male. Put the two of them together on an isolated island in the middle of a raging storm, and the outcome was predictable.

He'd surprised himself. Even with the possibility of sex off the table, he still wanted her close, content to hold her in his arms, touch her soft skin, and kiss her sweet lips. Sure, he wanted to take the physical relationship further, but he had his personal standards— no unprotected sex, not ever.

She muttered something unintelligible in her sleep.

He smoothed her hair back from her face, soothing her, easing her restless dreams. She'd opened up and revealed her innermost secret. Hard to imagine she struggled with alcohol addiction. Not that he blamed her. She was dealt a poor hand. Losing your parents was hard at any age, but to have them vanish without any explanation must have been hell. No wonder she took to alcohol as an escape.

He'd had a few run-ins with drugs and alcohol after his parents' accident. If it hadn't been for Angus, who knew what would have happened? His adoptive father took Russ under his wing and guided him through his grief. Instead of drinking, Russ focused on sports. Hard to be an all-star athlete if you were drunk or stoned.

Athena had mentioned an aunt who supported her. And there was her dog. He smiled. The longhaired, tail-wagging mountain of a beast was quite a character. If Otis hadn't darted across the trail in front of him, Russ wouldn't have crashed his bike. He wouldn't have met Athena until the confrontation in the lawyer's office. And wouldn't that have been a shame? He yawned, his muscles relaxing, as he tucked her head under his chin and closed his eyes.

****

She awoke slowly, feeling rested for the first time in ages. She stretched and opened her eyes. The bed beside her was empty. The only indication Russ had slept there was the slight indentation on the pillow. An image of him holding her close, and the steady reassuring beat of his heart, rose before her. She touched her lips, swollen from his passionate kisses.

A rush of heat seared her cheeks. What had come over her? She'd begged him to stay and make love with her. Even worse, she'd told him about her drinking problem. Instead of recoiling in disgust from her sordid tale of weakness and regret, he'd told her he admired her.

Sitting up, she threaded her fingers through her hair, grimacing at the tangled snarls. Talk about bed head. The curtains were open, and bright sunlight streamed through the window, revealing a clear blue sky. The branches of the towering cedar and Douglas fir trees were still. The storm had passed, and the day was beautiful. The ocean would be calm, and they could row the rubber raft to the *Minerva* and sail back to Vancouver.

A tinge of regret tightened her chest. She should be thrilled she was leaving Shelter Island and all the disturbing memories, but leaving the island meant saying goodbye to Russ. She almost wished the storm would return so they'd be forced to spend another day—and night—together.

She quashed the ridiculous idea. There was no future with Russ. Not for her. Not in the way she wanted. She promised him she'd sign over her rights to Angus Crawford's fortune. In exchange, he'd agreed to search through Angus's house, office, and personal files and see if there was anything that would explain what happened to her parents.

She was a fool if she thought he was helping her for any reason other than he wanted Angus Crawford's business and the money, and he was prepared to do anything to get them. She needed to face the truth. His kindness last night involved greed, a way to stay on her good side and ensure she didn't change her mind.

They were both using each other. He wanted Angus's estate. She wanted answers to her parents' disappearance. He had access to Angus's personal files that no one else had. Classic *you scratch my back, I'll scratch yours*. Quid pro quo.

Yesterday's upsetting events returned full force…the box of photographs, her uneasiness at being in Angus Crawford's cottage, the shock of seeing her old home after all those years… She shoved off the covers and slid out of bed.

Her clothes were folded neatly on the dresser. She'd left them dripping wet and hanging in the bathroom to dry. Someone—Russ—had retrieved her clothes from the bathroom. She picked up the clothing and, clad in only the oversized T-shirt, she scurried down the hallway to the bathroom for a shower.

Much later, filled with determination to leave the island, she stepped out of the steaming shower, toweled dry, and dressed. Without bothering to look at her reflection in the fogged mirror, she forked her fingers through her short curls, and opened the bathroom door and stepped into the hall.

And stopped.

Male voices echoed from the living room.

She inched down the hall. Nearing the front room, she slowed her steps.

An unfamiliar man's voice filtered from the room. "Like I told you, Mr. Crawford, this place takes a lot of upkeep. Mowing that lawn keeps me hopping."

Russ responded, but she couldn't hear what he said.

He must be talking to the caretaker. Russ had said the caretaker would stop in to check on them. She turned to head back to the bedroom but paused. She had to face Russ some time. Maybe the situation would be less awkward if they weren't alone. That way he couldn't bring up any embarrassing details of the previous night. Inhaling a deep breath, she about-faced and strode into the room.

Russ was clad in the faded jeans and rumpled T-shirt he'd worn the previous day. His feet were bare, and his dark hair mussed as if he'd just climbed out of bed. He stood in the middle of the large room.

A rush of desire kicked her in the stomach.

She must have made a sound because he swung toward her and smiled. His dimple popped out, and his golden eyes crinkled at the edges.

Her pulse skyrocketed.

"There you are." He beckoned to her. "Come and meet Rick Menzies. He's the caretaker I told you about."

A tall, thin man with long, shaggy blond hair jolted up from the couch. A smile broke out on his youthful face. He didn't hide the fact he was sizing her up.

Russ clapped his palm on Rick's shoulder. "We can thank Rick that we were warm last night. He's the guy who makes sure the generator has enough diesel to keep the furnace running and the hot water flowing."

At the mention of just how warm they'd been during the night, a flush of heat soared up her neck.

"Russ was just telling me about you, Ms. Reynolds." Rick held out his hand. "Nice to meetcha."

Her gaze shot to Russ. "He…he was? What did he say?"

"I told Rick how you and I came onto the island to check out Angus's cottage, and then the storm came up, and we were forced to spend the night."

"Oh, that." For a heartbeat she'd been afraid he'd told the caretaker her true identity. Remembering her manners, she grasped Rick's callused, bony hand and shook. "Nice to meet you, Rick."

"Right back atcha, Ms. Reynolds." His boyish face lit up in a welcoming smile.

"Please, call me Athena." She tugged her hand, but he tightened his grip and held on for a moment longer than was polite. A second tug, and he released her hand.

"Athena. Pretty name for a pretty lady." He grinned.

She ignored his blatant flirting. "So, you're the person who looks after this cottage."

He stood straighter, and his chest puffed out. "You betcha. I'm in charge of this cottage, the grounds, the whole friggin' island. Believe you me, this place keeps me busy."

She studied his long, lanky build and the peach fuzz on his pointed chin. He was younger than she'd expected. Why would a young guy like him want to live alone on the isolated island? "How long have you worked here?"

"Almost two years." He shrugged his narrow shoulders. "The dude before me worked for Mr. Crawford for years, but he got too old or something." He grinned. "I was couch surfing at a friend's place when I saw the ad online." His grin widened. "I called Mr. Crawford right away, and I got the job."

Russ jerked his thumb toward the direction of the kitchen. "I just put a pot of coffee on, Rick. You're welcome to join us."

"That would be righteous." Rick beamed. "Thank you." He followed Russ out of the room.

She trailed after the men into the kitchen. A bank of overhead fluorescent lights illuminated the huge room and the mile-long granite countertops. Expensive-looking glass-fronted cupboards extended above the counter. The entire room, including the state-of-the-art stainless-steel appliances, gleamed. "This room is so modern, and the appliances are new. Why would Angus have spent all that money on renovations? I thought he didn't visit the island."

Rick's smooth brow furrowed. "Where'd you hear that? Mr. Crawford came out here every couple of weeks." He flipped his long golden hair over his shoulder. "He liked to keep the place up." He patted the gleaming countertop. "I installed this a few months ago." He grinned. "The new tile floors were put in last year."

"Angus came here every few weeks? I didn't know that. He traveled on frequent business trips, but not to Shelter Island." Russ set the coffee pot he was holding on the counter with a bang. "Are you sure?"

"Of course. He'd call me midweek and tell me he was comin' and to make sure the generator was filled with diesel and food was in the fridge."

"What did he do when he was here?" Russ asked.

"No idea," Rick said. "He liked his privacy, so I stayed away. My place is on the east coast of the island, but sometimes I'd see him walking on the beach or sailing in that beauty boat of his."

Her heart slammed into her ribs. "Was he alone?"

"Sometimes he had a lady friend with him, but most times it was just him. Though once I recall seeing him with a big, red-haired dude…young, rough-looking, lots of tattoos…" His upper lip curled. "Not the sort of guy I'd expect a man like Mr. Crawford to know. But mostly, I kept out of his way."

Russ filled three mugs with coffee and handed her a cup and gave one to Rick. He leaned his hips against the counter and sipped from his own cup.

The fragrant smell of dark roast filled the room.

She crossed to the large teak table with a matching set of eight chairs in front of a bay window with a view of the ocean and sat down. Russ had told her Angus never visited the island after her parents had gone missing; yet Rick said Angus visited often. Why had Angus kept his trips secret? What had he been up to? "When was the last time Mr. Crawford was here?"

Rick scratched his head. "Let me think." His eyes lit up, and he smiled like he'd figured out the answer to a challenging math question. "Sometime last September. I remember because the season-opener hockey game was on the TV, and I was upset because I had to come over here and open the house. I didn't want to miss the game. The Canucks are looking good this year, and I wanted to see the new lineup. They have this new defenseman who's supposed to be—"

"You're sure it was September?" Russ asked.

Rick nodded. "Like I said, the season starter was on."

Russ shot her a look and turned back to Rick. "That must have been right before he died."

The caretaker nodded. "That makes sense, because the next thing I knew a lawyer called me and said Mr. Crawford had passed, and you—" He nodded at Russ. "—were the new owner."

She sipped her coffee and digested the news. Why were Angus's trips to the island secret? Was that when he locked himself in his study and looked at the photos of her? She shuddered. Russ's deep voice drew her out of her disturbing thoughts.

"Do you live alone, Rick?"

Rick's face flushed red. "Well, once in a while I have a female guest spend a few days, but never longer than that." He wrinkled his brow. "Mr. Crawford didn't mind me having guests. It's okay with you, isn't it?"

Russ nodded. "Of course. I'm sure you get lonely out here."

"It's not too bad. This place keeps me busy, and I have my podcasts I listen to. I love the true crime shows." His pale-blue eyes lit up. "I'm writing a book about this island. That's why I wanted this job, though I didn't tell Mr. Crawford that. I didn't think he'd like the idea. He was prickly whenever I brought up the couple's disappearance." His wiry body vibrated. "But you know what I'm talking about, all that stuff that went down years ago? Those people who went missing? No one knows what happened to them." He bounced on the toes of his scuffed, suede boots. "How cool is that?"

Her hand jerked, and coffee slopped on the table. Rick's prurient interest in her family's tragedy was an example of why she'd changed her name and moved away from the west coast. Everyone wanted a piece of her. Growing up, reporters had hounded her and Clara for juicy tidbits. The police, social services, doctors, and neighbors had regarded her with too much pity, too much seriousness. Their solicitousness and curiosity were overwhelming.

An awkward silence descended, and the hum of the refrigerator and the distant pounding of the surf grew louder.

Russ cleared his throat. "You clean this cottage, right?"

"You bet. I dust and vacuum once a week whether the place needs cleaning or not. That's what Mr. Crawford paid me for. That, and keeping the grounds looking good."

Russ cut in. "What about that house on the north side of the island? Do you clean it too?"

"I keep the dust down and get rid of the mice." His cheeks flushed red. "Wait a minute, are you worried about that broken window? That just happened a few weeks ago. We had a real big blow, and a branch broke the glass. I'da fixed the window by now, but I had to order a pane from the mainland, and the glass hasn't arrived yet."

"How often do you check on the house?"

"Once a week or so." Rick chewed on a ragged cuticle. "When I first came to the island, I asked Mr. Crawford if I could move into the house. I mean, the place was old, but I figured that's where those people lived." He shrugged. "You know, maybe I could soak up their vibes. Living in the house, sleeping in the rooms where the O'Flynn family lived, would help with my book. Maybe even get me a documentary. That sort of authenticity sells."

The room spun in dizzying circles. He was talking about *her* family, *her* nightmare, as if her life were a true crime television show.

"And what did Angus say?" Russ asked.

"He got all weird and said I couldn't live there, so I moved my stuff into the caretaker's cottage." He picked a piece of lint from his sleeve. "You're not going to fire me, are you? I'm sorry about the window. I should have boarded it up until the glass came, but—" He shrugged. "I got busy and forgot. I won't do it again. I promise."

Russ stared out the window, his jaw working.

Rick hung his head. "Look, I need this gig, Mr. Crawford. I can't leave here yet; not 'til I'm finished researching my book."

"I'm not firing you." Russ set his cup on the counter. "I haven't decided what I'm going to do with the island. For the time being, I want you to continue to keep an eye on the place and fix that window. Can you do that?"

Rick grinned and pumped his fist in the air. "Awesome!" His gaze shifted to her, and his smile faded. "I know this is none of my business, but that house freaks me out. I can't imagine why Mr. Crawford insisted I keep it neat and tidy." He shivered. "It was almost as if he was expecting that family to walk in the front door." Another exaggerated shiver. "I mean, they're dead, right? Everyone knows that. Ghosts don't—"

"Don't you have work to do?" Russ's voice thundered.

Rick's face paled. "Yeah. Sure." He shuffled his feet. "Those branches the storm brought down need picking up. I better get on that."

Russ nodded. "Good idea."

As if he were a kid freed from the principal's office, Rick wheeled around and almost sprinted out of the room.

His boots pounded down the hall, and the front door closed with a bang.

All was silent.

Chapter 25

Russ rubbed the back of his neck, kneading the pads of his fingers into the painful knot of muscle. He looked out the window, watching as Rick trudged across the lawn toward a garden shed, his long blond hair tangling in the wind.

The handyman opened the shed door and dragged out a red wheelbarrow. Tugging on a pair of work gloves, he picked up a fallen branch and tossed it into the wheelbarrow.

Russ glanced over his shoulder.

Athena stared at her clasped hands on her lap. Her shoulders drooped, and her face was pale.

He drew out a chair, set it beside her, and sat. "That couldn't have been easy."

She kept her gaze on her hands. "I've faced people like that my whole life. It's what happens when your family's tragedy is all over the news. I'm used to it. It doesn't bother me. Not anymore."

He snorted. "Liar."

Her head snapped up.

"I saw your face when Rick mentioned the book he's writing." Unable to resist, he clasped her hand. Her fingers were icy. "I can't imagine how upsetting it is to hear people talk about something so horrible, as if your personal tragedy is entertainment."

"I guess tragedy is exciting, unless something bad

happens to you." Her lower lip trembled. "Do…do you think he knows who I am?"

He tightened his grip on her hand. "I don't think so."

A shudder rippled through her slight body. "What if he figures it out? What then?"

"That's not going to happen."

Her laugh was brittle. "Come on. He's writing a book on my family. He must have seen a photo of me. The newspapers were full of them. He's not stupid."

"I'll make sure he doesn't."

"And just how are you going to do that?"

"I don't know. I'll tell him that if he tells anyone, I'll fire him, or sue him, or something. Whatever I have to do to keep him quiet." He meant every word. He no longer questioned his motives. She'd been through enough, and he was prepared to go to any lengths to protect her.

"You heard him." The corners of her mouth tightened. "He's determined to write his true crime book. He won't stop just because you fire him. Once word gets out that your father left me his estate, the media will go crazy. It'll all come back…the questions, the harassment—" She shuddered. "I couldn't stand it."

The pain etched on her face cut like a knife. "You're a lawyer, so you know this already, but once Angus's will is probated, it becomes a public document that anyone can access."

She rubbed her arms as if she were chilled. "I…I forgot about that." Her throat worked as she swallowed. "So, anyone curious about the details of the will can read about them?"

He nodded.

"Damn."

He shoved back his chair and stood, drew her to her feet and enfolded her in his arms. "We'll figure this out...together."

She stiffened, as if all the muscles in her body contracted at once, but in the next heartbeat, she softened and sank into his embrace.

"What if we made a public statement before the will is probated? That way this won't blow up in your face." His mind whirled as he worked out the details. He wanted to do whatever he could to ease her distress. "*We'll* control the story. *We'll* decide when and how the information comes out."

Her brow furrowed, and she chewed on her bottom lip.

Distracted, he stared at her mouth. Fantasies of kissing those plump lips swamped him like a tidal wave.

"I don't like the idea. I've worked so hard to keep my life private, but I don't see another option." She shrugged. "Who knows? It just might work." For the first time that morning, the corners of her mouth lifted in a smile. "What's with the *we*? Are you planning to help?"

"Of course. I have your back. We're in this together, remember?"

Her smile widened, and her blue eyes sparkled. "You continue to surprise me, Russell Crawford. Thank you."

Unable to hold off any longer, he kissed her, a deep, tongue-down-her-throat kind of kiss, bursting with all his hunger and desire.

She kissed him back.

Hallelujah!

All too soon, she freed her mouth from his. The light in her eyes dulled. "Let's go check out those photos. I can't help the feeling I'm missing something."

He smoothed a wisp of her silky hair off her forehead. "Are you sure you want to do that?"

"Angus took those photographs for a reason. The answer's in that box of pictures. I just know it."

He studied her for a long moment, and then nodded. "Okay. Let's do this."

****

For all her bravado, she hesitated on the threshold of the study and stared at the dozens of photographs strewn across the floor.

Russ edged past her and headed for the cabinet. "Maybe there's something else in here that will give us some answers." He opened the door wider and peered inside.

She moved into the room, her knees quaking. One photo after another blasted her, and she fought for breath. The walls closed in, sucking the oxygen out of the small, windowless room. She needed air, space, a drink, room to process the nightmare before her, but she held steady. Angus had taken the photos and stored them in this room. She wouldn't rest until she knew his reasons.

"Here's something." Russ dragged out a small cardboard box. He lifted the cardboard flaps, rummaged in the box, and tugged out a handful of glossy papers. "More photos."

Her feet were glued to the floor. "Are—" She swallowed. "—are they like the others?"

He sifted through the photographs. "You're the star

in every picture." His brow furrowed, and he shuffled more photos. "I don't think you're going to like this."

"What is it?" Her heart pounded.

He handed her a photo. "Take a look."

Her breath whooshed out in a blast of air, and the picture fell from her nerveless fingers and floated to the floor. Her legs wobbled, and she would have fallen if he hadn't grasped her arm and held her steady. "That's my house. The picture was taken in my backyard last summer. The rosebush I planted in June is blooming in the background. You can see it." She met his gaze. "Angus followed me to Calgary?"

All those times when she'd sensed she was being watched, she'd dismissed her unease as the result of an overactive imagination. But now there was proof that someone had been watching. But Angus Crawford? The thought of that dignified old man, sneaking around, hiding in the bushes, spying on her, taking his invasive photos, didn't make sense. Had he hired someone to take the pictures? "Are...are there more photos like that?"

He nodded. "Yeah." He handed her another one.

Her breath caught in her throat. "This—" She struggled to swallow over the fist-sized lump in her throat. "—this was taken in December. I...I'd just put up my Christmas lights."

He tugged the photo from her fingers. "Are you sure about the month?"

She nodded. "Positive. I always put up the lights on the second weekend in December. It's a tradition. I buy eggnog and play Christmas music."

"You know what this means, don't you?"

She shook her head. "No." But that wasn't quite

true. Something twigged in her brain—something about the photo, but she couldn't put her finger on her disquiet.

"Angus died in September." His mouth tightened. A tiny pulse ticked in his firm jaw.

Her breath whooshed out. "Oh my God." She gulped. "If Angus was dead when this photo was taken—"

"Someone else took the picture and stored it in this box." He finished for her.

She stared, her mouth gaping, her breath frozen in her throat.

"Did you hear me?" He brushed her arm, his fingers a light caress. "Someone, other than Angus, was spying on you."

She rubbed the goose bumps prickling her arms. "Who?"

He shook his head. "I don't know, but trust me, we'll get to the bottom of this."

"Did...did you find anything else in the cupboard?"

"No. Just the box with the photos."

She chewed on her bottom lip. There had to be something. She'd bet her life the answer to the disturbing photographs was in this room. She zeroed in on a large watercolor painting on the far wall.

Mounted in an ornate wooden frame, the painting presented a vivid scene of stormy skies, waves crashing on a rocky beach, fingers of foaming seawater frothing over a lopsided stack of washed-up logs. On a bluff in the background, towering cedar trees swayed in the wind.

Her heart stuttered, and she stumbled back a step

when she spotted the familiar signature in the lower right corner. "My...my father painted this picture."

Russ's shoulder brushed hers as he edged closer. "I saw the one he painted hanging on the wall in the living room at your old house. He was a talented artist."

"Why would Angus have one of my dad's paintings?"

Russ shrugged. "He liked it?"

There were other paintings hanging on the white walls, but her father's painting was the largest one. An idea popped into her brain—a wild thought—but she couldn't ignore it. Her hands shook as she lifted the painting from the hook. A small, metal safe was set into the wall behind where the painting had hung. Her breath gusted out in an explosion of air, and the heavy painting clattered on the floor.

"What the hell?" Russ leaned closer. "How did you know that was there?"

"I...I didn't, but I've read more than my share of mystery books. There's always a safe hidden behind a painting." She spun the knob. "How do we open it?" The clicking of the dial was loud in the little room. "We don't know the combination."

He stuffed his hands in the front pockets of his jeans. "I suppose we could get a locksmith out here. He should be able to figure out a way to open the safe."

"I don't want to wait." She tapped her foot on the hardwood floor. "I want to know what's in this safe now." She stopped tapping. "We'll figure out the combination ourselves."

He snorted. "You *have* read way too many books. We're not safecrackers."

She studied the combination dial. She wasn't

leaving the island until they opened that safe. "I don't suppose Angus had any dynamite or other explosive devices hanging around?"

He choked. "What?"

"I'm kidding."

He blew out a breath. "You watch too many movies."

"Probably." Her teeth worked her bottom lip. "I suppose we could try random numbers and see what happens. I mean, what would that hurt?"

"There are thousands of possibilities. Even if we spent all day trying, we wouldn't get the combination right."

She bounced on her toes and grinned. "I've got it! I know the combination."

"Right." He chuckled. "The combination's one, two, three, four." He smacked his forehead with the palm of his hand. "Why didn't I think of that?"

A trill of excitement rippled along her spine. "I'm the focus of all those photographs. For whatever reason, Angus was fixated on me."

The furrow between his dark brows deepened. "How does that help us figure out the combination?"

"It's my birth date. It has to be."

"Go ahead." He smirked. "Give it a try."

Her cold fingers slipped on the rough metal as she spun the dial. Cursing, she tried again. Her next attempt failed. Biting back her disappointment, she spun the knob, clicking each number with care. She tugged on the door, but the safe still wouldn't open.

Russ blew out an audible breath. "Even if your birthdate is the combination, there are hundreds of permutations of those numbers. We could be here all week."

His shoulder brushed hers, and an instant zing of awareness slammed into her like a shot of adrenaline. She swallowed hard, fighting to concentrate, and attempted a different combination of her birthdate numbers.

And another. And another.

The tips of her fingers grew sore, and her wrist ached, but she didn't quit. She wanted answers, and she refused to stop until she found them. She worked the dial again.

Another series of numbers. And another. And yet another.

"Looks like this is going to take time." Russ crossed to the door. "I'll make more coffee. We're going to—"

A quiet metallic click resonated, and the safe door swung open. "Yes!" She pumped her fist in the air. "Oh, yes. That's what I'm talkin' about."

Chapter 26

He let out a whoop and swept her into his arms, capturing her mouth in a hard kiss. Before she could respond, he lifted his lips and grinned. His golden-brown eyes flashed. "You did it!" He planted another kiss on her mouth. "You're really something, you know that?"

"It...it just made sense. I..." Her voice trailed off as their gazes met and held.

The air sizzled between them.

Her heart thumped like a drum. His eyes transformed to liquid molasses, the pupils dilating until she felt she was being drawn into his very soul. She tore her gaze free. "Let...let's see what's in the safe." Heart pounding, she swung back to the safe and opened the door wider. A stack of tattered envelopes bound by a string sat in the middle of the small safe. She withdrew the packet, and her fingers shook as she untied the knot.

There were five envelopes, each addressed to Angus Crawford at a West Vancouver address.

Her knees turned to water, and she sagged against the wall.

"Athena? What is it?"

Russ's voice sounded distant as if he were miles away rather than mere inches. The writing on the envelopes blurred, and she blinked to clear her eyes. She trailed her finger over the faded ink. Twenty-three years had passed, but she recognized the handwriting. Why would her mother write these letters to Angus Crawford? Were they rental payments? He was the island's owner. Her parents would have made arrangements to pay for leasing the small plot of land where they'd built their house. But why would Angus keep rental payment statements in a safe?

"What are those? Letters?"

She held up the packet of envelopes and swallowed over the boulder blocking her throat. "They're…they're from my mother, and they're addressed to Angus."

His eyes widened. "Your mother wrote Angus letters? Why?"

"I…I don't know." She lifted the flap of one envelope and slid out a thin sheet of paper and opened it flat. Her mother's neat handwriting covered the page. Her heart stuttered at the first three words—*My Dearest Love*.

"I…I need to be alone." She tottered on wooden legs out of the small room and down the hall to the front door. Flinging open the heavy door, she stepped outside and headed for somewhere private where she'd have the courage to read the words her mother had written to the man Athena had hated above all others.

****

Russ found her sitting on a rocky headland overlooking the small bay. The sun was setting, casting a pink glow over the shimmering ocean. The storm had passed, and the sea had calmed. Waves lapped at the gravel shoreline below, the gentle ebb and flow a soothing melody.

Seagulls screeched and dove into the froth of the incoming tide, their raucous cries echoing off the surrounding forest and rising, rocky headland. The rain-washed air was fresh with the heady scents of fish, ocean, and forest. In the bay, the *Minerva* rocked at its moorings.

When she stumbled out of the study clutching the envelopes, she'd looked beaten, her face ashen, her eyes dull and lifeless. He'd wanted to stop her, to demand she tell him what was in those letters. But she was so shaken, he was afraid if he touched her, she'd shatter. So, he'd stood aside and let her go. Finally, worried about her, he'd gone looking.

She must have sensed his presence because her body stiffened, but she didn't look up.

He settled on a large boulder several feet away, giving her space, and fixed his gaze on the sun as it sank beneath the horizon. Rich hues of orange, crimson, and purple painted the evening sky.

"How long have you known?" She broke the silence stretching between them.

His heart ached at the sadness etched on her pale, heart-shaped face, but he didn't bother pretending he didn't know what she was talking about. "The possibility occurred to me when I first learned the terms of Angus's will, but I wasn't certain until I saw the den with those boxes of photographs. Why else would Angus have all those pictures of you?"

She nodded and slapped the papers on her lap. "It's all in these letters, every sordid detail. My mother loved him. Can you believe that? She loved Angus Crawford."

A hundred platitudes struggled to break free of his tangled tongue, but nothing he said would ease her pain, so he tightened his mouth and kept silent.

"They…they had an affair, and…and my mother got…pregnant. With *me*." Her voice was thick with unshed tears. "He refused to marry her, said he wasn't ready to settle down with a child."

He flinched at the raw pain burning in the blue depths of her eyes.

"He broke her heart."

"That's why he left you the majority of his estate. It's the only thing that makes sense." He smoothed his hands over his thighs. "You were his daughter. He was trying to make amends for abandoning you."

"My…my poor mother." Sadness coated her words. "How horrible for her to live on *his* island and raise *his* child, all the while knowing he'd rejected her." She rubbed her forehead as if her head ached. "Why would she do that? Why would my father, my *real* father—the man who raised me—want to live here?"

"I don't know. It doesn't make sense, but they must have had their reasons." He stuffed his hands in his pockets to stop from reaching for her.

She looked at him with wounded eyes. "Did you know Angus wanted me to live with him?"

He blinked. "What?"

She nodded and toyed with the stack of letters, alternately creasing and smoothing the thin papers. "It was just before my parents vanished. I overhead them talking. Dad was out fishing. Mom and I were in the garden picking peas. When Angus showed up, she sent me to the kitchen for a glass of water.

"I was nervous because he hardly ever came to the house." She mashed the pads of her fingers to her temples. "I came back with the water, and they were arguing." She exhaled a shaky breath. "I hid behind the garden shed so they wouldn't see me, but I heard them."

She twisted her hands together on her lap. "They were talking about me. He wanted me to live with him in Vancouver. I didn't understand why he would even ask. I mean, he was just our landlord." She blew out a breath. "Mom refused, and he said something about getting his lawyer involved. Their voices grew louder, and Mom told him to leave." She rubbed her temples. "After he left, Mom was crying, but she refused to tell me what was going on."

A raven cawed, the bird's haunting cry resonating through the forest. The heavy scent of wet earth filled the yawning void.

He cleared his throat. "Angus must have loved you very much."

"Loved me?" She snorted, her lip curling in a sneer. "He broke my mother's heart and deserted her when she needed him the most. When he realized he wasn't going to have any other children, he wanted me, his heir, someone to carry on his bloodline. That's all I was." She planted her hands on her hips. "He was so desperate for an heir that when that didn't work out, he adopted you." She gasped and slapped her hand over her mouth. "I…I'm sorry. I shouldn't have said that."

He flinched at her harsh words, made all the worse because of their ring of truth. She was right. Angus had wanted an heir, someone to follow in his footsteps and run his business empire. That's why he'd adopted Russ. He'd always suspected the harsh reality, but he'd hoped somewhere, deep inside, Angus loved him like a father loved his own son.

"I'm glad he's dead." Her outrage blasted the

peaceful evening air like a fusillade of bullets. She kicked a rock, and the pebble shot off the cliff and bounced and tumbled to the beach below.

"Hate him all you want, but he was your biological father. That'll never change. He made a mistake. We all make mistakes. Looks to me like he was trying to make amends." He grimaced. Why was he defending Angus? The man had made his feelings about his adoptive son clear when he wrote his will.

Bottom line—Russell wasn't blood. Athena was. That astounding revelation explained everything. He'd suspected Angus had secrets, but this startling development was more than a simple secret. Hell, the revelation that Athena was Angus's biological daughter was an atomic blast, an implosion that shook the very fiber of his being.

"Was my father aware of their affair? Did he know I wasn't his child?" The bitterness had left her voice, replaced by a deep, aching sadness.

He shrugged. "You may never know."

"I wish my parents were here. There's so much I'd like to ask them." She spread her hands on her lap. "Why were the circumstances of my birth a secret? Why didn't my mother tell me? I had a right to know."

"I'm sorry." He grimaced. *Sorry*? A useless word, a meaningless platitude that rolled off the tongue, but did nothing to help. But what else could he say? He *was* sorry, both for her and for him. Sometimes life sucked, but you had to make the best of a bad situation.

"Russ?"

His name on her lips drew him out of his dark thoughts. "What is it?"

"Is it too late to sail to Vancouver?" She gestured

toward the glistening bay. "The storm's passed. The water looks pretty calm."

"The *Minerva* has night running lights. We can leave whenever you want."

"Good. The sooner I get off this island, the better."

"There's something I have to show you first." He swallowed and searched for the right words. "There was something else in the safe other than those letters. Something you missed."

Her brow furrowed. "What is it?"

He dug in his pocket and tugged out the thin gold chain he'd found hidden in a crack at the back of the small safe. "I found this."

She lifted the bracelet from his palm and studied it. "This is a baby bracelet. Why would Angus Crawford have a baby bracelet?"

He'd asked himself the same question.

She sucked in a sharp breath. "I don't believe this." Tears slipped from beneath her lowered lashes and trickled in a silver path down her pale cheeks. Her tear-glazed gaze met his. "This...this is *my* bracelet."

"Yours? Are you sure?"

"It has to be." She held up the thin chain and pointed at the ID plate. "My name's engraved inside this heart. Why would Angus have this?" She closed her fingers around the chain and squeezed until her knuckles stood out white and stark.

"Like I said before, he loved you. That explains all those photographs in his cottage and the baby bracelet. Even though he couldn't claim you as his child, he thought about you and wanted to be close to you in the only way he could."

A tear trembled like a tiny diamond, caught on her

long eyelashes.

Enough common sense remained in his brain that he didn't give in to his desperate desire to gather her in his arms and kiss away the shimmering drop. Spending the night holding her in his arms was a mistake, one he couldn't take back. Touching her now, when she was so vulnerable, would compound his error. They were involved in a business deal. That was all this was, nothing more, nothing less. Just business.

Really? If you believe that, you're a damn fool.

He gritted his teeth and ignored the snide inner voice. Now that the truth of her parentage was out in the open, their agreement had become far more complicated. She was Angus's daughter, and as such was the rightful heir of his estate. Russ's claims would be kicked out of court. If he wanted her to follow through on her plan to sign over her share of Angus's estate, he had to keep their relationship on an impersonal level. For the time being, it was hands off. But when she was hurting, he struggled to remember his vow to remain unmoved.

She sniffled and wiped her face with her sleeve. "This is all too much."

He fished in his back pocket and tugged out a tissue and dabbed at her tears. His fingers tingled as they grazed the silken softness of her smooth cheek. He studied the rich fullness of her mouth and ached to kiss those sweet lips.

She licked her bottom lip with the tip of her pink tongue.

His breath gusted out in a whoosh at her innocently sensual gesture. His blood thickened and headed due south.

She shot to her feet, the letters and necklace clutched in her hand. "Let's leave now. Please?"

He forced his gaze from the rich softness of her mouth and that pink tongue. "Um, sure. Whatever you want. We'll leave right away."

Chapter 27

While Athena gathered her few possessions and washed their coffee cups and tided the cottage, Russ left in search of Rick. He wanted to talk to the caretaker and make sure the guy repaired the broken window in Athena's family's old house. With the recent storms, he was concerned about water damage. It was nice he cared about the place, but she wouldn't return. Never again would she walk through that familiar door and step into the past. The memories were too painful. She had to move on with her life and put the past behind her.

Yeah. Sure. Like that was going to happen. She swiped at the sudden dampness in her eyes. She couldn't move on until she knew what happened to her parents. Hopefully, Russ would be able to help her find answers.

She'd pulled herself together by the time he returned.

He locked up the cottage, and she followed him down the path to the beach where they'd left the rubber dinghy. The last rays of the setting sun lit the top branches of the tallest cedars on the headland in a golden glow. The ocean rose and fell in rhythmic, gentle waves.

"What did Rick say?" She slipped on a fluorescent-yellow life jacket.

Russ shrugged into a salt-stained PFD. "He won't let any strangers on the island, and he promised not to talk to any reporters."

"Do you think he's figured out who I am?" She tightened the waist strap.

He shook his head. "I don't think so. But it's only a matter of time."

Russ was right. Her physical appearance had changed in over twenty years, but she still possessed her distinctive red hair. In his research into the O'Flynn family, Rick would come across a photo of her from a newspaper article or television newscast and make the connection. Once he did, the proverbial cat would be out of the bag. And then her life would once again become a circus. Heart thudding, she helped Russ lug the rubber raft to the water's edge.

He held the raft steady while she jumped in, scrambled to the stern, and sat on the small bench seat facing the bow. He shouldered the raft into the surf and settled on the middle seat. Hefting the oars from the oarlocks, he used quick, sure strokes and rowed the small boat through the breaking surf to the calmer waters of the small bay.

The raft rose over the crest of a wave and sank with a thump into the following trough. Gripping the canvas straps on the gunnel, she held on tight. Leaving the shores of Shelter Island filled her with mixed emotions. She'd hoped revisiting her old home would answer the questions that had plagued her for so many years. Instead of peace of mind, her brief time on the island had raised even more unsettling issues.

Russ had shoved the sleeves of his long-sleeved T-shirt over his elbows. The tendons in his tanned forearms bulged, and the muscles in his biceps flexed. A look of intense concentration was fixed on his handsome face, as with each powerful stroke, he dug the oar blades deep into the blue-green water, shooting the little raft ahead.

"Here we are." He shipped the oars. "Hold on until I secure the raft to the ladder." Grabbing the painter, he slipped the coil of rope through a metal cleat on the *Minerva*'s shiny hull. With quick efficiency, he tied a bowline. "Okay. You're all set to board." He held the raft steady as she struggled out of the bobbing dinghy and clambered up the ladder to the *Minerva*'s deck, wincing as her knee protested the awkward movement.

Minutes later, he climbed aboard and secured the dinghy. Moving about the boat, he worked with calm efficiency, preparing to set sail.

She settled on the padded bench seat in the stern, resting her injured leg, and stared out at the deepening dusk. So much had happened in the past two days. Her entire foundation had shattered. Facts she'd held to be true were no longer her reality.

Angus Crawford is my father.

The shocking refrain echoed through her brain on an endless rerun, but no matter how many times she repeated the words, they were impossible to accept. That tall, remote man wasn't her biological father. Her mother didn't have an affair with him. The letters weren't real. They were part of some sort of elaborate hoax.

Deep down she knew the awful truth. Angus Crawford was her father. The question that haunted her was why did her mother move to Shelter Island? Did she still have feelings for Angus? Was that the reason?

Had her father known the truth about Athena's parentage? She crushed her hand to her stomach in a futile attempt to ease the painful cramping. Stars popped out in the clear velvet night sky, the rising moon a distant glow on the horizon. She inhaled the fresh sea air, fighting for calm.

Russ stood at the helm, feet braced against the boat's gentle rolling, his hands commanding the wheel. Under the reflection of the lights from the control panel, his cheekbones stood out stark and hard as if carved from granite in his tanned face.

She'd known him all of two days, but they'd been through so much, their time together felt longer. But she couldn't forget who he was and why he was helping her. They had an agreement. He wanted Angus's money, and she wanted his help in finding answers to her parents' disappearance.

Sure, there was an attraction. She grimaced. An attraction? More like an explosion of lust. She couldn't keep her hands off him. Just looking at him heated her blood. When he caressed her—or God forbid, kissed her—the rational world vanished in a blaze of desire. The previous night in the luxurious cottage, they'd almost made love, would have if the situation had been different. If she spent any more time alone with him, the inevitable would happen. And sex would be a complication. Her life was messy enough. She didn't need more problems.

It was time she went home. She missed Otis. He had to be wondering where she was. When she'd dropped him at the kennel, she'd promised she'd be back that night. For the past three years, it had been just the two of them. He was always there for her, ready to cuddle or offer his silent, unconditional love. Just thinking of him penned up in the kennel brought the sting of tears.

The red and green running lights of other vessels moored in the bay reflected on the calm ocean waters as the *Minerva* sailed into the small marina. Russ steered the craft into its slip and secured the lines, his movements swift and precise.

"Thank you for taking me to Shelter Island. I...I want you to know that nothing's changed. I'll have the lawyer send you the paperwork to forfeit my share of Angus's estate. Let me know if you find anything about my parents in his files." She headed to the ladder, desperate to get away before she did something stupid, like kiss him.

"Athena, wait. Please."

Her breath hitched in her throat, and she halted.

He sauntered toward her with an easy, lithe grace. "Where are you going?"

"To...to my car." She swallowed, pinned by the hunger blazing in his eyes. "I...I have to get home. My dog's waiting."

The toes of his boat shoes bumped her sneakers. The heat from his body filled the two inches of air separating them. He slipped a loose strand of her hair behind her ear, his fingers lingering, toying with the curl.

"I thought—" His strong, tanned throat worked. "—I thought you might stay."

"Stay?" The word came out as a croak.

"Yes. Stay the night." He pointed at the boat. "Here. With me."

Her throat closed tight, and even a single word

failed her. All she could do was stare into his heated gaze.

He grazed the pad of his thumb over her mouth, tracing the outline of her lips. "Don't think. Don't analyze this. Just say yes." His warm breath washed over her.

The rasp of his callused touch sent shivers rocketing through her.

Just say yes.

Was it that easy? Nothing in her life was ever easy. But maybe just this one time, with this man, love could be that simple. "I…"

He grinned, as if he sensed her weakening. "Say yes." His grin faltered. "I mean…I…I don't want to force you to do something you don't want to, but I think you do want this…us." He trailed his fingers along her skin, raising goose bumps.

She glanced at the parking lot. It was the weekend, and the small lot was full. Her rental car was jammed between a black SUV and a white four-by-four pickup truck. All she had to do was walk away from temptation and get in her car, and drive.

His face was expressionless, but the heat of desire sparked in his golden eyes.

Once she stepped off the boat, reality would set in, and the situation between them would never be the same. But here on this sailboat, they existed in a protected bubble, separate from the rules and expectations of normal life. She inhaled a deep breath and took the plunge. "Okay."

He stilled, and his eyes widened. "Okay?"

"Yes." She stared into those hazel irises and trembled. "I think so."

"You think so, or you're sure?"

"What's the difference?" Why was he asking so many questions? Why wasn't he kissing her?

"A lot." He backed up a step. "You don't have to do this. You get that, right? I'll help you no matter what."

She rose on her tiptoes and planted a kiss on his mouth. Fire flamed to life, her analytical brain shut down, and a desperate ache took over.

He groaned deep in his chest.

His tongue teased the seam of her lips, and she opened, welcoming his taste.

Their breaths mingled.

His hand settled on her hip, and he tugged her closer. His other hand cupped the back of her head.

The world spun in a dizzying spiral, and she shut her eyes. They'd kissed before, but those kisses were like hot chocolate on a stormy evening, or crisp autumn air. This kiss was different. Hot, fiery, passionate, and demanding. For the first time in forever, her mind was locked in the present. She wanted the kiss to last forever.

His callused hands roved over her body, awakening a raging hunger. He drew back, and she opened her eyes.

Swirls of emotion reflected in his handsome face…lust, desire, and something else, something softer, something she couldn't identify. "Athena." Her name lingered on his lips as if he savored each letter. "Please tell me this is what you want."

Her heart fluttered. She could trust him. He'd stop if she told him to. No questions asked. But that wasn't going to happen. Not a chance. "I hope you were telling the truth about those condoms."

The corners of his mouth twitched. "You bet I was." He claimed her mouth again with a ferociousness that staggered her.

She was gasping for breath when he broke off the kiss.

Without a word, he slid his arms under her hips and lifted her, holding her close to his chest. He strode across the gently rolling deck and along the companionway to the hatch. With surprising ease, he maneuvered down the ladder and carried her past the tiny galley into the cabin. He set her gently on the double berth.

She mewed in protest at the loss of his warmth. Her breathing was rapid and shallow, and her heart raced like she'd run a marathon.

He flicked on the bedside lamp, and the cozy space was bathed in a warm, golden light. Locking gazes with her, he tugged his T-shirt over his head. The muscles in his chest and arms flexed as he undid the metal snap on his jeans. He unzipped the zipper and shoved his jeans over his lean hips. They pooled at his feet, and he kicked them aside. His boxers were next.

She licked her parched lips, but she didn't look away, couldn't, not even if the world around her erupted in a nuclear explosion. His tall, athletic, masculine body with his sculpted pecs and taut abdomen, and the hunger radiating from his blazing golden eyes set her blood on fire. She lounged back on the bed and opened her arms. "Come here."

He stretched his long body beside her, and his heated gaze raked her. "You're overdressed." His voice was low and husky.

"I'd better fix that." Her fingers trembled as she struggled to tug her shirt over her head.

He brushed her hands away. "Let me." Once her arms and head were free of the clinging cotton shirt, he wadded it into a ball and tossed the shirt on the floor. He grasped the waistband of her leggings and slid them over her hips. They met the same fate as her shirt. He undid the clasp on her bra and slid the silk straps off her shoulders.

She shimmied out of her panties.

"You're so beautiful." His heavy-lidded gaze was scorching. He groaned and drew her against him and kissed her.

Her tongue fluttered against his. She writhed with a deep, aching need and crushed her swollen and aching breasts against the hair-roughened skin of his chest. An ache built throughout her body, centering between her thighs.

She tasted his skin, slid her hands down his body, pressed the full length of her bare skin against his, and shivered at the contact. Yet it wasn't enough. The feel of him, the taste of him... She needed him closer, against her, above her, inside her...everywhere. Right now. Right this instant.

He raised his head and licked her dark, swollen nipple, taking the turgid peak between his teeth and tugging.

Gasping, she arched, but just as the pleasure became too intense, he shifted his attention to the sensitive skin on her neck. She released a throaty moan.

Chapter 28

He licked her salty skin, thrilling in her response. His chest heaved as he struggled to draw in breath.

Her cheeks were flushed, her eyes shining.

The hot steel of his arousal quivered against the softness of her belly.

Oh man.

He lurched up and wrenched open the top drawer of the built-in dresser beside the berth. Grasping a small foil packet, he tore it open and removed the condom.

"Let me." She seized the condom, curled her fingers around his shaft, and slid on the sheath.

Her touch was fire. Gritting his teeth, he hung on to what little control remained. He calculated interest rates, recited baseball stats, recalled the rapid onset of global warming, world hunger, anything to slow the rush of excitement and prolong the pleasure. Touching her, caressing her soft skin, discovering the places that brought her pleasure, was almost enough.

Almost.

Her breathing escalated until she was gasping, begging for release.

The spark within him grew to a raging inferno. He traced soft, sensuous circles on the sensitive skin of her lower belly and dipped lower, tangling in the nest of auburn curls between her thighs. Panting, his body on fire, he focused on her needs, driving her higher and higher.

She arched beneath him. "Russ…yes…please."

His name on her sweet lips was his undoing. He rose above her, his erection prodding her swollen entrance. Perspiration gleamed on her brow. Her hair was tangled, but she'd never looked more beautiful.

Slow down. Make this good. For her.

Too late. He was lost. "Sorry. I can't…." The thought trailed off as a bolt of excitement sizzled through him, and he plunged into her with a single, deep thrust.

She moaned, the primal sound thick with passion.

The muscles in his arms corded, the veins bulging as he held himself immobile and stared into her eyes. "Look at me, Athena." His command was a hoarse rasp. "I want you to watch me when I take you."

She met his fervid gaze. "I am looking." She lifted her hips, and her inner muscles clenched.

"Yes, sweetheart, yes." A groan exploded out of his mouth, and he thrust into her, again and again.

She convulsed around him.

The friction built to a crescendo, and he stiffened, his breath rasping, coming apart, and he spilled into her. As the exquisite sensations faded, he collapsed on top of her, his heart pounding like a speeding locomotive.

Minutes—or was it hours?—later he levered his body off hers and settled on the bed beside her. He gathered her in his arms and drew her close, nuzzling a gentle kiss on her shoulder.

The only sounds in the cozy space were their tortuous breathing and the gentle lap of waves against the hull. The musky scent of sex settled over them.

He relaxed, each limb deliciously heavy. His

eyelids drifted closed, and he was on the verge of sleep when she spoke so quietly, he had to strain to hear.

"I hope we won't regret this in the morning."

"Wh...what?" He leaned back, but her eyes were closed, the light too dim to read her expression. "What did you say?"

"Nothing." She rolled onto her side, so she faced away from him and tugged the rumpled blankets up to her chin. "Let's get some sleep. This has been a long day. We'll talk in the morning."

Get some sleep?

As if he could sleep after *that* statement. Did she regret making love? Because he sure as hell didn't. The sex had been great. He grimaced. More than great. Something about her drew him in, something he hadn't found in any other woman, but whatever the attraction was, he wanted more.

The question was—did she?

He'd known making love to her was a mistake. Sex would complicate an already complex situation. But he couldn't stop. No man could have, not when she was so open and willing. A gentle snore broke through his turmoil.

Her brow was furrowed, and her eyelids fluttered. Her legs twitched, and her kiss-swollen mouth opened. She moaned as if she were in the throes of a nightmare.

He leaned over, turned off the light, and drew her closer until her bottom nestled against him, her back against his chest. He closed his eyes and tried to stop thinking.

****

Her eyes popped open, and in a nanosecond, she transitioned from the fog of sleep to stark reality.

Russ sprawled beside her on the bed, lying on his back, naked, snoring lightly. The hard lines of his face had softened, providing a peek into what he'd looked like as a young boy.

Unable to resist, she smoothed her hand across his chest, and just like that, she wanted him. Again. That was crazy. Making love with him was supposed to be a one-time occurrence, an itch that needed scratching, and once scratched, forgotten. They had separate agendas. Getting emotionally involved would make a challenging situation more difficult. But it was too late. She was already in too deep. The truth of the matter was that sex wasn't enough. Not for her. She wanted the whole nine yards—love, marriage, babies…a forever life.

Together.

Forever.

With him.

Certain heartbreak faced her if she stayed. He was attracted to her. He even liked her. That was obvious, but she was a fool if she thought there was anything more between them. Not on his part. Better to get the hell out of there before it was too late, but deep inside, she knew with a sinking heart she was doomed. She already cared far too much.

The bone-deep ache for a drink settled over her like an all-too-familiar friend. She closed her eyes, imagining a tall frosty glass, ice cubes clinking, the smooth, tart alcohol sliding down her throat, tendrils of warmth spreading through her body…oblivion. Her mouth watered.

She had to get off the boat.

Now.

She shoved back the covers and slipped out of bed, careful not to wake him. Scrambling into her rumpled clothes, she tiptoed out of the cabin and snuck up the ladder. Shoes in hand, she crept across the deck and climbed overboard. Jumping onto the pier, she slipped on her sneakers and bolted.

Fumbling with the key fob, she unlocked the rental sedan, opened the driver's door, and collapsed on the seat. God help her. She loved him. Her breath sawed in and out. Sweat dampened her brow, and small beads of perspiration slipped between her breasts. The keys fell from her nerveless fingers.

Heart thundering, she retrieved the key fob from the floorboards and inserted the key in the starter. The car rumbled to life, and she pressed a button to roll the windows down. Fresh morning sea air wafted into the car. She leaned her head against the headrest and closed her eyes.

"Hey, where are you going?"

Her heart jumped at the words, spoken quietly, but so near, and her eyes flew open.

Russ leaned in the open window, his eyes narrowed, a furrow between his dark eyebrows. His hair was rumpled, and he hadn't bothered to fully dress when he chased after her. He wore jeans, but no shirt, and his feet were bare. The jeans were half zipped and threatened to fall down. "I thought we had a deal."

Memories of the shared intimacies of the previous night rose before her. Blood rushed to her face. "Deal? What deal?"

"Don't you remember? I promised to help you find out what happened to your parents." He threaded his long fingers through his hair, mussing the shiny locks further. "I told you. I'm a person of my word. I thought you were too."

Disappointment doused her spurt of hope like a water bomber pouring retardant on a forest fire. He hadn't come after her because he cared. He was worried she'd renege on her offer to sign over Angus Crawford's estate. His actions had nothing to do with his heart and everything to do with money. "Don't worry." Her voice was wooden, devoid of her inner storm. "I'll hold to my end of the bargain. You'll get your company and the money, just like I promised."

The planes of his face hardened, and his lips thinned. "I wasn't talking about the estate. When I make a deal, I keep my word."

She snorted. "You'll do anything to gain control of Angus's business. That's what this is all about—money and power. Isn't it?"

His eyes flashed fire. "Look who's talking? You'll do anything to find answers to your parents' disappearance, even sleep with the enemy. You don't care who you use." Anger was there, hot and controlled, but his voice remained cool.

The bitter words hung in the air.

She punched the button, and the windows slid closed. Jamming the car into gear, she sped off. The car's back wheels spurted gravel. She glanced in the rearview mirror as his tall, lean form receded in the distance. Tears filled her eyes. The road ahead blurred, but she kept driving, uncaring if she crashed.

Chapter 29

Russ stood in the middle of the gravel parking lot, watching her car disappear around a bend as dust and gravel settled around him in a thick cloud. He scrubbed his hand over his whiskered cheeks, struggling to make sense of her sudden departure. No, not departure. She hadn't just left, she'd fled as if the hounds of hell were after her, as if she were afraid. Of what? Him?

He stumbled to the wire fence enclosure and leaned against it. She'd enjoyed last night. No doubt about that. A vision of her flushed face and scream of release rose before him. She'd wanted him, and he'd damned sure wanted her. Hell, he still wanted her with a deep-seated ache that floored him.

He'd agreed to help her solve the mystery of her parents' disappearance. What more did she want? But she'd raced away and left him—literally in her dust. His jaw ached from grinding his back molars. The worst was how much he cared. He hadn't wanted to. Hell, he didn't know her, not really. He'd taken her sailing with the intention of finding out her plans for Angus's estate. She'd thwarted his scheme by offering him everything he'd ever wanted. And then some.

Her generous offer had blindsided him. Even more ground shaking—he'd fallen for her. Not because she was willing to sign over Angus's fortune, but because her selfless act showed her true nature. She wasn't the conniving bitch he'd imagined. Far from it. Even more surprising, she'd battered through his defenses and wormed her way into his heart. But just when he realized how much he cared, she'd fled and left him standing in the parking lot like a fool, his heart shredded on the ground, crushed beneath her cold disdain.

The roar of an engine echoed from down the road, and his heavy heart lightened. She was coming back! He grinned.

A blue SUV rounded the corner, and the driver pulled into an empty slot.

Russ's smile faded, and the breath he'd been holding seeped out. His knees sagged, and he stumbled a step.

The driver of the vehicle climbed out, grabbed a travel bag from the passenger seat, and slammed the door. He strode toward Russ. "Hey, Russ. How's it goin'?"

"Hey, Joe." He cleared his throat. "Going for a sail?"

Joe grinned. "You bet. After that storm yesterday, it's a beauty of a day." He held up a canvas fishing rod case and a tackle box. "I'm hoping to catch dinner."

The words washed over Russ like meaningless sounds. "Good luck."

Joe narrowed his eyes and stepped closer. "Say, is everything okay? You seem... I don't know... distracted." He waved his hand at Russ. "And you're not really dressed."

Heat flooded Russ's face, and with the fire came a flicker of anger. Who the hell did she think she was? She had no business treating him the way she had. He'd

226

agreed to her fool's quest. He'd promised to search Angus's house and office and look for any mention of her parents and what might have happened to them. Did she still want him to do that? Or didn't she care about that either?

"Russ?"

He forced his focus to his friend. "What's up?"

The corners of Joe's mouth twitched. "Oh, I get it. Your hangdog expression has something to do with that hot redhead I passed on the road. She was driving like a bat out of hell. I don't think she even saw me." He clicked his tongue. "What happened? Did she dump you?"

"Something like that." The words strained between his clenched teeth.

"Oh, man. Sorry to hear that." An awkward silence settled between them. Joe cleared his throat. "You know what they say, right? Plenty of fish in the sea." He hefted the fishing rod case. "Speaking of which, I'd better get going. I won't catch any fish standing here." He patted Russ's arm. "Take care, man." He trotted toward the pier, calling over his shoulder, "Hey, if you're around when I get back, maybe we'll cook up some fish and have dinner and a few brewskis. You in?"

"Sure. That sounds great." Even to his own ears, his voice sounded brittle.

"Catch you later." Joe's heavy footsteps faded in the distance.

Russ stared down the empty road.

She wasn't coming back.

He tightened his hands into fists. If she wanted to keep relations between them strictly business, he could do that. Damn straight he could. The lady wanted business, that's what she'd get.

He about-faced and stomped back to his boat.

****

The second Athena's plane touched down at the Calgary airport, she used her cell phone, searched online, and found an AA meeting in the basement of a dingy office space downtown. Sipping a cup of bitter coffee loaded with two heaping tablespoons of sugar and a dollop of creamer, she sat on a hard metal chair and listened to the sordid tales of the other drunks.

She didn't like being there, felt too exposed, but she had to attend a meeting. If she gave in to her craving, one drink would lead to two, and then three. She'd drink until she passed out. And, riddled with guilt and disgust, she'd drink again, just to silence the inner voices.

When the meeting was over, she called her aunt and asked her to come over. She had questions to ask, hard questions about Athena's biological father and how much Clara knew. The drive to Athena's house would take Clara an hour, allowing plenty of time for Athena to stop by the kennel and pick up Otis.

When he spotted her, he whined and pranced around her feet like a puppy, slobbering, thrilled to see her.

Guilt flooded her. She shouldn't have left him, shouldn't have gone to Vancouver. Hell, she shouldn't have done a lot of things.

Arriving home, she unlocked the front door and stepped into the house.

Otis blasted past her, raced to his food dish, and crunched kibble, pushing his metal bowl across the linoleum, his tag dinging against the metal, and leaving a trail of hard, crumbled chunks of dog food.

She plodded down the hall to her bedroom and tossed her purse on the bed. Her body ached with a deep-seated exhaustion, and all she wanted was a shower and sleep. But first, she needed answers, answers only Clara could provide.

Fifteen minutes later, she stepped out of her bedroom, freshly showered and wearing clean jeans and a blouse.

The doorbell rang.

Otis lifted his head from his mat on the floor in the living room and let out a woof. Scrambling to his feet, he raced for the front door.

She threaded her fingers through her wet hair and opened the door to her aunt.

Otis barked in joy. Clara was one of his favorite people. His tail wagged, and his mouth hung open in a wide doggy grin.

"Hello, Otis." Clara petted his furry head. "How's my boy?"

Otis's tail swept the floor, and he stared adoringly at Clara as she rubbed his ears.

Clara looked up, and her eyes narrowed. "What's going on?" She clasped Athena's hand. "Are you okay?" She leaned closer and sniffed. "Are you drinking again?"

"No. I haven't had a drink in—" She paused. How long ago was her last drink? Three days? Four? She couldn't remember.

"Athena?"

"It's true. I haven't had any alcohol, not since we last talked. I promised you I wouldn't." Her heart tugged at the older woman's loving concern. Clara was her number-one supporter. "I'm fine." Her lie filled the entryway. She was fine, unless a broken heart counted. "I...I found out some disturbing news, and I need to ask you a couple of questions."

"Certainly. Anything you want, dear. I'm anxious to hear what that lawyer in Vancouver had to say."

Athena gestured down the hall. "Let's go into the kitchen and talk. I'll make coffee."

A thousand questions painted Clara's lined face, but she wheeled around and walked with a slow, jerky gait down the short hall to the kitchen.

The afternoon sun streamed in thinly slatted light through the kitchen window blinds, painting the tile floor in bright stripes. The sun glinting off the gleaming countertops was too bright for Athena's tired eyes. She hadn't gotten more than a few hours of sleep the previous night. Her face heated as she recalled the reason for that lack of sleep.

She'd gone into Russ's arms knowing exactly what she was doing, but sometime during their long night of loving, she'd realized she was developing feelings for him, deep feelings. That realization terrified her and, like a coward, she'd run. Shoving those unsettling thoughts aside, she filled the coffee pot with water, poured coffee grounds into the machine, and set the switch to brew.

Clara sat on a wooden chair at the table, her age-spotted, arthritic hands clasped on the table.

A car horn sounded on the street, the coffee maker gurgled, and the earthy scent of perking coffee filled the air.

Otis wandered into the room and settled on the

floor beside Clara. His tail beat like a metronome.

"I missed you too, boy." Clara petted the big dog's dark head. "Were you lonely in that kennel? No other dogs to play with?"

Otis plopped on the floor with a grunt and rolled onto his back, exposing his belly.

"You're such a big baby." Clara chuckled and rubbed his stomach.

Ecstasy was written across the dog's face.

Athena didn't want any distraction from the difficult conversation she was about to have, so she pointed at the back door with the inset doggie door. "Time to go out, Otis."

The dog regarded her with sad, soulful eyes, but he stood, stretched, and trotted out the door.

Athena opened a cupboard, removed two mugs, poured steaming coffee into the mugs, and toted them to the table. Opening the fridge, she retrieved a container of milk. Two spoons and the sugar bowl followed.

Clara added a teaspoon of sugar to her cup and stirred. "Are you going to tell me what's going on? Because I can tell something's got you upset." She grabbed a handful of tissues from the box on the table and wiped her hands.

Athena stared into the steamy swirl of cream-scented coffee in her mug. All the way home from Vancouver, she'd thought about this conversation. She wanted answers. That's why she'd called the one person who'd know the truth. But now that Clara was seated in front of her, Athena's courage wavered. Did she want to know? Her stomach rolled over. But could she live with never knowing about her past? Inhaling a breath, she faced Clara. "Angus Crawford is dead."

Clara's gasp filled the kitchen. "Dead? How…how do you know?"

"The lawyer I met with told me. That's why she was looking for me. She's in charge of Angus's will."

"What?" Clara slumped on her chair, her hands pressed to her chest. "Angus is dead?"

Athena nodded. "According to the terms of his will, he left me the majority of his money and his company." She swallowed and pushed on even though Clara's face had drained of color and tears pooled in her eyes. "The only asset he didn't leave me was Shelter Island. He left that to his adopted son."

"He left the island to Russell?" Clara wrung her hands.

Athena sucked in a sharp breath. "How do you know Russell Crawford?"

"I don't." Clara's face flushed. "Not at all. Your…your mother must have mentioned him, or maybe I read about him in the paper." She fiddled with the tissues in her hands, tearing off tiny strips that littered the floor.

The skin on the back of Athena's neck prickled with the certainty Clara wasn't telling the truth. But why would her aunt lie? No, she was tired and on edge and reading guilt in the older woman's actions where there wasn't any. "I met Russell Crawford at the lawyer's office."

Clara dabbed at her damp eyes.

"He offered to take me sailing for a couple of hours, but the weather turned, and we had to shelter off Shelter Island and—"

"Wait a minute. You were on Shelter Island?"

232

Clara blew out a shaky breath. "I…I thought you didn't want to go there. Why did you go with Russ?"

"It's a long story." Athena grimaced. As much as she loved her aunt, she wasn't prepared to reveal everything that had happened while she was on the coast, especially any details involving her complicated relationship with Russell Crawford. Instead, she gave her the edited version. By the time she was finished, Clara's mouth was open, her cheeks were flushed, and she was fanning her hand in front of her face as if she were having a hot flash.

But Athena wasn't finished. Not nearly. She gulped a swig of coffee for courage. "We found a box of old photographs in Angus Crawford's cottage. The box was filled with dozens of photos—all of me. Most were taken when I lived on Shelter Island, but some were from when we lived in Regina, Ottawa, and even here in Calgary. One was as recent as last December."

Clara's hands fluttered about her hair, fussing with her short gray curls. "Oh, my goodness."

Athena tugged the envelopes she'd found in Angus Crawford's safe from her back pocket and tossed them on the table. They landed with an ominous thump.

Clara's gaze met Athena's. "What's this?"

"Look at them."

The furrow between Clara's gray eyebrows deepened. She picked up the top envelope and studied the front. Her hand shook, and she dropped the letter like it burned. "Where…where did you get these?"

"They were stored in a safe in Angus's cottage on Shelter Island." Athena patted the top envelope. "What do you know about them?"

Clara shoved the stack of envelopes away as if it

were a coiled heap of venomous snakes.

"Aren't you even going to read them? They're from my mother to Angus Crawford."

Clara's face paled even further, and her mouth opened and closed, but no words escaped.

The truth punched Athena like a blow to the stomach. "You knew." Her accusation hung in the air, swelling and gaining in power with each second of strained silence.

Tears glimmered in Clara's eyes. "I—"

Athena shoved her chair back and shot to her feet. "You knew Angus Crawford was my biological father, didn't you?"

A single tear slipped from Clara's eye, slid down her lined cheek, and trembled on her chin. "Yes, I knew."

"Are you kidding me?" Athena slammed her palm on the table. "All these years you've known that bastard was my father." Her breath blasted out. "Why didn't you tell me?"

Clara tugged another tissue from the box and blew her nose. "I…I promised your mother I wouldn't tell you. I swore I'd keep her secret." She sniffled again. "You have to understand what things were like back then. The…the situation was…difficult for your mother, for everyone."

The *situation*.

Clara was talking about her. *She* was the situation. Athena bit hard on the tender skin on the inside of her cheek, fighting to control her outrage. "Tell me everything."

"All right. I'll tell you." Clara looked like she'd aged a dozen years in the span of a few minutes.

A thick lump blocked Athena's throat, making swallowing difficult. How could she browbeat Clara? She adored the old woman. She could never repay her for her years of selfless love. Clara had taken in a traumatized young girl who'd lost everything and offered her a home filled with warmth and compassion. But Athena had to know the truth. No matter the cost. "I'm sorry to put you though this, Aunt Clara. I know it's not easy." She clasped Clara's cold hand. "My parents are gone. They've been gone a long time. Please. It's time the truth came out."

Chapter 30

Clara wiped her streaming eyes. "Your father, William, and your mother went on a few dates, but their relationship wasn't serious, at least not on your mother's part. They were just friends. She met Angus Crawford at a party in Vancouver hosted by close friends, and the second she saw him, she fell in love." Clara blinked back tears. "Do you believe in love at first sight, Athena?"

"Of course not." She tore her gaze from Clara and stared into her mug to hide her lie. An oily scum floated on the surface of the cooling coffee. She hadn't believed in love at first sight. That was the stuff of romance novels, but then she met Russ. Now she wasn't so sure.

"Your mother loved Angus with all her heart. And he loved her." Clara's voice cracked. "Their…their affair lasted six months."

A knot twisted in Athena's stomach at the thought of her mother loving the tall, spare, dour Angus Crawford. "What happened?" Though she knew, oh, she knew the ugly truth. The letters had revealed all the sad details.

"If you read those letters—" Clara pointed a shaky finger at the stack of envelopes. "—you know the rest. Your mother became pregnant. Angus wasn't ready to settle down. He offered her money for an…an abortion, but she refused." Clara sought Athena's gaze. "She loved you even then."

Athena wiped her face, surprised at the dampness.

"His rejection broke her heart." Clara blotted her damp eyes with the soggy tissue. "But the good Lord has a plan, and in the end, the situation worked out for the best. William loved your mother. He offered to marry her and help her raise you. He didn't care that you weren't his biological child." Her lips trembled in a shaky smile. "He was a good man, and he was head over heels in love with your mother. He'd have done anything for her." She huffed out a shaky breath. "She grew to love him, and they were happy. You saw them together. You know that. They had a good relationship."

Athena's head throbbed. Was this sordid story of love and rejection really her life, or was she in the middle of a soap opera? "So, Dad knew about me? I mean—" She clenched and unclenched her fingers. "He knew Angus Crawford was my father."

Clara stared out the window. "That didn't matter to him. He loved you and your mother with all his heart."

Athena couldn't dispute her aunt's claim. Her father had loved her. In countless ways he'd shown her the depth of his love. He'd comforted her when she was frightened, tended to her scrapes and bruises, and read to her even when she was long past the age of needing a bedtime story to fall asleep. Grabbing her cup, she lurched to her feet and crossed to the sink and dumped the cold coffee. She hefted the coffee pot and refilled her cup. Setting her cup on the table, she topped up Clara's cup from the pot and sat.

She scooped two heaping tablespoons of sugar into

her cup and stirred. The clatter of the metal spoon against the ceramic cup added to the pain in her throbbing head, so she stopped stirring. In the ensuing silence, she asked the question that had haunted her since she'd discovered her mother's letters. "Why did Mom and Dad move to Shelter Island? Angus Crawford owned the island. Wouldn't Mom have wanted to be as far away as possible from the man who'd broken her heart?" She wrapped her chilled hands around the hot mug.

Clara's hand shook as she poured creamer into her cup. A puddle of white slopped onto the table. She grabbed a handful of tissues and mopped up the spill. "You...you were only a few months old when Angus reappeared. He was having second thoughts, and he wanted to be part of your life. No matter what your mother said, he wouldn't leave her alone. He was determined to be your father." She lifted her mug with both hands and sipped.

Athena drummed her fingers on the pine tabletop. She wanted to grab her aunt by the shoulders and shake the truth out of her, but one look at the elderly woman's pale, stricken face, and she gripped the edge of the table and held back. "Go on. Tell me the rest."

"Angus wanted to acknowledge you as his daughter. Your mother and he argued for months over your custody." Fresh tears filled Clara's eyes, and she tugged more tissues from the box and mopped her face. "He was rich and powerful. Your parents realized they couldn't win a custody battle. His team of lawyers was too good." She sniffled and dabbed her eyes. "They reached a compromise. Your parents agreed to move to Shelter Island where Angus would have limited access to you. In return, he promised not to tell you or anyone else that he was your biological father."

Athena's heart stalled. "My parents moved to Shelter Island because of *me*? I thought living off the land on an isolated island was their dream. I thought they were like hippies or free spirits."

"The situation worked out. Before long they realized they liked living on the island. Fortunately, Angus was a busy man, and his visits were infrequent." Clara's mouth tightened. "Once he won, he lost interest in them. And in you." She placed her hand over Athena's. "Your parents loved you. They never regretted anything, not you, nor living on the island. Not for one minute. You must believe that."

Athena struggled to digest this news. The tale was too incredible not to be true. The letters she'd found in Angus Crawford's safe backed up Clara's story. Her heart ached at the pain her mother must have suffered in loving a man, discovering she carried his child, and then being cast aside. To rub salt in the wound, she'd been forced to live in close proximity with her ex-lover, forever under his control.

Her memories of her parents' relationship were filled with laughter and affection. They'd loved each other. And they'd loved her. No question. Clara was right. They'd enjoyed living on the isolated, rugged island. She flattened her palms on the table. "Do you have any idea why Angus would have had all those photos?"

Clara shook her head. "I suppose he wanted to keep an eye on you as you grew up."

Athena nodded. That was the conclusion she'd drawn. The thought of Angus Crawford creeping around and spying on her was unsettling to say the least, but his actions were also sad. He'd missed out on a relationship with his daughter, and the only way he could connect with her was through stolen photographs.

She met Clara's gaze. "There's something else I have to show you." She fished in the front pocket of her jeans and tugged out the baby bracelet and set the fragile chain on the table. "I also found this."

"What is it?" Clara stared at the chain.

"I think it's my baby bracelet." She pointed at the inscription on the tiny gold ID plate.

Clara squinted at the engraving. "You'll have to tell me what it says. My old eyes aren't what they used to be."

"The name Margaret and a small heart are engraved on the ID plate." Athena picked up the fragile gold bracelet and rubbed the cool metal between her fingers.

"You found that bracelet in Angus's safe with the letters?"

Athena nodded.

"Your mother must have given the chain to Angus as a keepsake after you were born." Clara struggled to her feet. "Maybe he cared more for you than we thought. Why else would he have taken all those photos? He kept your mother's letters and your baby bracelet all these years in his safe. They were important to him." She pushed out her bottom lip. "That must be why he left you his estate. He didn't have to leave you a penny. No one knew you were his biological daughter. He could have endowed everything to Russ."

Athena had heard enough. She jumped to her feet and planted her hands on her hips. "Angus Crawford gave me the creeps. He still does, even if he's dead. I've always known he was involved in what happened to my parents. That's why he left me his estate—guilt. That's the only reason."

The doggie door burst open, and Otis squeezed through the opening. Tail wagging a mile a minute, he trotted to Athena and laid his shaggy head on her lap as if he sensed her distress.

She buried her face in his soft fur, breathing in his musky dog smell.

"I'm sorry, dear, but I'm having a hard time processing all this." Clara wrung her hands. "We've talked about this. Angus didn't harm your parents. What would he gain?"

"I don't know, but you can be damn sure I'm going to find out."

Clara's cup clattered as she set it on the table. "Be careful, my dear. You may not like what you learn." She pursed her mouth. "Sometimes the truth is worse than the not knowing."

Chapter 31

Athena leaned back from the desk and stretched her aching back. Her eyes were bleary from staring at the computer screen for the past four hours. She should take a break and walk Otis.

As if sensing her thoughts, his tail thumped from his bed on the floor by her feet. He sat up and whined.

She patted his head. "I know, boy. You want to go for a walk, don't you?" She studied the computer screen. "Give me ten more minutes, and we'll go."

He whined again, a plaintive whimper.

She scratched behind one floppy ear. "I promise." She held out her hands, fingers splayed, as if he could count. "Ten minutes. Okay?"

He plopped back down on the floor with a heavy thud and laid his head on his front paws, looking miserable and dejected.

Guilt flooded her. He enjoyed his walks, but she had to finish her work. She stared at the document on the flickering computer screen. Her boss had sent her a preliminary case as a sort of test to see if she was ready to return to work. So far, the project wasn't going well. She was too distracted, too shattered by all she'd learned over the past weeks.

Ten days prior, she'd contacted Jennifer Smythe and informed the lawyer of her intention to sign over Angus Crawford's inheritance to Russ. Jennifer had tried to talk her out of giving up millions of dollars and a thriving business, but Athena had insisted.

Reluctantly, the lawyer had drawn up the paperwork and couriered Athena the documents. They'd arrived the following morning. She'd signed the papers, stuffed them in a return envelope, and shipped them out that afternoon.

She hadn't heard from Russ, but she hadn't expected to. *Really?* Her inner voice chided. *So why do you keep your phone at your side and check the call display every ten seconds?* She assumed he was happy. He hadn't hidden how much he wanted Angus's business. Now he was the sole owner of Crawford Industries. And he was rich.

Lucky him.

Not so much her. All she thought of was Russ. Day or night, he was on her mind. She'd lost track of how often she'd awakened, tears dampening her pillow and the sheets tangled around her legs, a deep-seated ache in her heart. During the day, she was exhausted and restless and couldn't concentrate as images of his tall, lean body, engaging grin, and golden eyes flashed before her.

Her focus wandered to the window and the tangled leafy branches of the lilac bush outside. Eight days before, the bush had been covered in brilliant purple blossoms, the sweet, flowery scent drifting through the open window. Now the flowers had withered and dried to brown, seed-filled stalks.

She forked her fingers through her shaggy hair. Man, she needed a haircut. Studying her fingernails, she frowned at the short, ragged tips. A manicure wouldn't hurt either. One positive ray of light illuminated her otherwise bleak existence—she hadn't had a drink. Not a single sip of alcohol. She was on a record-breaking roll. It wasn't easy. She'd had cravings, lots of them, but somehow, she'd dug deep and resisted the thirst assailing her.

So far.

The peal of the doorbell jolted her out of her dark thoughts.

Otis scrambled to his feet and bolted, scrabbling across the hardwood floor in his eagerness to greet whoever was at the front door. His excited barking echoed throughout the small house.

She heaved to her feet and plodded to the door. Ever since she'd returned from Vancouver, Clara had become a frequent visitor. She brought trays of home-baked cookies, squares, and fruit pies—all from a woman who hated baking. It was as if she thought her extra dose of kindness would make up for her years of hiding the truth. So far, Athena had gained two pounds, but her inner pain was just as raw.

With a smile fixed on her face, she opened the door. "Nice to see you again, Aunt—" Her words died in her throat.

Otis flung his immense hairy body at the visitor, his tongue licking whatever bare patches of skin he could reach.

"Hey, there, boy." Russ leaned down to pet the beast attacking him.

Like the sucker for attention he was, Otis stopped trying to climb into the man's arms and flopped on the tiled floor and rolled onto his back. His long tail thumped as he exposed his belly, begging for a rub.

Russ set down the brown leather briefcase he was

holding and knelt and threaded his fingers through the dog's wiry fur. "How have you been, Otis?"

Otis's eyes rolled up in his head in ecstasy.

Disgusted at her dog's traitorous behavior, Athena snapped, "Otis, sit." Biting back an expletive when he ignored her command, she grabbed the ungrateful animal's collar but froze when Russ switched his attention from the dog to her.

He was even better looking than she remembered. His tousled dark hair was longer and curled along his neck, reminding her what it felt like to run her fingers through the silken strands. Her heart bounced in her chest as she stared into the rich, golden-brown depths of his eyes. A hundred memories flashed before her...his passionate kisses...his sensuous touch...his scent... She shut the torrid thoughts down and tore her gaze from his, but she was too late. His image was seared into her brain. Unable to resist, she turned back and stared, drinking him in.

He grinned. His eyes twinkled, and the dimple in his cheek deepened. He scratched Otis behind his ear. "He's such a handsome boy. What type of dog is he again?"

The dog stared at him adoringly. A thin stream of slobber dripped to the floor.

"He's a little bit of everything." She grimaced. She should have left Otis in the kennel. "But mostly, he's a big pushover."

Russ laughed.

Her heart thudded even harder against her ribs at the rich, familiar sound.

He stood, ignoring Otis's protesting whines. "Are you going to invite me in?"

"Why should I?"

His smile faded. "Because I drove all the way from Vancouver, and we have to talk." The determined set of his jaw made clear he wouldn't leave until he had his say.

She opened the door wider. "Come on in." Better to get this over with than to turn him away and spend the next days wondering why he'd come.

"Thanks." He stepped across the threshold, and his hip grazed her arm.

Her skin tingled from the brief contact, and she jerked back, shaken. Their extended separation hadn't cooled her ardor.

Not. One. Bit.

Tall and muscular, all virile male, he dwarfed her floral-patterned living room furniture. "Nice place."

"Um…er…would you like coffee or something?" She bit her lip. What the hell was she doing? Why was she playing the good little hostess? She should demand to know why, after two, long, unendurable weeks of silence, he showed up looking impossibly handsome, grinning, and petting her dog as if nothing had happened. In spite of her agitation at his unexpected arrival, part of her—the weak part—was elated he was there.

He stuffed his hands in the front pockets of his faded jeans. "Coffee would be great. Thanks."

Her legs were rubbery as she stumbled down the hall and into the kitchen. She nearly dropped the coffeepot twice before she finished filling the glass pot with water, set it on the machine, and hit the Brew button. She stared out the window as the coffee maker gurgled, and the comforting scent of dark roast filled the air.

A robin swooped over the yard and landed in the long grass.

She frowned. Mowing the lawn was another job she'd put off.

A butterfly flitted from one yellow flower head to another. The swishing sounds of the next-door neighbor's sprinkler and children's laughter filtered through the glass.

How could the neighborhood be so normal when her inner world was imploding? The skin under her arms dampened, and she tugged at the collar of her shirt, loosening the too-tight neckline. Why was he there? To thank her for signing the transfer papers? That task could have been accomplished in a phone call or a text. He didn't have to drive a thousand kilometers.

When the coffee finished brewing, she filled two mugs with the fragrant brew, added a teaspoon of sugar and milk to each cup, and carried the steaming cups through to the living room.

He was sprawled on a chair, his long legs stretched out, his feet, clad in black leather boots, crossed at the ankles. The briefcase was on the floor beside the chair. Otis was curled at his feet.

She stepped over the traitorous beast and set a cup on the oak table beside Russ's chair.

"Thanks for the coffee." He smiled, and that deadly dimple she remembered so well made an appearance.

She gulped. Was he aware of the devastating impact of his dimple? Of course, he was. Women probably went gaga over that sexy indent all the time. "I didn't know how you liked your coffee, so I added cream and sugar." Hopefully her tone made clear she hadn't cared enough to pay attention to how he took his coffee. But of course she knew. She hadn't forgotten one second of their time together. He liked his coffee strong and black. She placed her mug on the coffee table and perched on the sofa facing him, her body strung tight, her nerves vibrating.

The awkward silence swelled and grew until it was a living entity hovering over the room, sucking out all the oxygen.

She couldn't stop looking at him, studying every detail. Alcohol wasn't her only obsession.

Shadows lurked in his hazel eyes. His normally swarthy face was pale, his five o'clock shadow heavy. Dark smudges underlined his eyes. Tension radiated off him in palpable waves.

She wasn't the only one who was nervous. Despite his relaxed posture and easy smile, he was as uncomfortable as she was. She rubbed her damp palms on her thighs and swallowed. "Wha—"

"I—"

They'd both spoken at the same time.

And stopped.

He cleared his throat. "Sorry. Go ahead. What were you saying?"

She shook her head. "You first."

He rubbed Otis behind the ears and met her gaze. "I had to see you."

Her heart skipped a beat. "You...you did?"

"I talked to Jennifer Smythe. She told me what you did." He smoothed his hands on his jeans. "I don't know what to say. Thank you for signing over Angus's estate. That means a lot to me."

Her heart sank. She was right. He wanted to thank

248

her. That's why he'd come, not because of love, but gratitude. "I told you I didn't want his money or anything else connected to that man."

His dark gaze pierced her. "Does that include me, Athena?"

She sucked in a breath, and once again an awkward silence settled between them. What was he talking about? She hadn't seen or heard from him in two long weeks. They'd made love, and that was it. No contact. She wasn't surprised. Not really. She'd known all along he was using her to obtain Angus's estate. What she hadn't counted on was how much his callousness hurt.

Otis's ears pricked. His head tilted to the side as he scrutinized first her and then Russ as if he were trying to figure out what was going on.

Russ shifted on his chair and re-crossed his feet.

She gripped the edges of the seat cushion, her fingers digging into the soft fabric.

The throb of a motorcycle roaring down the street seeped through the living room window.

He withdrew a folded piece of paper from his shirt pocket. Leaning forward, he set the paper on the table in front of her. "This is for you."

She released her death grip on the cushion and picked up the paper, unfolded it, and spread it flat on her lap. The paper was a legal document. She skimmed the contents. Her heart stuttered, and she reread the document.

And read it again.

The paper dropped from her fingers and fluttered to the floor. "What is this?" The question was rhetorical. She knew exactly what the legal document was.

Chapter 32

His smile dimmed. "That's the deed to Shelter Island."

"I don't understand. Shelter Island wasn't part of our deal." The craving for a drink howled through her like a ravenous beast, and all she could think of was a big glass of red wine. She licked her dry lips. That clear ruby color, the aroma of black currants and alcohol, the smooth, fruity tartness sliding over her tongue, the warm buzz... She gripped her mug and sipped the now-lukewarm coffee, grimacing at the bittersweet taste.

He pushed to his feet, stepped over Otis's stretched-out body, and crossed to the couch. Bending down, he picked up the deed. "Take it, Athena." He laid the paper on her lap and sat beside her and clasped her hand. "You may not be interested in returning to the island now, but that'll change once the shock of everything you've learned this past month wears off. Shelter Island is part of your heritage."

Her hand tingled with tiny needles of awareness where her skin brushed his. She tried not to breathe, tried not to inhale his scent—a tantalizing mix of fresh spring air and spicy cologne. She stared at the legal document as if it were a killer bees' nest. "I told you. I don't want the island, not now, not a year from now." Shelter Island represented sadness and inexplicable loss. She'd never return to its rugged windswept shores, never witness the sad desolation of her old home, never again encounter the ghosts of the past.

"I came here today because I wanted to give you that deed and thank you. But there's another reason." His Adam's apple bobbed. "Part of our deal was that I'd help you find what happened to your parents."

She tugged her hand free and tucked a lock of hair behind her ear. "I know in my heart that Angus Crawford murdered my parents. What difference does it make if I find proof? They're…they're dead." Tears burned her eyes, but she persevered. "He's dead. The law can't touch him. Nothing will change that."

His brow furrowed. "I thought you wanted answers."

Unable to sit still a second longer, she exploded off the couch. "You don't get it, do you? Your father did something to my parents. I know it." She thumped her fist over her heart. "I know it in here. I don't have to prove his guilt to anyone. Not anymore." She huffed out a breath. "I'm done. Do you hear me? I'm done."

Otis raised his shaggy head, and a soft whine escaped his mouth.

Russ rested his elbows on his thighs. "I understand. You're afraid of what you'll find. Anyone in the same situation would be."

"I'm not afraid." She held his gaze, hoping he didn't detect her lie. "It's time to move on. I can't live in the past. I've wasted too much of my life doing that already." Maybe she wasn't lying. Maybe for once she was telling the truth, a truth she needed to hear. It was long past the time she should let the tragedy go and get on with her life.

Russ rose in a single, fluid motion, a determined

251

look in his hazel eyes. "Bullshit." He moved toward her, each slow step bringing him closer.

"What?" She backed up a foot, and another, until her hips bumped the wall and there was no escape.

"You heard me. I call bullshit."

Her gaze bounced around the room, seeking escape. "I…I don't understand."

"Finding answers is all you've thought of for the past twenty-three years." He halted a hairsbreadth away. "Think about it, Athena. Ask yourself why you've waited all these years to seek out the answers. You didn't need me for that. You could have asked any number of people to help you."

She raised her hands as if to ward him off, but they fluttered helplessly in front of her. Words died in her throat.

"Do you want to know what I think? You're afraid to find out the truth." His mouth thinned. "You're terrified you'll discover Angus is innocent, and your parents abandoned you. They sailed away and left poor, sweet Maggie all alone."

Her legs threatened to give out, and she braced against the wall. "No. That's not true. They wouldn't have done that." Her shoulders shook with a gut-wrenching sob. "They never would have left me."

"Then let's find out what really happened. Together." The light of earnestness shone deep in his eyes.

Was he right? Was she afraid to learn the truth? She shuddered. What if her worst fear was true, and her parents had chosen to abandon her? Could she live with the knowledge she'd been cast aside like an old pair of shoes? She licked her dry lips, wishing she were sipping on a glass of wine, beer, vodka…anything to slake her thirst and help her forget.

"Asking for help isn't a weakness, Athena. Sometimes, it's the strongest thing you can do."

His husky voice washed over her like melted chocolate.

The air between them pulsed. Her body swayed toward him like a plant seeking the sun.

Grasping her chin with two fingers, he turned her to meet his intense gaze. "Let me help you." He caressed her cheek, his warm, callused thumb eliciting another shiver. "Please let me help."

Her heart thundered against her ribs. "I…I don't know."

His warm breath gusted against her cheeks. "Together we'll find the answers."

"I…" She shook her head in frustration. Why was this so difficult? She'd spent her life wondering what happened that fateful day on Shelter Island. He was offering to help her find those answers. "Okay."

He nodded. "Before we start, there's something you should know. After you ran away from me at the marina, I—"

"I didn't *run* away."

The corners of his mouth twitched. "After you *left* the *Minerva,* I sailed back to Shelter Island and searched Angus's cottage."

Her irritation faded, and curiosity took over. "Did you find anything?"

He smiled, and the creases at the outer corners of his hazel eyes deepened. "I discovered a box of papers in the attic." He tugged at his shirt collar. "The box was filled with notes concerning your parents' disappearance."

"Angus confessed?" Her breath hitched in her throat. Her knees turned to rubber, and she swayed. She grabbed Russ's arm to hold steady.

"Hey, take it easy. Maybe you should sit down." He gripped her elbow and steered her to the couch.

Her legs gave out, and she plopped on the cushions.

"Do you want me to get you a glass of water?" He hovered over her.

"Please. Tell me what Angus wrote."

"The papers aren't what you think." He stuffed his hands in his front pockets. "They're reports from a private investigator Angus hired to find out what happened to your parents." He strode across the room and retrieved the leather briefcase from the floor. Unsnapping the metal clasps, he flipped open the flap, revealing several thick file folders.

She ached to rip the briefcase from his grasp, but she kept her hands clasped on her lap. "That doesn't make sense. Angus already knew what happened."

Russ held out the case. "Read the files. You'll see what I mean."

"I don't need to read them. I know what he did."

He settled on the couch beside her. "Think with your brain and not your heart. You've said it yourself. Why would Angus pay someone to investigate if he already knew what happened to your parents?" He patted the briefcase. "The private investigator didn't work cheap, and over the years, Angus paid him a lot of money. He hired him right after the incident and kept him on the payroll until a few years before Angus's death." He huffed out a breath. "Angus was careful with his money. He wouldn't throw cash away on a whim."

A thousand snarky responses trembled on the tip of her tongue, but she bit them back. Maybe Angus was innocent, and she'd blamed the wrong person all these years. Was that possible? Tears burned her eyes.

"Hey. It's okay." His arm curled around her waist, tugging her closer. "This isn't easy. None of what's going down is."

A sob hiccupped in her throat, and she burrowed deeper into his comforting embrace. Tears streamed down her cheeks and soaked the soft flannel of his shirt.

The light had faded, and the room darkened before she raised her head. The compassion shining in his eyes caused a fresh sting of tears, but she swallowed, refusing to cry anymore. "I've always been certain Angus was responsible for what happened. All these years, I've hated him. I've—" Her voice broke.

He rubbed his palm over her back, kneading the tense muscles with the pads of his strong fingers. "You were a child when your parents left. How could you know who was responsible?"

"You don't understand. It had to be him." She blinked back tears. "He was the only other person on the island that day."

"He was the only one you *saw*. There are lots of bays and inlets on that island. Someone could have landed a boat in any one of them and rowed ashore, and you wouldn't have known."

She shook her head, refusing to accept his calm reasoning. "I would have seen a boat. I would have…" Her voice trailed off as doubt clouded her thoughts. Could she be wrong? Was it possible that for all these years she'd blamed the wrong person? Had someone else been on the island that day? Someone who wanted to destroy her family? Unease trickled down her spine, and she shivered.

Chapter 33

Athena's tears had dried, but her face was wan and pale. Lines of strain bracketed her mouth. Her hand holding the papers trembled as she read through the files.

Watching her torment was the hardest thing he'd ever done. No woman had provoked such a fervent desire to protect. He wanted to slay dragons, to battle her enemies, to topple empires, anything to erase the shadows dulling her blue eyes. More than anything, he wanted to be the man who rescued her from the demons of her past.

The fourteen days, sixteen hours, and thirty-two minutes he'd stayed away were the most difficult hours of his life. His very essence demanded he go to her, but he'd fought the raging desire. She was vulnerable, reeling from the shocking discovery that Angus was her biological father. She needed time to come to grips with her new reality.

His decision to return to Shelter Island and search the property for clues to her parents' mysterious disappearance had been a Hail Mary. He hadn't expected to find anything. Years had passed. The police investigators had gone over the island with a fine-toothed comb. What chance did an untrained dude like him have of uncovering new clues?

He must have done something right, because after

three long days of scouring every inch of the stone-and-cedar cottage and searching all the outbuildings, he'd found a dust-covered cardboard box of files in the attic. The box, covered by a mildewed cotton sheet, was hidden behind a stack of other boxes filled with old clothing, vinyl records, and dated household accounts. It was labelled *Russell's High School Yearbooks*.

He'd ripped off the tape sealing the box and, instead of old yearbooks, he'd tugged out investigative reports, stacks of them. Once he read through them and understood their significance, a wave of relief washed over him. The papers were proof that his father wasn't involved in Athena's parents' disappearance. He was convinced of Angus's innocence. The challenge was to persuade Athena.

"I've got it." Her eyes shone with excitement, and a flush stained her pale cheeks. She waved a paper in the air.

"What are you talking about?"

"There is someone who might know what happened." She handed him the paper. "Read this. I can't believe I didn't think of him before."

When he finished skimming the paper, he arched his brows. "You've lost me."

"Did you read it?"

"Of course, I did."

She pointed at the third paragraph on the piece of paper. "The answer's right there."

He breathed in her sweet floral scent, and his blood heated as he remembered the slide of his fingers over her soft skin, her moans of excitement, her hot breath gusting against his chest…

"You were right."

258

Her words snapped him out of his fantasy. "Really?" He smirked. "Can you repeat that?"

"Repeat what?"

"What you just said."

She wrinkled her brow. "You've lost me."

"I believe you said I was right." He grinned. "I don't think I've heard you admit that before."

She stared at him for a heartbeat, and then she giggled. "I hope you enjoyed the moment, because I guarantee you'll never hear me say those words again."

Her laughter curled around him like a caress.

Their gazes connected and locked.

The moisture dried in his mouth as he lost himself in the pull of her vivid blue eyes. His heart jackhammered in his chest. Oh man. If the mere sound of her throaty laughter wreaked such havoc, he was doomed. He ripped his gaze from hers and focused on the paper in his hand. "Okay. Tell me what I'm missing." He held up the paper. "I don't see what's in here that has you so excited."

"It's just like you said." Matching red patches flushed her cheeks. "There was someone else who could have been on the island."

"Who?"

"JD Burroughs. He worked the supply boat. My parents paid him to deliver supplies to the island every month. That's how my correspondence courses arrived. He transported food, building supplies, mail, everything we needed."

Her excitement was contagious, and he sat forward on the edge of the cushions. "Was he on the island that day?"

"I don't think he was due to deliver the next

shipment for another week, but I could be wrong. It's been a long time."

He blew out his breath. "So, what makes you think he was on Shelter Island the day your parents disappeared?"

"This." She grabbed the paper out of his hand and held it up as if she were hoisting a prize. "It says here the police interviewed JD Burroughs, but he had an alibi. He was delivering a shipment to another island that day."

He rubbed the back of his neck. He'd read the passage mentioning JD Burroughs, and he'd dismissed him just like the police and the private investigator had. The man had no motive to harm the O'Flynns. More importantly, on the day of the couple's disappearance, he wasn't on Shelter Island. "But you don't believe that. You think he was lying."

She nodded. "It's not what's written in the files, but what's missing that's important."

"I'm sorry, but I don't see where you're heading with this. He had an alibi. The police checked him out, and they cleared him."

She blew out a breath. "JD had a contract with my parents to deliver supplies to Shelter Island once a month. Over the years, my father and he became friends. They were both avid sailors. Whenever JD stopped at the island, Mom invited him for supper and to stay the night.

"He and Dad drank beer and talked for hours about sailing." The corners of her mouth curved, and her eyes took on a wistful look. "JD brought sales brochures and the latest yachting magazines. Dad's dream was to one day own a Hansard 750."

He whistled. "Your dad had good taste. The Hansard 750 is still the top-of-the-line catamaran. Every weekend sailor I know would kill to own one." He flinched at his choice of words, but fortunately she was too wrapped up in her thoughts to notice.

"Dad never got the chance to fulfill his dreams." A sob hitched in her throat.

He fought the urge to enfold her in his arms and kiss away her tears. "I still don't get it. What's JD got to do with your parents' disappearance? From what you've said, they were friends."

"In his interview with the private investigator, Burroughs said he was delivering supplies to another customer that day." She paused. "He wasn't."

His brow furrowed. "How do you know?"

She glanced up, her blue eyes intense. "I wasn't feeling well that day, and I was supposed to be resting in my room, but I wanted a drink of water, so I went to the kitchen, and I overheard my father talking on the radio phone. He was making plans with JD to try out a sailboat JD was trying to sell him." She stared at him triumphantly. "They arranged to meet that afternoon."

He rocked back, stunned at her revelation. "Are you sure? This happened a long time ago, and you were just a kid. How can you be certain you're thinking of the same day?"

"I haven't forgotten one second of that day. I've relived it over and over a million times. I remember *everything*." She threaded her fingers through her tangle of shiny red curls. "Every little detail."

He studied her flushed face. True memory or wishful thinking, she certainly believed what she was saying. Her parents disappeared a long time ago. She was just a child when the nightmare happened. Could her memories of the distant past be trusted? "How come you never told anyone this before?"

"Because I just remembered." She tapped the paper in her hand. "What's written in this report reminded me of the phone call."

"Athena—" He hated to puncture her enthusiasm. "—you've wanted for so long to find out what happened to your parents. Do you think it's possible you imagined the phone call? Or you have the day wrong?"

Her face fell, and the light in her eyes vanished.

Way to go, buddy. What's next? Are you going to tell her there's no Santa Claus?

She clutched the pillow to her chest. "Do you think I made this up?"

He rose to his feet, aching to touch her, to take back his words, but he didn't. He was afraid—terrified if he enfolded her in his arms he'd kiss her, and once his lips stroked hers, he wouldn't be able to stop. She wasn't the only coward in the room.

She had too much going on in her life. The last thing she needed was some guy coming on to her. He stiffened his spine and stayed a safe distance. "Look, it's not that I don't believe you. I just think that—" He faltered. Ugh, he was digging an even deeper grave, but shovel in hand, he plowed on. "—that you want answers so desperately you'll—"

She cut him off. "I'll what? Lie? Make things up?"

"For years you were certain Angus was responsible for your parents' disappearance. Now you're saying this JD Burroughs had something to do with what happened." He swallowed. "Don't you see? You're grasping at straws."

Hurt mixed with anger flashed in her expressive eyes. "I didn't say JD did anything wrong. I just think it wouldn't hurt to talk to him and see if he remembers anything that could be helpful."

"Are you sure that's what you're doing?"

"You think my sudden recall of memory is a bit too convenient, is that it?" Her eyes flashed fire.

He kept silent. He'd said more than enough.

They stared at each other in an explosive silence like two combatants facing off.

The dull throb of a headache pinged in his right temple. He was responsible for the devastation on her face, and that unmanned him.

She gave a mirthless laugh. "You know, I believed you when you said you were here to help." Her lip curled. "I'm a fool." She wheeled around and strode from the room as if she couldn't get away fast enough.

"Son of a bitch." His curse punctured the air. He pounded his fist into his other hand, ignoring the pain, and he stormed across the room and kicked the stack of file folders, sending papers flying. He inhaled several deep, calming breaths, shoved his hands in his pockets, and with a resigned sigh, stomped out of the room.

Chapter 34

The door to her bedroom was ajar, and he tapped lightly.

She didn't respond.

Ignoring the warning claxons blaring through his brain, he nudged open the door. The curtains over the window were closed, but faint streaks of afternoon light leaked around the edges.

She lay on her back on the bed, staring up at the ceiling, her arms at her sides, her hands clenched into tight fists. Tears glistened on her cheeks.

A lump filled the back of his throat. She'd been so excited when she recalled the supply boat operator's long-ago telephone conversation with her father. And how had he responded? He'd doubted her. He tugged at his shirt collar, his face heating. Doubted her? Hell, he'd as good as told her she was imagining events.

A stronger man would walk away and leave her in peace. But where she was concerned, he was weak, and his feet didn't budge. He couldn't leave her. Not like this. Before he talked himself out of doing something stupid, he crossed the room, sat on the bed, and drew her into his arms. Her body was stiff and unyielding, but she didn't fight him. After a minute, her stiffness eased, and she relaxed and nestled against him like a child seeking comfort.

But she wasn't a child.

Far from it.

The soft curves of her breasts and the sweet roundness of her ass were proof of her womanhood. His blood heated, and his heart rate quickened. He ached to take this further, to claim her once again and hear her throaty moans of surrender, but he refused to take advantage of her vulnerability. He wanted her. Hell yeah. But the next move had to be hers.

The room darkened, and his arms grew weary, but still he held her.

Otis padded into the room, his nails clicking on the hardwood floor. He laid his bristled chin on the edge of the bed and whined. When he didn't receive the response he wanted, he barked.

Athena backed out of Russ's embrace and sat up, leaning against a pillow. Her hair was a tousled cloud around her tear-stained face. "Why are you still here?" Her limpet-blue eyes searched his.

Because I want to make love to you. Right here. Right now. She'd never looked more beautiful. He breathed deep and fought the desire raging through him like an out-of-control wildfire. He tightened his lips, kept silent, and erupted off the bed as if he'd been scalded.

Otis barked again.

Athena patted the mattress. "Come on, boy. Come here."

The oversized, gangly dog leaped onto the bed in a single bound. The bed bounced under the impact, and he licked Athena's tearstained face.

She shoved him away. "Stop, Otis."

Otis circled three times on the mattress before settling with a plop, his head resting on Athena's lap.

"I'm sorry I doubted you." Russ's voice was a rough croak. "Let's talk to this JD Burroughs. He might remember something."

Her fingers threading through Otis's fur stilled. "You'll help me?"

He nodded, unable to speak around the boulder stuck in his throat.

She stared into his eyes as if seeking answers to an unspoken question. Finally, she nodded. "Okay."

The choking lump in his throat dissolved, and he grinned, uncaring he was acting like a schoolboy who'd just been noticed by the most popular girl in class.

****

The small car-and-passenger ferry steamed through the aquamarine waves toward the wharf. As the rugged, forested hills of Hornby Island neared, butterflies danced in Athena's stomach. She gripped the rusted metal railing and breathed in fresh sea air laced with the acrid tang of the diesel exhaust spewing from the ferry's tall, black smokestack.

Other passengers, who, like her, had left the boat's warm interior and braved the cold wind and damp air, crowded the railing.

A trio of Pacific white-sided dolphins caroused through the rolling wake off the ferry's stern. Seagulls circled high overhead in the clear, robin's-egg-blue sky, shrieking and diving into the white-crested waves. The ferry's horn blasted a single long, lonely wail announcing the boat's arrival.

She glanced at the tall, handsome man leaning against the railing beside her, and her heart skipped a beat.

The wind ruffled Russ's thick, dark hair and

reddened his cheeks. His eyes were hidden behind dark sunglasses, his expression unreadable.

Once he'd agreed to her plan, he was all in, and he'd helped her track down JD Burroughs. An Internet search and three phone calls confirmed JD had sold his supply boat years ago and retired. The man who'd bought the business knew the old sailor's current address.

She could have phoned JD and asked him her questions. That would have saved them the long trip, but she wanted to meet him in person so she could see his face when she asked him if he'd been on the island the day her parents disappeared. That was the only way she could be certain he was telling the truth.

The kennel was overbooked, and she didn't have anyone with whom she could leave Otis, so instead of flying, they drove. The three of them. In Russ's small, red, two-door sports car.

The dog thought the road trip was a terrific idea.

She wasn't so certain.

They'd crammed the massive, shaggy dog into the small back seat where he alternated between staring out the window, panting and drooling, or curling up on the seat and sleeping. Dog hairs floated in the air, slobber painted the side window, and muddy dog prints marked the leather seat.

Throughout the long, ten-hour trip from Calgary to Vancouver, she and Russ took turns driving, stopping only for take-out meals, gas, and Otis's numerous pee breaks.

Russ didn't seem to mind. Another plus in his favor. He liked dogs. A lot. And he *really* liked her dog. A bubble of laughter filled her throat as she recalled the time they pulled into a picnic area along the side of the highway. In an effort to burn off some of Otis's energy, Russ had found an old wool sock and played tug of war.

The dog yapped and tugged on the sock like a puppy, his teeth bared in mock battle. He was so excited playing the game, he'd peed all over Russ's boot.

She'd held her breath, waiting for Russ's blast of anger, but instead of cursing and yelling, Russ had burst into peals of laughter.

Otis yapped and bounced around Russ's feet, oblivious of the faux pas he'd committed. Even now, she couldn't help chuckling at the memory.

When they had radio reception, they listened to music and watched the endless miles pass. They followed the Trans-Canada Highway out of Calgary and into the foothills. Climbing higher, they ascended into the Rocky Mountains and to the Rogers Pass where they drove through five long avalanche tunnels.

The rugged, snow-covered peaks of the mountains were stunning. Coniferous forests climbed the mountainsides, frozen lakes and ice-choked rivers filled the narrow valleys, and melting snowbanks lined the sides of the road.

As if they'd agreed ahead of time, they didn't talk about Shelter Island, the unsettling events on the *Minerva*, or their relationship. If they even had a relationship. She wasn't so sure about that.

Once they reached Vancouver, they drove straight to the ferry terminal and caught a ferry to Nanaimo on Vancouver Island. From there, they'd driven thirty minutes along the Island Highway to Comox and boarded the small car ferry to Hornby Island.

In all those long hours, she hadn't been able to keep her gaze from Russ's handsome face. The incongruity of his rugged features offset by the softness of his mouth intrigued her. All too well, she recalled the sublime feeling of those lips pressed to hers—lips that could be demanding and insistent one minute, and achingly tender the next. And then there was that damn dimple. When he grinned, and his dimple deepened in his lean cheek, she melted.

She tore her gaze from him and focused on the approaching shore. This trip could be a waste of time. Her memory might be faulty. Maybe JD Burroughs was telling the truth, and he had been delivering supplies to another island.

Maybe.

Or just maybe she was right, and JD delivered his supplies to the other island, and then stopped at Shelter Island. The possibility that he might know something about what happened that fateful day made the trip worthwhile. The ferry bumped against the dock with a jolting thud, and she staggered.

"Careful." Russ gripped her arm and held her steady. "Are you ready for this?"

"I…I think so." She swallowed. Was she? What if JD didn't know anything? Worse, what if he was the one responsible, and he was a murderer? Were they about to confront a coldblooded killer? She thrust her fears away. "I'm driving."

"Shotgun." Russ's laughter followed as they threaded their way through the tightly packed vehicles on the ferry deck.

"What are you talking about? You're the only passenger."

He pointed at the sports car. "I don't think so."

Otis sat perched on the front bucket seat, his head stuck out the open passenger seat window, his long pink tongue lolling.

She grinned. "Looks like you lost your seat." She opened the driver's door and slid behind the wheel.

Russ shoved his sunglasses onto the top of his head, opened the passenger door, grabbed Otis by his collar, and dragged the resisting animal off the front seat. "Nice try, boy, but that's my spot." He flipped the front seat forward and, grunting with the effort, lifted the heavy dog and shoved Otis into the back.

With a smug smile, Russ settled into the front passenger seat, dispelling a cloud of dog hairs.

She bit her bottom lip to stifle a giggle, but he must have heard her because he slid her a stern glance.

"Are you laughing at me?"

"No. Of course not." But too late, her chuckle spilled out. "Okay, maybe just a little."

He grinned, and the devastating dimple made an appearance. The tiny crinkles beside his eyes deepened.

Her laughter stilled. Dear Lord, he was pretty. Especially when he laughed. She stared into his hazel eyes and bathed in the searing heat. For a moment, she forgot where she was, forgot to breathe.

A car behind them honked, breaking the spell.

He slipped his sunglasses over his eyes. "Let's go."

Heart fluttering, she drove off the ferry ramp and bumped onto the road leading from the ferry terminal to the interior of the small island. As she negotiated the winding roads beneath towering cedar and Sitka spruce trees, she peered through the filtered afternoon sunlight, studying the road signs.

"There it is." Russ pointed to a narrow gravel lane branching off the main road. "That's the road we're looking for."

She steered the car onto the lane. The houses were set back from the road amidst dense, old-growth rainforest and lush emerald-green meadows. They bumped over a single-lane bridge spanning a small creek clogged with moss-covered rocks and tangled, leafy ferns.

The road grew rougher, and she slowed as she steered around deep, water-filled potholes. They hadn't seen another house for the past kilometer. A forest of tall trees and thick brambles lined both sides of the road. "Are you sure this is the right road?" She steered around another yawning hole.

He studied the map on his phone. "I think so. That guy I called said Burroughs lives at Number Sixteen, Gable Island Road." He pushed his sunglasses up his nose and peered through the mud-spattered windshield. "There. Turn there."

She swung the car onto a long, winding driveway shaded with towering coniferous trees and pulled to a stop in front of a mobile home protected by a rusted, moss-covered metal roof.

A small wooden addition, sided in faded silver-gray cedar slats, protruded from one side of the narrow trailer. A sagging, cedar-planked deck extended from the front. A wild tangle of weeds filled what had once been well-tended flowerbeds. The rusted hulk of a car, tires flat, windows shattered, and weeds growing inside, sat in the middle of the front yard like a giant lawn ornament.

Her heart sank. "Do you think anyone lives here?"

Russ nodded at a shed on the far side of the weed-filled clearing. A white, late-model pickup truck was parked under the sagging, moss-covered roof. "Looks like someone's home."

Turning off the motor, she opened the car door and climbed out. An air of desolation hung over the small, rundown mobile home. A row of grime-encrusted windows lined the front. She narrowed her eyes at a flicker of movement behind one of the windows. Someone was watching them. She shivered and rubbed the goose bumps on her arms.

"This'll be okay." Russ clasped her hand and squeezed. "No matter what you find out, you won't be alone. I'm here with you."

Warmth from his soft touch and his words radiated through her. "Let's do this." She pushed through the weeds, avoiding mud puddles and fallen branches, to the sagging porch. Climbing the rickety steps, she crossed the deck to the screened front door, drew in a deep breath, raised her hand, and knocked.

Chapter 35

The door swung open. A tall, heavyset, gray-haired man stood framed in the doorway.

The first thing that struck her was the smell, and she reeled back from the sickly-sweet stench of stale alcohol radiating off him in palpable waves.

"What do ya want?" His eyes were sunken, the whites threaded with red, and his nose glowed under a myriad of broken veins.

He was a drunk. She recognized the all-too-familiar signs. He'd probably had a beer for breakfast and a lunch of whiskey with a rum chaser. "JD Burroughs?" The years had been hard on him. His once-thick dark hair had thinned to greasy strands and dulled to a dingy gray. His muscular build had softened beneath layers of fat.

His bleary eyes, buried in a sea of wrinkles in his weathered face, studied her with suspicion. "I'm not interested in whatever it is you're sellin'."

He started to close the door, but she held out her hand and stopped him. "Wait, JD. It's me."

He blinked. "Do I know you?"

"It's me, JD. Margaret O'Flynn."

His eyes widened, his efforts to think through his alcohol haze almost comical.

"Maggie?" He opened the door wider and stepped onto the porch. "Well, I'll be. My goodness. Look at you. You're all growed up." A wobbly grin wreathed his face. "Damn, if you don't look just like your mama. What are you doin' here? How did you find me?" His gaze swiveled past her, settling on Russ, and he reeled back, grabbing the doorframe to steady himself.

Russ stepped onto the weathered deck and extended his hand. "Hi. I'm Russ."

JD's smile bared nicotine-stained, crooked teeth. "You're Maggie's husband?"

Heat flooded her face. "Er…no…um…" She ignored the teasing glint in Russ's hazel eyes. "Russ is a…er…he's a friend."

"A friend, is he?" JD cackled. "So that's what they call 'em these days."

Russ snorted, and she shot him a lethal look.

Suppressing an obvious grin, he said, "I'm sure you're wondering why we're here, Mr. Burroughs. Maggie has a few questions she'd like to ask you."

The old man's gaze swiveled. "You do, do you, Maggie?"

"I'd like to talk to you about my parents." Was it her imagination, or did JD's grizzled face lose some of its ruddy color?

"Your parents? Terrible thing, but that was a long time ago. I don't remember much."

His warm spittle sprayed her face, and she reeled back. "Please. We've come a long way. This won't take long."

A nerve twitched beneath his left eye. "If we're gonna be relivin' old times, we'll be needin' something to celebrate seein' you again, won't we? Helps with the memory, if you know what I mean." He winked. "Right, Maggie?"

She flinched as if he'd struck her. Did he know about her drinking problem? No way. How could he? She hadn't seen him since she was a child. He was drunk, that's all. When people were inebriated, they said and did things they didn't mean. She inhaled a steadying breath. "Don't worry about us. We don't want anything to drink." He was already well on his way to being drunk. She'd never get the answers she wanted if he was hammered. Besides, then there'd be two drunks, instead of just one.

"You sure?"

She nodded.

"What about your *friend*?" His gaze switched to Russ. "Do you wanna drink?"

Russ shook his head. "No thanks."

JD shrugged. "Suit yourselves, but I'm sure you won't mind if I indulge." He opened the trailer door. "I'll be right back." He disappeared into the dark interior.

"Are you going to be all right?" Concern softened Russ's hazel eyes.

Her face flamed at the certainty he wasn't referring to the emotional meeting with JD. Russ was worried she'd succumb to her craving and have a drink. "Don't worry. I've got this." The lie slid off her lips.

He leaned close and brushed a stray curl behind her ear. His warm breath fanned her cheek. "I don't doubt that for a minute."

She beamed under his approval, praying her smile didn't look as goofy as it felt.

"JD's quite a character." A furrow formed between his dark brows. "I wonder if he knows anything."

"He seems nervous, but his anxiousness could be

because our visit surprised him, and he's been drinking." She smoothed her hand over her hair. "I don't remember him being much of a drinker, but I was just a kid."

"He likes his booze now, that's for sure."

The door opened, and their host appeared, carrying a beer bottle.

She stilled. The frosty amber bottle, beaded with condensation, looked like heaven itself. She could smell the sweet, yeasty hops. Her mouth watered, and she licked her lips.

JD held up the bottle. "You sure you two don't want one? Plenty more in the fridge."

Her hand trembled with the bone-deep ache to rip the bottle out of his hand and down the contents in a single gulp. But she dug deep, swallowed back the insatiable thirst, and shook her head. "No thanks, JD. I don't drink." Not a complete falsehood. She *didn't* drink. At least, she hadn't for the past eighteen days.

JD's eyes narrowed. "Really? Huh." He lifted his bottle and gulped a giant swig. "Ahhh." He swiped his mouth with the back of his hand. "You two don't know what you're missin'."

She stared at the beer, unable to look away. The beast inside her demanded to be fed, but she held to her resolve and resisted. As if sensing her struggle, Russ looped his arm around her waist, lending her added strength by his nearness. She tore her gaze from the beer long enough to shoot him a grateful look.

"Is that your dog in the car?" JD leaned in, his ninety-proof breath leaking through his teeth.

She winced and followed the direction of his gaze.

Otis had climbed into the front passenger seat, and

his head and half his body hung out the sports car's open window.

"That's Otis."

"Nice lookin' pooch." JD guzzled another slurp. "Let him out if you want. I don't mind. I like dogs."

Glad to put distance between herself and the yeasty smell of hops, she hustled over to Russ's vehicle and opened the door.

Otis bounded out, his body wriggling with excitement. He galloped over to the porch and greeted JD with sloppy licks on his hands and face.

JD chortled and petted him. "Hey there. Aren't you a handsome boy?"

A squirrel chattered from somewhere in the surrounding trees.

Otis's ears pricked to attention, and his nails skidded across the deck as he raced off.

Athena perched on the edge of a wobbly wooden chair. "You were a good friend of my parents, weren't you?"

Burroughs nodded his grizzled head and took a long pull of beer. "Your father was the only man I ever met who liked sailin' as much as me."

"Dad loved to sail, that's for sure." She sorted through the multitude of thoughts clogging her brain, struggling to find the right words to ferret out the truth without flat-out accusing him of lying all these years.

An awkward silence settled over the trio.

A huge black raven croaked from the top branch of a towering cedar.

Otis's booming bark echoed from deep within the forest.

Finally, JD spoke. "I was real sorry to hear about

your parents."

Unbidden, tears filled her eyes, but she blinked them back. "Thank you." She had no idea why she thanked him, but over the years she'd learned that thanking people was the expected response when someone offered condolences. "Do you remember anything about the day they disappeared?"

He choked on a swallow of beer. "Me? I don't know nothin'. Only what I saw on the television news."

Her heart sank. She'd been so certain he could help. They'd traveled all this way for nothing.

"I need another beer." He tossed the empty bottle into a large, metal oil barrel filled to the brim with broken beer and liquor bottles.

"I'll get it." Russ strode to the door and opened it. "You and Maggie talk."

The older man looked as if he were going to argue, but he shrugged. "Beer's in the fridge."

"Got it." Russ nodded, and the door closed with a slam behind him.

She sucked in a breath. "I was just a kid, but I remember overhearing my father talking to you on the phone. He was asking about a boat you were selling. He wanted you to bring it to Shelter Island so he could try it out."

JD's pupils were the size of quarters in the shadowy blue depths. "Yeah? Your dad was interested in boats. That's pretty much what we always talked about."

"You were supposed to bring the boat by on the day my parents disappeared. Did you?" She gripped the arms of her chair and held her breath, her heart pounding.

JD scrubbed his hands over his whiskered cheeks. "Why are you askin' me all these questions?" His eyes narrowed. "I told the police years ago I don't know nothin' about what happened to your parents. That hasn't changed. I still don't know nothin'."

"You weren't on the island that day?"

A slew of unnamed emotions crossed his craggy face. "Like I said, I can't tell you nothin'."

"Can't or won't?"

She jerked around.

Russ stood behind the screen door, a beer bottle in his hand. He shoved open the door and handed the bottle to JD. "Well, Burroughs? Are you going to answer the lady's question?"

Chapter 36

JD's age-spotted hand shook as he grasped the bottle and downed half the contents in one long swallow. Wiping the back of his hand across his mouth, he fixed her with an unfocused look. "There's nothin' I can tell you."

Distracted by the sickly sweet reek of alcohol, it was a heartbeat before his words sank in, along with a sudden, overwhelming exhaustion deep in her bones. This was another dead end. Pushing up from her chair required an insurmountable effort. "I'm sorry we bothered you, JD."

"Hey, no problem." He struggled to stand, a relieved smile plastered on his wet lips. "It was sure good to see you."

She shifted to leave, but hesitated. Something was off. She couldn't put her finger on her unease, but her intuition buzzed. "Look, JD, I'm desperate to find out what happened. If you know anything, anything at all, I'd really appreciate you telling me." In spite of her best intentions, her lower lip trembled. "You…you don't know what it's been like…all these years…not knowing if my parents are alive or dead. Thinking maybe they abandoned me, or…or worse."

"Awww. Maggie girl, I'm sorry." He wobbled and grabbed onto the back of his chair. "I wish I could help you, but—"

"Isn't it time you stopped lying?" Russ's voice was laced with steel.

"Lying?" JD spluttered. "What the hell you talkin' about?"

Russ strode to the door, flung it open, and stepped inside the trailer. He was back in a second with a camera in his hand. "This is yours, isn't it?" He tossed the camera to JD.

"Hey. Careful with that." JD grabbed for the camera, fumbled, and the bulky box slipped, but he caught it by the thin leather strap before the camera hit the deck and hauled it onto his lap. He clutched the expensive-looking camera in both hands.

"What's going on?" She studied the large digital camera. The attached telephoto lens was at least six inches long. Her mouth dried, and her heart skipped a beat.

"You should see the photos in his living room." Russ sneered. "Lots of close-ups of whales and bald eagles. JD here is pretty good with a telephoto lens."

"The camera's not mine. It belongs to my son. He took those photos." A hint of pride crept into his rough voice. "He sells them at the island market. He's real good at taking pictures."

"It was you, wasn't it?" She glared at JD. "You took all those pictures of me."

"I told you. My son—"

Russ advanced until he loomed over JD. "We saw them, JD. We found the boxes of photos in Angus's cottage. Your son would have been a baby when the early ones were taken. Admit it. You took those photographs."

JD's shoulders sagged, and he shrank, all his

bluster vanishing. He regarded her with hollow, red-streaked eyes. "Angus told me to take them. I didn't want to, but—" He licked his lips. "—he paid me good money. I didn't see how they hurt anyone. I mean, it wasn't like you were naked."

Her head spun. "Angus paid you to take pictures of me. Why? What did he want?"

"I never asked." He chewed on his bottom lip. "Why would I? It was easy money. I...I had to pay child support and—" He shrugged. "I wasn't doin' nothin' wrong. I mean, I was real careful. You never knew I was there, so what was the big deal?"

Russ leaned over JD and placed his hands on the back of the chair, crowding the old drunk. "The big deal is you violated a young girl. Creeping around in the bushes and taking pictures." Russ's lip curled in a sneer. "That sort of thing gets you arrested."

JD's florid face paled, and his chair squeaked as he shifted in a futile attempt to escape the confines of Russ's arms. "It wasn't like that."

"Okay. Tell us what it *was* like."

He shot her a pleading look. "All I know is that when I made my deliveries to the island, Angus wanted me to take pictures of you." Beads of sweat popped out on his forehead. "I'm sorry, Maggie girl. I never meant to hurt you."

She rocked back on her heels and stared at the forest, but she wasn't seeing the trees. JD had taken the photographs for Angus. Clara had suggested Angus wanted to acknowledge she was his daughter. Since he couldn't do that, he'd hired JD to take photos so he could follow her life, if only from a distance.

A lump swelled in her throat. Maybe Clara was

right, and Angus regretted his poor choices. Maybe he had loved her. Looked at from a different angle, that room on Shelter Island with the boxes of photographs of her could be interpreted as a father showing his love for the daughter he could never acknowledge.

Or not. She shuddered.

"What about this, JD?" Russ tugged a small, plastic-wrapped white package out of his back pocket and tossed it on the deck at JD's feet. It landed with a thump. "How do you explain that?"

JD's eyes widened, and he scrambled to his feet, nearly dropping the camera. "What the hell?"

She stared at the rectangular package. "Russ, what is that?"

"Go ahead, JD. Tell her. Explain why you have a packet of cocaine hidden in the back of your freezer."

"You were snooping in my house?" JD's offended expression would have been comical if the situation weren't so dire.

"Cocaine?" Her voice squeaked. "You have drugs in your house?"

"It's not what you think. It's not mine." He snatched the white packet and stuffed it in the front pocket of his pants. "I don't use drugs."

"Whose is it then?"

JD licked his lips, and his gaze skittered around as if he were searching for an escape.

"You might as well tell us, JD. We're going to find out." Russ backed away, giving the older man space.

JD's gaze flicked from Russ to her and back again. He scrubbed his fingers through his thinning hair. "If we're goin' there, beer ain't gonna cut it. I need somethin' stronger, but I'm all out of the hard stuff."

He lurched to his feet, set the camera on the table, and fished in the front pocket of his baggy, stained jeans. Tugging out a set of keys, he staggered across the deck.

"Where are you going?" Russ asked.

"I told you. I want whiskey. There's a store just down the road a ways."

Russ stepped in front of JD, blocking him. "You're not going anywhere in your condition."

"What the hell you talkin' about? I'm fine." JD snickered. "Believe you me, I've driven in a lot worse shape. Besides, the store's not far, and there's next to no traffic on this island."

Russ snatched the keys out of his hands. His gaze met hers, and he shrugged. "I'll go. Just give me the directions."

"Are you sure, Russ?" she asked. The last thing JD needed was more booze, but the stubborn set of his chin made clear he wouldn't reveal anything more until he had his whiskey.

"As long as you're okay with staying here with JD." Russ arched his brows.

She grimaced at his all-too-obvious ploy to provide her with an opportunity to talk to JD alone. Though she doubted she'd learn anything worthwhile. The man was a drunk. He probably suffered from alcohol-related dementia, but maybe he'd be more forthcoming if Russ was gone. "I'll be fine. JD and I'll catch up on the old days."

Russ nodded and headed down the steps.

"Make sure you get the good stuff. None of that cheap crap," JD hollered after him.

Russ climbed into the car. The engine roared to life, and he drove out of the yard.

JD staggered back to his chair and plopped down. "So, what do you wanna know?"

A frisson of unease tickled her spine. Was it her imagination or were his eyes more focused than they'd been a minute ago? She swallowed. "You know what I want. Tell me the truth about what happened that day."

His brows bumped together in a scowl. "I gather you know your mom and Angus Crawford were lovers, and he fathered you."

Her mouth fell open. Had everyone but her known the truth of her parentage? "I just learned of their affair. A few weeks ago, I found letters from my mother in a safe in Angus's cottage on the island."

The corners of his lips twitched. "Did you know they continued their affair even after you were born?"

"What?"

He smirked. "That's why your mother moved to the island. She wanted to be close to Angus."

"What are you talking about? She married my dad—" She shook her head. "—I mean, William O'Flynn. They loved each other. She wouldn't have cheated on him."

He rubbed his hands together. "That may be what she wanted you to believe, but she wasn't tellin' you the truth. Anna and Angus screwed around for years. Oh, they hid their relationship from you and William all right, but they were always sneakin' off to be alone."

She narrowed her eyes. "How did you know about their affair?"

"I saw them." He rubbed his hands together. "One time when I was creepin' around taking pictures of you, I came across them kissing." He shook his head. "Could have knocked me over with a feather."

She collapsed on a chair, almost knocking it over. "My father didn't know about their affair?"

He picked up the beer bottle and rolled the amber glass between his hands. "Not until that last day."

"What happened?" Heat swelled in her chest, and tears blurred the warped boards at her feet.

"William didn't know about Anna and Angus's affair. He didn't even know you weren't his kid. Poor sap." He smacked his wet lips. "The news was a real blow."

The world spun, and she clutched the sides of her chair and held on. "When...when did he find out the truth?" Clara had told her that her father knew she wasn't his child before he married her mother, and he'd married her anyway. Had her aunt lied? Or was JD spinning tales in his drunken stupor?

JD set the beer bottle on the table and sat back, crossing one leg over the other. "You were right. I arranged to meet William that afternoon so I could show him a boat I wanted to sell. The *Silver Shadow* was a top-notch catamaran. She was fast and sleek and could turn on a dime. As soon as William saw her, his eyes lit up."

He grinned, exposing crooked, yellow teeth. "I knew right then I'd made the sale, but he wanted to try her out and see how she handled on the water. So, I—" The words slurred, and spittle sprayed. His eyes glazed over, and he seemed to lose his train of thought.

"What happened?" Her heart stuttered. No matter how painful the truth, she had to know.

He blinked and refocused, as if surprised she was still there. "Don't you remember? You...you weren't feelin' so well, so you were restin' in your room. Your mother wanted to wait 'til you woke up so you could all go for a sail, but you know your father. He was as excited as a kid with a new toy." His eyes were bleary. "He wanted to try the *Silver Shadow* out before dark. He didn't want to wait."

He scrubbed his hand over his chin, the rasp of whiskers loud. "They were supposed to be gone an hour, two at the most." He picked up the bottle, leaned his head back, and guzzled. "I guess I shoulda been more careful. I forgot I had a bunch of pictures for Angus that I took the last time I was on the island." The lines in his face deepened. "They were on the boat, hidden, I thought, but William found them."

"Dad found photos you took of me?"

"There were other pictures too." His ruddy cheeks flushed. "I took some of Anna and Angus in…shall we say…a compromisin' situation?" He grimaced. "Nothin' too racy, but enough to get the point across. I figured the photos might come in handy."

His gaze settled on her. "You have to understand. I needed money real bad, and Angus was rich. He could spare a few extra thousand." He studied the beer bottle. "I knew he'd pay big bucks if I threatened to show the photos to William or sell them to the media. His shareholders wouldn't be impressed if the president of the company was exposed as having a fling with another man's wife. Add in a bastard child, and the press'd skewer his balls."

Bastard child!

He was talking about her. She was the bastard. The word tasted foul on her tongue, and her stomach roiled. "You blackmailed him."

"I wouldn't use that particular word, but that was

the general plan."

"What did my dad do when he found those photographs?"

"William told me he confronted Anna. She confessed to the affair and admitted you were Angus's brat." He winced theatrically. "Ouch. I gather the fight got pretty ugly."

She blinked back tears. Her father deserved the truth, not the lies and betrayal he'd been faced with. No wonder he was angry. The urge to give in to grief was overwhelming, but she inhaled a steadying breath. This nightmare wasn't over. One glance at JD's face told her more shocks were still to come. "You'd better tell me the rest."

"You sure you want to know?"

No. She definitely did not want to hear any more. The ugly story was killing her, but she had to finish this, had to finally face the truth, no matter how awful. "Tell me."

"All righty then." He sat up straighter. "Bear in mind, I got all this from William after I fished him out of the ocean."

Chapter 37

The birds stopped chirping, and the wind in the branches stilled as if the world and all its creatures waited for JD's next shocking revelation. The air was charged with something indefinable, and ordinary, everyday sounds took on an ominous note.

"Are you saying Dad fell overboard, and you rescued him?" Athena's headache ramped up. Following JD's rambling story was like sinking into quicksand. The more he revealed, the more confusing the story. "What happened? Did the catamaran capsize?"

"William told me that he and Anna were so wrapped up in their argument they didn't pay attention to the wind and ocean currents. They got caught up in Deadman's Banks."

She sucked in a breath. Everyone who lived on the islands in the Salish Sea feared Deadman's Banks where massive volumes of water squeezed between the headlands and were expelled in fierce spouts. If an unwary sailor sailed too close to the treacherous rocky shoals, they risked being swept against the rocks by the force of the dangerous riptides.

She shivered as she recalled the tales her father told her of the many sailors over the years who'd drowned in those unforgiving waters. "Dad wouldn't have risked the Banks. Not in a vessel he didn't know." Her father had been a cautious sailor. He never took unnecessary risks. "He knew better."

JD tightened his mouth into a thin line. "He was mighty upset. Who could blame him after what he'd just learned? By the time he realized where they were it was too late. The waves caught them, and the boat capsized." He fumbled for the beer bottle and upended it over his open mouth, sucking back the dregs.

She shifted on her chair, wishing she were anywhere but where she was. All too vividly she visualized her parents' terror as their boat overturned, throwing them into the freezing waters of the North Pacific. "Go...go on." She hardly recognized the thin squeak of her voice.

"They weren't wearin' life jackets. When William surfaced, he treaded water, fighting the undertow, but he couldn't see your mother."

The sun disappeared behind a cloud, and she shivered in the sudden chill. What was taking Russ so long? She needed his calm, reassuring presence with a bone-deep ache. "What happened, JD?"

"William tried—" His face crumpled, and he faltered as a sob shook him. "He tried to reach Anna, but he'd hit his head on somethin' when the boat capsized, and he was hurt bad." He smoothed the palm of his hand over his greasy hair. "A wave caught him, and he was washed farther away. It...it was gettin' dark, and...and..." He buried his face in his weathered hands.

She struggled to digest his horrifying tale. "What about my mother? Was she okay?" But she knew she wasn't. She'd never seen her mother again after that fateful sailing trip.

He fixed bloodshot eyes on her. "He tried to save her. I believe that. God knows he loved her. He'd forgive her no matter what she'd done. But the current was too strong, and he—" His throat worked. "The first I knew they were in trouble was when they were late gettin' back. I had a feelin' somethin' was up.

"I launched your parents' ketch so I could run a search grid, but—" He stopped and stared into the darkening forest, his throat working.

Her brain felt like it was stuffed with gauze, as she fought to make sense of his unbelievable tale. Her parents drowned? Impossible. Even if the seas were rough and the currents strong, they were both good swimmers.

He tossed the empty beer bottle at the can but missed, and the bottle crashed on the hard-packed ground and broke. "I need whiskey. Where the hell's that man of yours?"

"Tell me the rest." Her voice was wooden.

His eyes narrowed. "You sure you can handle it? You're lookin' a mite peaked."

"Just tell me."

"I found William, but there was nothin' I could do. He'd lost too much blood." He pinned a beseeching gaze on her. "I think he was hangin' on just so he could make me promise I'd save your mom. I left him there on the boat and searched for hours." He forked his fingers through his gray, stringy hair. "By the time I found her, it was too late." He winced and pressed his swollen knuckles into his lower back. "Her body washed up on shore later that night."

She couldn't speak, could barely think. Terrifying images of her parents struggling against the cold ocean currents and finally losing their battle assailed her. She shuddered, swallowing back nausea.

The rumble of a well-tuned car engine filled the twilight, and Russ drove into the yard.

Otis barked and raced across the weed-filled lawn, greeting Russ as if he'd been gone for weeks instead of an hour.

Russ climbed out of the car and petted Otis. He stepped around the excited beast and approached the porch, a bottle in his hand. "Your directions weren't great, JD. I ended up on an old logging road before I realized I was lost. Luckily, someone came by and—" He stopped. His gaze fixed on her. "What happened?"

A lump filled her throat, and tears pricked her eyes. She gripped her chair tightly, so she didn't run into his arms and dissolve in tears.

JD lurched out of his chair. "I gotta take a piss." He stumbled across the deck and disappeared inside the trailer.

The slamming of the screen door released her from her stupor, and she shot from her chair and into Russ's arms, almost knocking him off the porch. The tears she'd been holding back burst free.

He held her tight. "What's going on? What happened?"

The awful words spilled out. "My…my parents…they're dead." She backed out of his arms and wiped her tears with her sleeve.

He set the whiskey bottle on the table and sat down, patting the chair beside him. "Tell me what JD said."

She stumbled over to the chair and collapsed. Inhaling a breath, she recounted the shocking tale.

The fine lines at the corners of his mouth grooved deeper, and by the time she was finished, his face was a thundercloud. "I'm so sorry. I know this wasn't what you wanted to hear." He brought his lips to hers and kissed her, tender, close-mouthed.

She shrugged out of his embrace. His sympathy would be her undoing. As it was, she was barely holding on to her sanity.

The screen door banged open, and JD plodded across the deck. His gaze went straight to the bottle on the table. He rubbed his hands together and licked his lips. "Got the good stuff, I see." He cackled and reached for the bottle.

Russ shot to his feet and gripped JD's arm, stopping him. "No way, old man. You're not getting another drink until we're done."

"What the hell you talkin' about? I told her everything I know. What more do you want?"

Russ tightened his grip. "I'm not convinced you're telling the truth."

JD scrubbed his gnarly hand through his hair until the thin strands stood up in greasy gray clumps. "Of course I am, I—"

"What happened to the *Silver Shadow*?" One final squeeze and Russ released his hold on JD. "How come the catamaran was never found?"

JD rubbed his arm and averted his gaze. "I dunno. I guess the hull was crushed against the rocks. Deadman's Banks will pulverize any vessel. All that'd be left would be bits and pieces, and those would wash away in the currents."

Chapter 38

"So, you're telling us that neither the police nor their trained divers found any evidence of the boat because the *bits and pieces* washed away?" Russ injected steel into the question. JD was lying. Russ had suspected something was off the second the old man opened the door. That was why he'd offered to get JD a beer. He'd wanted a chance to check out his place, to see what he was hiding. And that's when he found the camera. And the cocaine.

The story of the capsized catamaran was unbelievable. The old man was lying through his rotten teeth. He glanced at Athena, and his heart lurched at the translucent paleness of her skin. Dark circles rimmed her eyes, and her sea-blue irises were hollow with wounded hurt. Anger punched a hole in his gut, and he pinned hard eyes on JD and slid the bottle of whiskey closer. "Have a drink. Maybe that'll loosen your tongue."

JD grabbed the bottle, twisted off the cap, and slugged back a swallow. He coughed and sputtered, his eyes watering. Wiping his mouth with the back of his hand, he set the bottle on the floor beside him. "I tried to save your parents, Maggie. Really, I did. You have to believe me."

Her mouth tightened, but she remained silent.

Otis galloped across the clearing, his tongue

lolling, tail wagging.

A butterfly fluttered in the air, highlighted by a shaft of soft light from the setting sun, and the dog skidded to an abrupt halt, swerved, and gave chase, oblivious to the thick tension on the porch.

"Now tell us what really happened to the O'Flynns' boat." Russ rubbed the burn in his gut. JD's story stunk like rotten fish. "The truth this time."

JD swilled another slurp of whiskey. "No one knew about the *Silver Shadow*. The boat wasn't registered. I won it in a poker game, under the table, so to speak." He wiped his mouth. "Everyone figured Anna and William left the island on their ketch. The Coast Guard found pieces of a smashed boat, but when the broken parts weren't a match to the O'Flynns' boat, they didn't connect them to your parents' disappearance." He closed his eyes, looking like he was about to pass out. "And that's all I can tell you."

Russ had had enough. He gripped JD's scrawny arm and squeezed until the old man was forced to open his eyes and meet his gaze. "Oh, I think you can tell us the rest."

JD sputtered and opened his mouth to protest, but no words escaped.

"Not good enough." Russ tightened his grip. "Try again, old man."

"Come on, JD. You owe me the truth." Athena's face was pale and pinched. "Tell us what you know."

The seconds ticked by, one sonorous beat after another.

JD exhaled, his shoulders sagged, and his body deflated. "Okay, okay. I'll tell you the rest, but then I want you both outta here."

Russ released his hold on JD's arm. "Start talking."

JD reached for the bottle, but Russ got there first and held it out of reach. "You get another drink when you tell the truth."

JD stared at the bottle and licked his lips. He dropped his hands to his lap and blew out a shaky breath. "Like I said, William was hurt bad. I tried to stop the bleedin', but I was too late." He turned pleading, bloodshot eyes on Athena. "Your father knew he was dyin', and he knew Anna was gone. He pleaded with me to keep you safe." He swiped beads of sweat from his forehead. "He loved you. That's why I told the cops what I did, Maggie girl. To protect you from the awful truth."

"So, you thought it was better I believed my parents had deserted me all these years?" Athena's face was so pale she looked as if she were about to pass out.

Russ ached to take her in his arms and soothe her grief, but he couldn't. Not now. Not when they were so close to getting answers. He caught her eye and sent her a silent message. *Be strong, my love, be strong*. His heart leaped into his throat. *My love*? Where the hell had that come from?

Focus, damn it!

If he was going to get this drunk old man to tell the truth, he had to concentrate. "Why didn't you call the authorities? If William and Anna O'Flynn's deaths were an accident like you say, why didn't you call the Coast Guard?"

JD chewed on a ragged cuticle. "I…I wanted to. Really I did."

"So, what was the problem?" Russ tried not to snarl, but he was losing the battle. He ached to plow his fist into the deceitful man's face. He stuffed his hands into his pants pockets. As much as he wanted to find out the truth, hurting JD wouldn't help.

Tears glistened in JD's puffy eyes. "I'm sorry, Maggie. I hated lying to you." JD chewed on his lip and searched the lengthening shadows. "But like I said, I didn't have a choice. If word got out, Angus—"

"Don't bring Angus into this." Russ rubbed the knot in the back of his neck. Had he stumbled into an alternate universe? Nothing JD said made sense. Angus couldn't have been involved in this nightmare. No way.

JD stared at the bottle of whiskey and licked his lips. "Any chance of me havin' another drink?"

"Not until you tell us what you know. Once we're done, you can drink your face off as far as I'm concerned."

Athena lurched forward, a gamut of emotions flitting across her ashen face—fear, dread, sorrow... Her blue eyes shone with unshed tears. "Please, JD, tell us the truth. How was Angus involved?"

JD wiped his streaming nose with his sleeve. "You sure I can't have just one little sip?"

"Keep talking." Russ spat the words between his clenched teeth. The story was taking forever, yet not nearly long enough. He dreaded learning the extent of Angus's culpability in the senseless tragedy; yet, he had to know.

"Like I told you, my supply boat business wasn't doin' so good. My bitch of an ex was hounding me for child support, and I owed a lot of money to some pretty bad dudes." JD gnawed on a torn cuticle, drawing blood. "Angus offered me a shitload of cash to burn those photos of him and Anna." He waved a shaky hand at the rustic mobile home. "Enough to pay off my debts and buy this place. I needed the money. I didn't have a choice."

Russ tightened his hands into fists, relaxed his aching fingers, and clenched them again as he asked the question the whole convoluted nightmare circled around. "What the hell did you do, JD?"

"I—" JD opened his mouth, but snapped his lips closed when a rusted, red, four-by-four pickup truck careened into the yard, spraying clumps of mud and grass.

The vehicle skidded to a stop, and the driver's door swung open. A tall, thin man with a bushy red beard and wearing a red cap pulled low over his eyes jumped out and planted his hands on his hips. "What the hell's going on here?"

Chapter 39

Athena shot a look at JD. His weathered face had drained of color, and his body seemed to have folded in on itself. His hands shook as, with a furtive glance at Russ, he snatched the whiskey bottle and sucked down a long swig.

She swung back to the new arrival.

Even in the dimming light of encroaching dusk, the anger on the man's bearded face blazed like a torch. "I asked you a goddamned question." He stomped across the weed-infested grass, his heavy-soled black boots thudding the hard ground.

Otis raced out of the trees barking in greeting, his tail wagging.

The man stopped and glared at the dog. "Who the hell is this mutt?"

Otis's tail slowed its rapid swishing and slipped between his hind legs. His ears flattened, and he slunk down, making a beeline to Athena. He cowered behind her legs.

The man glowered. "Who the hell are you people, and why are you harassing my father?"

Athena backed up a step, her heart shuddering. This was JD's son?

Russ stepped forward, his body rigid, a friendly smile pasted on his face. "We're not causing any trouble. We're just asking your father a few questions."

His voice was pleasant, but his hands were fisted at his sides.

"Shawn. What…what are you doing here?" JD's voice trembled, his words slurring. "I…I thought you was in Vancouver."

"I was on the ferry when Randy Stevens gave me a call. Said you had some visitors. Thought you might need some help." Shawn clomped up the steps onto the porch. His lip curled in a sneer. "Looks like he was right. You're drunk." He turned accusing eyes on Russ and then her. "Did you buy him the whiskey?"

Athena gulped at the menace in his icy gaze. "I—"

"Wait a minute." His eyes narrowed, and he moved a step closer. "I know you. You're Maggie O'Flynn, or should I call you Athena Reynolds? That's the fancy name you go by now, isn't it?" Spittle sprayed from his mouth. "What the hell are you doing here?"

She blinked. He knew who she was? How was that possible? The red hat with the black design, the beard…it all clicked. She'd seen him somewhere. But where? Before she could fumble an answer, Russ moved closer, his shoulder brushing hers.

"We came here today to ask your father some questions," he said.

"You did, did you?" Shawn focused his scowl on JD. "And what have you been telling them, old man?"

"Nothin'." JD licked his lips. "I ain't told them nothin', Shawn."

"Really?" He snorted. "Why don't I believe you?" He ripped the whiskey bottle from JD and tossed it across the yard. It landed with a heavy clunk in the dark.

"Hey! Why the hell you gotta do that? That was

mine." JD's voice was a piteous whine.

Shawn ignored his father's outrage and faced Russ. "I know who she is—" He jerked his thumb at Athena. "—but I don't know you. What do you want with my dad?"

"Like I said, we're asking your father some questions. That's all."

Shawn's blue eyes narrowed. "Questions about what?" He tore off his cap and threaded his fingers through his long red hair.

Athena drew in a shaky breath. "JD was explaining what happened to my parents. Please, you have to let him finish."

Shawn spun toward his father. "You been runnin' your mouth?" He lunged to the table, snatched the camera, and dangled it by the strap. "What the hell, Dad?"

JD reeled back from his son's anger. "I haven't told 'em nothin', Shawn. I...I was just sayin' how Angus Crawford gave me the money for this place. That's all." The words slurred and ran together in a continuous stream.

"He's had too much to drink. He doesn't know what the hell he's saying. It's time you two left." Shawn's tone made clear his words weren't a request.

She frowned. Why was he so anxious to get them away from his father? What was the man afraid JD would say? "Please, let him finish. I need to know what happened."

The lines on his face beneath the ginger beard hardened. "I told you to leave. Now get the hell off our property."

Otis whimpered and licked her hand.

She shivered at the malice in Shawn's icy eyes. "There's no need to get upset. We're leaving." She crossed the deck, Otis shadowing her heels.

Russ didn't budge. "Hold on, Athena." He turned to JD. "Come on, JD. It's truth time. Let's cut the crap. You know who I am. You knew it the second you saw me. Am I right?"

JD's mouth opened and closed like a fish out of water. Finally, he inhaled a deep breath. "You're Angus's son."

Russ nodded. "Good. Now we're getting somewhere." He set his hands on his hips. "There's no way the events happened the way you described. You may have tried to blackmail Angus, but I knew my father. He wouldn't have paid you a penny for those pictures. Besides, I've checked his old bank records. There weren't any large withdrawals at the time the O'Flynns went missing."

A cold heaviness settled in her chest as a sickening realization struck her, and in spite of Shawn's looming presence, she blurted, "You killed them, didn't you, JD? You killed my parents."

JD wiped the snot leaking from his nose. "No, things happened just like I said."

Shawn held up his hand. "Shut up, Dad! You've said enough."

She ignored Shawn and focused on JD. "I'll tell you what I think happened." She moved closer to JD, invading his personal space, making him squirm. His sour stench gagged her. "The boat capsized, and Mom and Dad were washed overboard. My mother…drowned like you said, but Dad survived. But then you killed him. You had to. He found more than

302

photos on the catamaran. Didn't he?"

JD's bloodshot eyes widened.

She rushed on, determined to finish this once and for all, no matter the consequences. "You were a drug dealer. You're still one." She nodded at the bulge in his front pocket. "Dad found your stash of drugs. Isn't that right? That's the only thing that makes sense." She inhaled a wavering breath. "He was going to tell Angus, and Angus would have called the cops. You'd be arrested and end up in jail. You couldn't let that happen. All the money Angus paid you to take photos of me would be gone, wouldn't it?"

JD squeezed his hands together, his swollen, arthritic knuckles white. A dozen emotions crossed his stricken face…fear, regret, sadness, anger, and something more—something feral and deadly. "William shoulda kept his mouth shut."

"Let's go." Russ tugged her hand.

She shook him off and ignored the warning flashing in his eyes. "You killed my father, JD! I don't know how, but you killed him to shut him up." Her chest heaved as if she'd run a marathon, but the stricken look on JD's face made clear she'd spoken the truth.

Shawn leaned back against the deck railing and crossed his arms over his chest. "Go on, Maggie. What else do you think he did? Lay it all out."

She shuddered at the threat in his harsh voice, but she couldn't stop. The truth had to come out. "He hid their bodies where no one would find them, hoping the cops would think my parents sailed away on their ketch and left me." Tears filmed her eyes. All these years she'd lived with the hope her parents were alive, and one day she'd find them, and they'd be reunited. Now that dream was dead. She glared at JD, and a wave of revulsion and hatred flooded her. "You murdered my father."

"Let's go, Maggie." Russ's voice was firm, and he gripped her arm and steered her down the steps, not giving her a choice.

Once again, she shook free of his grasp. "I'm not finished." A sob hitched in her throat, but she swallowed back the lump and let her fury reign. "Do you realize the hell I've been through, JD? All these years I've wondered what happened, thinking my parents deserted me. Not knowing has eaten at me until it destroyed everything good in my life. And that's on you."

JD raised his grizzled head and turned bleary eyes on her, a pleading light in the rheumy depths. "I'm sorry, Maggie, but if your father told Angus about the drugs, I woulda lost everything. I needed that shipment. I needed the cash. I didn't mean to hurt anyone." Tears filled his eyes, and he blubbered. "It just sort of happened. William wouldn't stop talkin' about the drugs, sayin' he was going to the cops, and I had to shut him up. I…I found a rock, and the next thing I knew he was dead."

Shawn lunged at JD and slapped him across the face. "Shut up, old man. For once in your life, shut the fuck up."

JD's head snapped back, and the chair tilted and crashed onto the deck, throwing him onto his back. He sprawled, chest heaving, a string of drool escaping his gaping mouth.

She stared in stunned silence, shocked at the violent explosion.

Russ rushed to JD and helped him sit up. He glared at Shawn. "Why the hell did you hit him? He's your father, for God's sake."

Shawn hitched up his pants and sniffed. "He wouldn't shut up. He never shuts up." He glowered down at JD.

The package of cocaine lay on the deck where it had slipped out of JD's pocket when he fell.

"Shit, Dad. You showed them the drugs? What were you thinking?"

JD groaned and tried to scramble to his feet but collapsed on his butt. "It's not my fault." He jerked his chin at Russ. "He found the package in the freezer. I didn't tell 'em it was yours. I didn't, I promise."

Shawn smoothed his hand over his scraggly beard. "You just did, you stupid old man. You talk too goddamned much." He drew back his fist.

Russ stepped between father and son and held up his hands. "Don't hit him again."

Shawn's eyes narrowed to slits, and he jutted out his bearded chin, but he lowered his arm.

A bone-crushing weariness stole over her. "I need to know one more thing, and then we'll leave." She swallowed, but her mouth was devoid of moisture. "What...what happened to my parents' bodies? What did you do with them, JD?"

"Don't say anything more, Dad. Keep your friggin' mouth shut."

JD's red-rimmed eyes met Shawn's. A look of defeat deepened the lines on his weathered face. "It's too late, son. She deserves to know." With Russ's help, he stood on unsteady feet and leaned against the table. "I wrapped their bodies in a strip of old canvas your father had lyin' around and carried 'em to their skiff. Then I sailed to Sewell Island. They're buried there." He stared at his shaking hands. "I found a real nice spot under a tree on a hill overlookin' the ocean." His rank breath huffed out in a noxious cloud. "After I laid them to rest, I sailed the ketch to a remote location, opened all the valves, and scuttled her. A friend picked me up on his boat."

Her legs wobbled, and she grabbed the back of a chair for support. She finally had her answer. She knew where her parents were, where they'd been all these years. Clara was right—sometimes the truth was worse than the not knowing.

Chapter 40

The sun sank behind the trees, casting long shadows across the weed-filled clearing. Crickets chirped in the deepening dusk. An owl hooted from somewhere deep in the forest.

Otis stood at her side, his body tense, his gaze fixed on Shawn.

"You know we have to go to the police." Russ's steel-laced voice sliced through the tension-filled silence. "You murdered William O'Flynn. You're going away for a long time, JD."

"Wait." JD lurched toward Russ and grasped his arm. "You can't go to the cops."

"I can, and I will." Russ threw off his hand, gripped her elbow, and guided her down the steps. "Come on, Athena, let's get out of here."

"Stop right there!"

Startled at the command in Shawn's voice, she swung back.

Incredibly, he held a handgun—pointed at her chest. His eyes were savage, his mouth a thin, hard line.

Fear clawed her heart. The ground beneath her dissolved, and she felt as if she were falling. She clutched Russ's arm. "What...what are you doing?" Her voice was a thin squeak barely audible over her pounding heart.

Russ shoved her behind him, protecting her with

his body. He held his hands out in front of him in a placating gesture. "Put the gun down, Shawn. You don't want to hurt anyone."

"What the hell, Shawn. Don't shoot 'em." JD staggered across the deck.

"I can't let them go to the cops, Dad. You know that, right? You'll end up in prison like he said." He waved the gun in the air. "And they've seen the drugs. I'm not going down for that. No damn way."

"This is all your fault, Maggie." JD swayed and gripped the railing, his eyes sad. "Why couldn't you have left well enough alone? Why did you have to come here and stir up this old shit?" He tipped his head back and stared up at the darkening sky. When he looked back at her, he nodded as if he'd reached a decision. "I took those photos of you for Angus, just like I said. After you left the island and moved in with your aunt, I kept takin' pictures and sendin' them to him. And he kept payin'."

He sniffed. "He wanted to know everythin' about you, but I didn't tell him you'd changed your name or where you lived. If he knew that, he wouldn't have needed me. He could have hired someone else. The money was too good to give up.

"When my arthritis got too bad to be hidin' in bushes—" He nodded at Shawn. "—Shawn here took over." A note of pride crept into his voice. "He's a damn fine photographer." He puffed out his chest. "Just like his old man."

Her breath caught in her throat, and she peeked around Russ's bulk and glared at Shawn. "I saw you. You followed me to Vancouver." She remembered the bearded man with the red cap with the distinctive black logo vanishing in the crowd outside the lawyer's office. "It was you outside my house in Calgary, and again at Angus's cottage. I knew someone was there."

"That's funny." His cackle was at odds with the dull gray gun he held steady, his grip unwavering. "You never noticed all the other times I followed you, snapping pictures, peeking in your windows, watching everything you did." He smirked. "And I mean *everything*."

Her fury found a new target, and she scowled at Shawn. "You're still taking pictures. Why bother? Angus is dead. No one's paying you anymore."

His grin widened. "I was hoping I'd catch some pics of you naked. Those type of photos sell, especially if they're of poor, tragic little Maggie O'Flynn, all grown up."

Her breath rattled in her throat, and she shuddered.

Russ inched a step closer to Shawn.

"Stay where you are." Shawn pointed the barrel at Russ.

He moved another step. "What are you going to do? Kill me?" Russ sneered. "Are you willing to murder two people in cold blood, just like your father killed William O'Flynn? Tell me, does murder run in your family?"

"I told you that was an accident," JD said. "William was gonna call the cops. I would've spent the rest of my life in prison." His face darkened. "I wasted a couple of years in jail when I was a punk. I swore I'd never be stuck in a cage again."

Otis growled deep and low in his throat. His lips curled back, exposing sharp canines.

"Shut that damn dog up." Shawn pointed the gun at

Otis.

The evil intent in Shawn's eyes confirmed her worst fears. He was a cold-blooded killer and wouldn't hesitate to shoot. "Please don't hurt him." Tears burned her eyes. The thought of Otis getting hurt because of her was too much to bear.

JD's rheumy gaze settled on her. "Don't worry, Maggie. I like dogs. Otis is upset now, but once this is over—" The corners of his mouth tightened, and his gaze skittered away. "—the two of us'll get along just fine."

Shawn waved the gun at Russ. "Put him in the trailer."

Otis growled again. The ridge of hair along his spine rose, and his muscles bunched, ready to spring.

"Do it!"

Athena couldn't breathe, couldn't swallow. "Quiet, Otis." Her voice was a strangled whisper.

The night sounds of crickets and frogs were muted. Salt and the faint sewer scent of low tide carried on the light breeze.

Russ grabbed Otis's collar. "Come on, boy." He dragged the resisting dog up the steps and across the deck to the trailer door. Opening the screen with one hand, he shoved Otis inside and slammed the door and returned to Athena's side.

Otis whined and barked, his claws screeching as he raked the flimsy metal door.

"You don't want to do this, Shawn." Russ's voice was low, calm, and persuasive. "What happened with William and Anna is ancient history, but if you kill us, both you and your father will go to prison for the rest of your lives."

"I'm not stupid." Shawn spat a stream of saliva on the dirt at his feet. "The second you two walk outta here, you'll go straight to the cops."

"Don't do this. Please. We won't tell anyone." She fought for breath through her tight throat. "I promise."

"Maybe we should think about this, son." JD stumbled down the steps, almost falling, but he gripped the railing and managed to stay upright. "Maybe there's another way outta this."

"We're done thinking. I'm not going to jail." Shawn motioned with the gun. "Get moving."

"You're making a mistake," Russ said. "If we don't show up at our motel, people are going to wonder where we are. We took the ferry over. There'll be a record of our trip. Your neighbor, what's his name, Randy? He knows we're here. He'll tell the cops, and they'll come looking."

"We keep to ourselves on this island. No one's gonna tell anyone anything." A cruel smirk lifted the corners of Shawn's mouth. "Besides, they can look all they want. No one's gonna find you, or that fancy car of yours."

Otis's frenzied barking filled the night. The screen door banged as he lunged, fighting to reach them.

"That's right. Your dad's an expert at hiding bodies. Aren't you, JD?"

Ice flowed through her veins. They had to escape. They couldn't stand there waiting to be killed. She searched the dark yard for something—anything—she could use as a weapon. A stack of split firewood was piled under the eaves along the side of the trailer. If she could grab one of those chunks of wood, maybe she could throw it at Shawn and knock the gun out of his hand. She gulped.

She hadn't thrown a ball in years, but she had to act, and soon. She gauged the distance to the wood pile. Could she reach the stack before Shawn pulled the trigger? She slid Russ a glance.

His face looked as if it was carved from stone. His body bristled, and his muscles bunched, hands tightened into fists, ready to strike.

Shawn and JD were focused on Russ and seemed to have forgotten her. Now was her chance. Inhaling a deep breath, she inched sideways, one slow step at a time.

Shawn didn't shift his attention from Russ.

Another inch. And another.

A few more steps, and she'd be able to reach the wood. She shuffled another foot.

"Just where the hell do you think you're goin', Maggie?" JD asked.

Her heart stopped beating. "I…I—"

The trailer door blasted open in an explosion of animal, and Otis scrambled across the deck. With a single bound, one hundred and ten pounds of angry dog went airborne, and he rocketed past JD and into Shawn.

The gun fired in a deafening blast. Splinters of wood and plastic sprayed where the bullet embedded into the side of the trailer.

Too terrified to move, Athena stood, rooted to the spot.

Otis's paws dug into Shawn's thighs and chest, his teeth ripping at exposed flesh.

The man stumbled back, bellowing, swinging blindly with the gun. He crashed onto the ground, the dog snarling on top.

Russ lunged into the fray, seizing the gun out of Shawn's grip, and tossing the deadly weapon into the dark.

Swearing and gasping, Shawn grabbed Otis's collar and flung the dog aside.

Otis landed with a heavy thud and yelped.

Her blood ceased moving, her insides turning to concrete.

Russ tackled Shawn, and the two men wrestled, rolling over and over on the packed dirt.

Otis scrambled to his feet and charged. His teeth clamped onto Shawn's arm.

Shawn howled and punched Otis in the side.

Otis's cry of pain freed her from her paralysis. Adrenaline fired through her veins, and she fumbled among the weeds for the gun. Her hands shook as she grasped the weapon and lifted it, struggling to keep it steady, surprised at its weight. "Stop." Her voice was a thin whisper. She swallowed. "Stop!"

Russ clutched Shawn's shirt collar, drew back his fist, and punched the bearded man in the face.

Shawn's head bounced back, striking the ground with a loud whack. His eyes widened, went blank, and he groaned and collapsed in an unmoving heap.

Movement on the deck caught her eye, and she swung the gun toward JD.

He held his hands up. "Don't shoot, Maggie."

Arms trembling, she lowered the gun.

JD nodded at Shawn sprawled on the dirt and mud. "You didn't hurt him, did you?" Tears glistened in his eyes as he stumbled down the steps and crouched beside his unconscious son. He cradled the man's lolling head in his arms.

She dropped the gun and flew to Russ. "Are you okay? Are you hurt?"

Russ staggered to his feet. His chest heaved, and his face glistened with sweat. Crimson drops stained his shirt. "I'm fine." He clasped her close. "Are you all right?"

Tears blurred her eyes, and she burrowed into his arms.

Otis whined, and she pulled free of Russ's embrace.

The dog sat before her, his front leg raised, and whined again.

"Poor Otis. You're hurt." She fell to her knees.

The dog whined piteously and licked her face.

"Let me take a look." Russ knelt before Otis and examined his paw. "It's not bleeding, and I don't think it's broken. He must have bruised his paw in the fight." He petted Otis on the head. "Good boy. You saved the day."

Otis's tail thumped the ground.

She wrapped her arms around his neck and hugged him. "You're a hero, Otis. You saved us. Good boy."

"Lucky dog." A teasing glint shone in Russ's golden eyes.

She looked up, and her heart stuttered. Blood-spattered, bruised, his hair a riot of wild curls, his shirt sweat stained and torn, he was everything she'd ever wanted, everything she'd dreamed of.

Tears filled her eyes, blinding her. She loved him, but because of that love, she had to walk away.

To protect him.

From her.

She was damaged, and he deserved so much better.

She loved him enough to want him to be happy. Blinking back tears, she pasted a bright smile on her face. "You did all right too, Russ. I guess that makes you a hero." She swore she heard her heart shatter when his face lit up, and he grinned.

Chapter 41

Russ steered the *Minerva* through the marked buoys and tucked into the small bay on the leeward side of Sewell Island.

Athena stood in the bow, staring out at the sea. Her hair flamed in the morning sunshine. She'd lost weight and was too thin. His heart ached at the dejected slump of her shoulders and her seeming frailty. A strong gale would blow her over.

Two weeks had passed since the incident with JD and his son. The police had arrested the pair and charged JD with one count of second-degree murder for the death of William O'Flynn.

Shawn was charged with two counts of attempted murder and possession of an illegal substance for the purpose of trafficking. Father and son were in custody awaiting trial and looking at spending the next decade or so in prison. Maybe, if they were lucky, they'd get to share a cell—a real father-son bonding experience.

Police investigators had travelled to Sewell Island and found William and Anna O'Flynn's graves exactly where JD had said they were. They'd dug up the bodies and transported them to the morgue at the Vancouver General Hospital and conducted autopsies. JD had told the truth. Anna O'Flynn died from drowning, and William O'Flynn's skull had been crushed by a blunt object.

When the police arrived at JD's trailer on Hornby Island, Russ and Athena had been separated and taken back to the mainland, where they'd been questioned for hours. He hadn't seen or heard from her until last week.

He'd tried to connect with her, but she'd shut him out, ignoring his countless phone calls and text messages. He'd even flown to Calgary and waited for hours in the cold on her doorstep. His heart had shattered when she'd pulled her car into the driveway, saw him waiting, and without a word, backed her car out and drove away.

Her silence made her feelings crystal clear. He'd fulfilled his part of their bargain, and she had her answers. She didn't need him anymore. Not that he blamed her. She'd never hidden the fact that theirs was a business agreement. He just hadn't believed her.

He'd tried to get on with his life. Once the transfer of Angus's estate was finalized, a ton of work at the office awaited him, but he'd lost his spark. He went through the day-to-day motions at work, but it was like he was in a daze. He didn't care about the business, profit margins, board meetings, nothing.

Seven days ago, she broke her icy silence and called and asked him to take her to Sewell Island. And like a goddamned fool, he jumped at the chance to see her again, and he'd agreed. She needed to reach the isolated island. He had a sailboat. Who better than good old Russ to take her?

Sucker.

She was using him…again. The sooner he accepted that, the better. He was angry—you bet he was—but, God help him, he loved her. She was still reeling from JD's shocking revelations, and in spite of her making her feelings—or rather, her lack of feelings—for him clear, he ached to ease her burden of pain. He'd stopped questioning the ridiculousness of his love. She'd claimed a part of his soul. It was as simple and as complicated as that.

He hadn't told her of his powerful feelings. Men didn't bare their souls. Not to anyone. At least, that's what Angus had always told him. Men buried their feelings and carried on. No matter how much it hurt. His mouth twisted in a grimace. He was a bloody coward, terrified that if he revealed how much he cared, she'd reject him.

Too late, buddy. She's already kicked you to the curb.

Brushing off the snide inner voice, he focused on the boat and checked the depth finder. Dropping the anchor, he allowed the boat to drift back as he paid out the chain. The boat shuddered and jerked as the anchor dug into the seafloor for the initial set.

Without having to be asked, Athena started the engine and slowly increased the revs.

Once the anchor was set, he secured the chain on deck by tying off the snubber. They worked together like a well-oiled machine, requiring little verbal communication. Good thing, since she'd hardly spoken to him since they departed Vancouver.

The next hours would be even more difficult. Would seeing the spot where her parents had been buried result in the closure she so desperately wanted? Or would this trip be the catalyst that drove her deeper into her grief and farther from him? He glanced at her pale face, hollow cheeks, and slender form, and a fierce protectiveness filled him. Whatever the outcome, he vowed he'd be there, broken heart and all. At least he'd stay until she stomped on his heart…again.

Yep. He was a goddamned fool, all right.

****

The ocean pitched and rolled, and Athena grabbed the safety straps and balanced on the wobbly stern bench seat. Sea spray chilled her face as Russ hefted the oars and rowed the rubber dinghy toward the nearby shore.

Unfazed by the rocking, Otis perched in the bow, tail wagging, panting with excitement at the adventure.

Russ powered the little craft through the breaking surf and onto the smooth sand, and Otis leaped out of the dinghy, splashed to shore, and raced down the beach, his back paws raising clumps of wet sand.

With less enthusiasm, Russ jumped out and held the raft steady while Athena clambered onto shore. She shrugged off her life jacket and studied the stretch of smooth, golden sand, breathing in the familiar scents of salt, fish, and rich cedar. They couldn't have picked a better day. The sky was a brilliant blue, and the afternoon sun was a warm caress on her back.

A forest of towering evergreens sat atop a bluff, and a bald eagle, its white head gleaming, perched on a branch high above the beach, surveying his kingdom.

She swallowed over the lump in her throat and fought the ever-present sting of tears. Ever since JD confessed the awful truth of the events of that long-ago day on Shelter Island, she'd struggled against an overwhelming darkness that threatened to engulf her and take her down. As soon as the police completed their investigation, she'd broken her sobriety. Giving in to the urge to drink was wrong in so many ways, but as she struggled to make sense of the past, she needed the crutch alcohol offered. More than she ever had.

Clara convinced her to seek counseling, and Athena had reluctantly agreed. To her surprise, she liked the counselor and had met with her three times so far. The intensive therapy sessions helped, and she'd cut back on her drinking, but she hadn't garnered the strength to quit.

Not yet.

Her life was a mess. No question. Russ's solicitousness made her even more aware of what she'd lost and what that loss cost her. The irony was too much to bear. At long last she'd met a man she loved, but her emotional baggage stood in the way of happiness. Her spirit was damaged, and she feared she'd never be able to love him the way he deserved.

Besides, what could he see in her? She was a woman who'd been sober seven days, a woman who'd probably drink again. Even if she didn't drink, even if she somehow managed to beat back the beast, she'd fight her demons forever. That was the thing with being an alcoholic—there wasn't a cure. Alcoholism was a lifelong affliction.

Russ was hurt by her feigned indifference, but shutting him out was the only way to protect him, even though keeping her distance was nearly killing her. She had to straighten out her life, stop drinking for more than a week, and heal her wounds before she could open her heart.

When she'd asked him to take her to Sewell Island, she knew seeing him again was risky. She could have hired a boat and sailed there herself, but she'd wanted Russ at her side, needed his strength and unswerving compassion. How else could she face this new nightmare? And so, she'd been selfish…and foolish.

She wasn't surprised when he'd agreed to her request. He was always there for her, always had her back. That was why, when this venture was over, she was walking away. He deserved so much better. She refused to saddle him with someone so flawed.

Otis barked and galloped across the beach, bounding over driftwood and snapping at clumps of bull kelp, jubilant to be off the boat.

At least he was happy with this adventure. She wasn't so certain, but her therapist had suggested visiting the place where JD buried her parents might bring her peace.

"Are you sure this is what you want?"

Russ's deep voice broke through her thoughts. "I…I think so." She chewed her bottom lip. "Thank you. Thank you for—" She coughed and cleared her throat. How could she express in mere words how much his being at her side meant? "Thanks," she said again. Not good enough, but all she could muster.

"There's nowhere else I'd rather be."

His words soothed her soul like warm honey, and she wanted nothing more than to fall into his arms. Steeling her heart, she inhaled a deep breath, squared her shoulders, and followed the faint indentation in the rocky ground up the hill.

Puffing from the steep climb, she wiped her damp brow. The past few days had been unseasonably warm, with little wind and no clouds. The drone of insects filled the air, and she swatted at a fly buzzing her face. The surrounding forest was ancient, the bark on the towering tree trunks thick and rough, scarred from winter storms. Old, twisted roots broke through the rocky ground like the humps of serpents.

Otis galloped past her and into the trees, searching for squirrels and rabbits.

"From what the police told me, the grave site should be over there." Russ pointed at a tall Sitka spruce tree overlooking the bay.

A carpet of yellow-and-purple wildflowers, leafy ferns, and emerald-green clumps of moss covered the rocky ground. The branches of the ancient spruce tree offered welcome shade from the hot sun.

Bees buzzed and butterflies flitted amidst the flowers. A raven croaked from somewhere deep in the forest. The sun filtered through the canopy of branches and dappled the clearing. Two identical, rectangular depressions, a mound of rich, black dirt piled beside them, were hollowed out in the ground beneath the tall spruce tree.

This was where JD had buried her parents, where their bodies had rested until the police dug them up two weeks ago. Tears stung her eyes, and she staggered and would have fallen if Russ hadn't caught her and held her close, enveloping her in his strong arms. She clung, breathing him into her soul, taking strength from his calm presence.

"You don't have to do this. Not now." He smoothed his hands over her back. "Not until you're ready."

She shrugged off his warm, comforting embrace, knowing that if she weakened now, she'd shatter into a million tiny pieces.

He stiffened, and the softness left his face.

She grimaced at the sour taste of self-disgust that

filled her mouth. She'd hurt him...again...but she had to do this next step on her own. Had to prove, if only to herself, that she was strong, that she could bear these next minutes.

She stared at the depressions in the ground, her feet rooted in place. Her heart thundered so loud the pounding drowned out the distant, surging surf. She swallowed back tears. All the years she'd wasted, praying her parents would miraculously appear, and they'd be a family again. Years of living with the fear she wasn't good enough, that her parents had abandoned her. The anger and hatred she'd harbored for Angus Crawford, the drinking to escape her pain...

The warm spring breeze ruffled her hair.

You can do this.

Breathing in deep, slow breaths, she placed one foot in front of the other and crossed the small, sunlit meadow and sank to her knees. Sobs wracked her as she clutched handfuls of the cold dirt.

Long shadows stretched across the ground by the time her tears eased, and a wash of peace unfurled deep within her belly, inching like liquid honey through her veins, dissolving the block of ice encasing her heart. She rose to her feet, her muscles stiff, and wiped the tears from her face with a tissue she tugged from the pocket of her shorts.

The long nightmare of never knowing what happened to her parents was over. She could let go of the hurt and uncertainty. Her parents hadn't deserted her. They hadn't chosen to leave. Sadness and remorse remained, but the burden of guilt she'd carried for so many years eased. She'd lost so much, but mixed in with the grief was a new, burgeoning hope.

Russ leaned against a tree trunk on the far side of the clearing, where he'd waited still and silent, while she worked through her grief. His face was in shadow and his expression impossible to read.

Otis lay beside him, his head resting on his front paws, his gaze fixed on her.

She wiped away her tears, smiled a tremulous smile, and crossed the clearing, and met Russ under the leafy branches of the statuesque Douglas fir.

"Are you okay, Athena?"

His rugged good looks tugged at her heart. His strong cheekbones and firm chin were offset by the surprising softness of his full mouth. Warmth flooded her, filling her with a sense of rightness. This wonderful man had been with her every step of the way on this difficult journey, always at her side, never demanding more than she was able to give. She took his hand in hers. "Call me Maggie."

"Maggie?"

"Yes, Maggie." She said the name aloud again. And again. "Maggie." It sounded different on her tongue, yet familiar and comforting, like she was shrugging into a comfy sweater. Her smile widened. "It's time I reclaimed my birth name, don't you think?"

"Maggie." He grinned, white teeth gleaming, dimple flashing. "I like the sound of that." He wrapped his arms around her.

Otis barked as if in agreement, as she snuggled into Russ's embrace, secure in his strong arms, relishing the closeness before reality set in.

"You're leaving, aren't you?" Russ's voice rumbled in his chest. "You're going back to Calgary."

She nodded. "I have to know everything. JD said

my father found out my true parentage just before he died, but Clara told me my father knew my mother was pregnant with Angus's child before William married her."

He smoothed a lock of her hair from her forehead. "Maybe JD wasn't telling the truth."

"He confessed to murder, blackmail, and drug smuggling. Why would he lie about whether William knew I was his child or not?" She inhaled a shaky breath. "I need to hear Clara tell me what really happened. I can't shake the feeling she's keeping things from me."

"I'll go with you."

"No." She swallowed. "This is something I have to do on my own."

He studied her, his golden gaze delving deep, and then he nodded. "Okay."

He leaned closer and kissed her on the lips, a deep, curl-your-toes kind of kiss—the kind of kiss love stories were written about. A kiss she'd spent her life dreaming of.

Biting back a groan, she kissed him back. Hard. Her chest was heaving and her body on fire by the time they broke apart.

He studied her with a heavy-lidded gaze. "Do what you have to do, Maggie. Just make sure you come back…to me."

Her heart thudded, and she nodded.

Chapter 42

She raised her hand and knocked on the shiny black door. A glow of lights shone through the beveled glass. It had taken all her strength of will to say goodbye to Russ and Otis at the Vancouver airport. Already she missed them.

Every time she closed her eyes, Russ's image rose before her. He was all she thought of, all she dreamed about. Unspoken words had burned in her throat, desperate to be set free, but she hadn't told him she loved him. How could she when the future was so uncertain and more secrets waited to be uncovered?

The door swung open, and a blaze of light streamed onto the porch. "Athena! What a pleasant surprise. I wondered when you'd get back from the coast."

Maggie gulped, at a loss for words. Mouthing the usual pleasantries seemed ridiculous, but she couldn't blurt out the real reason she'd come. Not yet. "My name's Maggie."

Clara blinked. "Maggie?"

Maggie nodded. "I've decided to reclaim my old name."

"It's about time." Tears welled in Clara's faded blue eyes. "Your parents would be so happy. They loved the name Maggie." Her brow furrowed. "Are you okay? You seem—" She waved her hand in the air as if searching for words. "—upset."

"I need to talk to you." Maggie swallowed back a lump and blinked against the sting of tears. This wasn't going to be easy.

"Of course." Clara opened the door wider. "Come in, my dear."

Stepping into the over-warm house, Maggie hung her coat in the hall closet, slipped off her shoes, and set them on the mat like she'd done hundreds of times. The normalcy of the simple actions gave her courage for the coming confrontation.

Clara fussed about like a mother hen, smoothing Maggie's hair, straightening the collar of her blouse, all while mouthing a steady stream of loving platitudes.

She followed her aunt through the small, tastefully decorated living room, past the television where a game show was playing, the canned laughter loud, and into the cozy kitchen. Drawing out a wooden chair, she sat at her usual spot at the antique, round maple table and clenched her hands in her lap.

Clara filled the kettle and set the old, dented pot on the stove to boil. Opening the pantry door, she removed a container, pried off the lid, and lifted out several cookies. She arranged them on a plate and set the plate on the table in front of Maggie. "I had a feeling you'd be stopping by, so I made these yesterday. Chocolate chip and macadamia nut—your favorite."

The sweet scent of rich milk chocolate filled the air, but Maggie's stomach roiled. She couldn't eat, not with so much resting on the next few minutes. She shoved the plate of cookies away.

"Eat up, dear." Clara tsked. "You're far too thin." The kettle whistled with a high-pitched shriek, and she tossed two tea bags into a dainty, rose-patterned china teapot. Lifting the steaming kettle, she poured boiling water into the teapot.

Maggie glanced at the familiar surroundings—the soft, butter-yellow walls, the golden oak cupboards, and the gleaming laminate countertops. The sunlight reflected like a yellow flame off the row of lush potted plants set on the windowsill. How many times had she sat in this same chair while she'd cried out her woes over a cup of tea and awaited Clara's sage advice?

Her aunt was the closest thing to a mother Maggie had for the past twenty-three years. Clara gave up so much to raise her orphaned niece, and never once complained. How could Maggie question her honesty?

Clara poured tea into two, dainty china teacups and set one in front of Maggie. She sank onto the facing chair, added two spoonsful of sugar to her own cup, and stirred. "Okay. Now tell me about your trip to Sewell Island. Did…did you find—" Her throat worked. "—what you were looking for?"

The concern on the older woman's face brought a fresh sting of tears, but Maggie steeled her heart. She was there to find answers. She inhaled a breath for courage. "Did you know that my mother and Angus continued their affair after I was born?"

Clara's face paled, and a heavy silence descended on the overheated kitchen. "What…what are you talking about?" Her actions were as good as a confession.

Maggie tapped her fingers on the tabletop, her nails clicking a rapid beat. "Come on, Aunt Clara, it's time you told me the truth."

Clara worked her bottom lip with her teeth,

chewing off her shiny, cherry-red lipstick. Her narrow shoulders slumped, and she looked every day of her seventy-four years. She set her cup on the saucer with a loud clatter. "Your mother and Angus knew what they were doing was wrong, but they couldn't stay away from each other."

Maggie picked up a cookie and crumbled it between her fingers. JD had told the truth. "My mother cheated on my father for years."

"She wasn't proud of her actions, but telling William of the affair would have devastated him." Clara's lips tightened, deepening the fine lines grooved around her mouth. "You've always been wrong about Angus. He was a good man, and he wanted the best for you. That's why he dropped his custody claim when the publicity over your parents' disappearance blew up all over the news. He realized the best thing for you was for him to keep his distance. If news of his affair with Anna and your true parentage came out, your life would have become even more of a circus." She met Maggie's gaze. "He loved you enough to let you go."

There it was again, the reference to the fact that Angus Crawford loved her. An image of his cold eyes and austere bearing flashed before her, and she shuddered. "He didn't want me until he realized he wasn't going to have any other children."

"That's not true. He watched over you from a distance and made sure you didn't want for anything. He even paid me—" Clara's hand flew to her mouth.

"*Paid* you?" Maggie's heart thudded. "For what?"

"Never mind. I shouldn't have said anything." Clara struggled to her feet, grabbed her cup, and shuffled to the counter, then refilled the cup with hot tea from the pot. "Whether he paid me or not isn't important. Not anymore. Your parents are gone. Angus is gone." There was a hitch in her throat. "They're all gone."

Maggie slammed her palms hard on the table. Cookie crumbs scattered, spilling onto the floor. "Why did you accept his money?"

Tears filled Clara's eyes and streamed down her seamed cheeks. "He…he paid me to look after you. I needed the money…I had to quit my job and move…"

Maggie sucked in a breath. "Why would he pay you—" Before the thought fully formed, she knew the answer. "You're not my aunt, are you?"

Clara's lips trembled. "When your parents vanished, Angus hired me to be your guardian. We both decided it would be easier if you assumed that I was your mother's long-estranged sister, a blood relation."

"That's all I was to you—" She sneered. "—a paycheck?" Maggie rubbed the burning knot in her stomach.

"No, it wasn't like that. I—" Clara must have seen the disgust on Maggie's face, because she stopped trying to defend her actions. "Okay, I'll admit that at first, looking after you was just a job, and Angus paid good money. But soon—very soon—I grew to love you." She sniffled. "I still do."

Maggie swept the cookie crumbs into a pile. She wanted to believe Clara, but this woman had lied to her for over twenty years. How could Maggie trust anything she said?

Clara set her cup on the table, pushed up from her chair, and plodded to a cupboard. Reaching to the top shelf, she removed a large, leather-bound book and plopped it on the table in front of Maggie. "Look through this photo album, and then tell me I looked after you just for the money." She heaved a heavy sigh and shuffled out of the room.

In the silence of the empty kitchen, Clara's plodding footsteps and the closing of her bedroom door were loud. The ticking of the clock on the wall and a steady drip from the faucet echoed in the tiny kitchen. The familiar scents of chamomile tea, fresh-baked chocolate chip cookies, and lemon furniture polish filled the air.

Brushing the cookie crumbs aside, Maggie slid the album closer. She wiped her palms on her leggings and lifted the cover. Color photographs of her as a child filled the page, starting in the first months after she arrived at her aunt's—she grimaced—Clara's place. She'd been a thin child, all gangly arms and legs, with a mass of shoulder-length, red frizzy hair. The sadness in the hollows of her blue eyes was haunting.

An ember of warmth melted the block of ice in her chest. Clara had welcomed her into her home, and her life, with kindness and compassion. Without her support, Maggie wouldn't have survived those first bleak months.

She flipped the page. Page after page of pictures tracked the major and minor events in her life…birthdays, Christmases, summer holidays, high school graduation, prom… Beneath each photo, written in Clara's precise script, was a caption and date. Tears filled Maggie's eyes, blurring the images.

The photographs weren't like the sterile, impersonal ones she'd found in the cardboard boxes in Angus's cottage. An irrefutable truth shone from every page and in every lovingly captured moment—Clara loved her. Looking after Maggie might have begun as a good-paying job, but no blood-related aunt could have cared for a niece more.

She looked up at the soft rustle of a footstep.

Clara stood in the kitchen doorway. Anxious concern shone from her pale eyes.

"How can I ever thank you?" Maggie patted the photo album. "All these years, you've looked after me and wanted only the best for me." She swallowed back tears. "I'm sorry I doubted you."

Tears gleamed in Clara's eyes, but a brilliant smile lit her wrinkled face, making her look years younger. "Don't thank me, Maggie. I'd do it again in a heartbeat. I only wish I'd told you the truth from the beginning."

Dozens of emotions rioted through Maggie. "I don't know what to think. My entire life has been a lie."

"You've had a lot thrust upon you these past months." Clara's veined hand patted Maggie's arm. "Why don't you take a holiday? Get away from everything and give yourself time to think?"

The words ignited a spark that flared into a flame. A holiday. What a great idea. Maggie leaped up and hugged Clara. "Thanks, Aunt…er…Clara."

Clara's forehead wreathed in furrows. "What did I say?"

"I have to go. I'm going on a trip…a sailing trip." She smiled at the perplexed expression on the other woman's face, but she didn't have time to explain.

She flew out of Clara's house, leaving the old woman standing openmouthed in her doorway. "I'll call and let you know where I am." She bounded down the porch steps and ran to her car. "Oh, and by the way, I love you, *Aunt* Clara."

Tears filled Clara's eyes. "I love you too, dear. Say hello to your young man."

Epilogue

Maggie closed her eyes and raised her face toward the burning yellow orb in the cloudless sky, reveling in the soothing warmth. *The Minerva* rocked in the gentle swells. A light breeze freshened and teased the tendrils of hair escaping her short ponytail. Gulls swooped overhead, their raucous cries and the lap of waves against the hull the only sounds in the clear afternoon. Sensing a presence behind her, she turned. Her heart skipped a beat, and an instant rush of heat and desire melted her bones.

The past months had wrought changes to Russ's handsome face. The tension carving the lines bracketing the corners of his mouth had vanished, replaced by a relaxed contentment that softened the harsh planes of his rugged features. "Won't be long now." He smiled, the golden lights in his hazel eyes sparking. "We're almost there."

She tore her gaze from his. The first hint of a bluish dark shape appeared on the horizon. "You're sure you're okay with this?"

A shaft of sunlight glowed across his face.

His smile widened, and the dimple she found so irresistible popped out in his lean cheek.

"I'm most definitely okay."

She returned his smile. Hard to believe she was so happy. The shocking events of the past seemed a distant memory; the ghosts that had plagued her finally laid to rest.

There was no longer any doubt. She'd completed a paternity test using skin cells from the inside of her cheek and hairs she found in a hairbrush Angus had used in his home in West Vancouver. The results weren't a surprise. Angus was her biological father, but William O'Flynn would always be her real father. He'd raised her, loved her, and in the short time she'd had with him, he'd laid the groundwork that helped her become the woman she was today.

With Russ's help, she'd issued a press release explaining the events of the past months and the details of Angus's will. The media had gone ballistic, and a feeding frenzy ensued. For a few days, life was a nightmare. But the reporters accepted her request for privacy and chased after JD and his son for the lurid details. The furor soon died down.

Since she and Russ had scooped Steve, his true-crime book about her family had lost its attraction, and agents and producers weren't interested. He'd quit his job as caretaker on Shelter Island and was on to other adventures.

The past months were like a dream. After leaving Clara's house, Maggie had stopped at her own home only long enough to pack a bag and let her neighbor know she was going away for an extended vacation.

She'd flown back to the West Coast, and Russ and Otis met her at the airport. Otis was ecstatic, and after she confessed her love to Russ, he was pretty happy too. One thing led to another and, before she had time to come to grips with her new dream life, she and Russ were married in a small city hall ceremony in downtown Vancouver.

Otis, freshly washed and clipped, had stood in as Russ's best man, the ring pinned to the dog's collar as he'd pranced, tail high, tongue lolling, down the short aisle.

Clara had flown out and walked Maggie down the aisle.

Tears of happiness had been shed by all, except Otis. He'd become so excited he piddled on the city clerk's glossy shoe. After much embarrassment and many apologies, he was forgiven.

They'd returned to Russ's penthouse apartment and enjoyed a salmon barbecue and several glasses of non-alcoholic champagne.

Otis ate a dish full of kibble and gnawed on a new beef-flavored chew toy.

It was the happiest day of Maggie's life.

Bar none.

In the months since then, they'd moved aboard the *Minerva* and had spent the past month sailing around the Salish Sea, through the Gulf Islands, and north to the remote, rugged islands of Haida Gwaii. Their days were filled with happiness as they sailed past schools of dolphins, spotted killer whales frolicking in the waves hunting salmon, and even had a memorable close encounter with a curious humpback whale.

At night, she and Russ snuggled on the berth beneath warm blankets, expressing their love. Otis sprawled on the floor beside them on his padded bed and snored the night away. Everything was so perfect, she feared she'd wake up one morning and discover her life was a wonderful dream, and all her happiness had vanished.

Her heart bled for the tragedy of her parents' untimely deaths. She hadn't wrapped her brain around that loss, but the heavy cloak of grief that had been her constant companion for most of her life had lightened. Knowing her parents hadn't deserted her, that they'd loved her until their unfortunate deaths, brought peace to her ravaged soul.

When she awakened in the middle of the night in the throes of a nightmare, tears streaming down her face and dampening her pillow, Russ held her in his arms until her tears eased, and she fell back asleep.

One hundred and eighty days.

One hundred and eighty unbelievable days sober.

A record.

One she had every intention of continuing. The urge to drink lurked like a shark, waiting for her to weaken and give in to her craving, but each day she didn't drink was a celebration. And with each passing day, the desire to imbibe eased.

They were sailing to Shelter Island and planned to live in Angus's cottage for the next few months as a sort of extended honeymoon. Russ had taken a leave of absence from work. He no longer wanted to run Angus's company, and he had plans to sell the business. At long last, he was going to follow his lifelong artistic dream and paint. Where better to find inspiring seascapes than Shelter Island?

"Penny for your thoughts."

Russ's deep voice broke through her musings, and she smiled. "I'm just thinking that it's been a long time since I've been so happy." Her smile widened. "And that's all because of you."

He smoothed a strand of hair from her face. "You

C.B. Clark

make me pretty happy too."

Unable to resist, she nuzzled her lips to his. The kiss deepened until they were both gasping for air, and her pulse pounded in her chest.

He pulled back and looked at her with passion-glazed eyes. "This probably isn't a good idea."

"What are you talking about? This is the best idea we've had, at least since last night." Her face heated as she recalled the loving they'd shared in the cramped berth below deck as the boat rocked at its moorings.

He slid his hand under the light cotton fabric of her shirt and caressed her stomach. "What about Junior? Won't making love risk harming him?"

She chuckled. "We don't have to worry about that for months. Besides, I'm sure *she* won't mind that her parents are in love and can't get enough of each other."

"Well, then…" He scooped her in his arms and carried her across the *Minerva's* polished wooden deck and down the hatchway to the berth.

Otis trotted behind.

She smiled in keen anticipation. Yesterday, before they set sail, she'd found out she was expecting. They hadn't been trying to conceive a child, but they hadn't *not* been trying either. The news was welcomed with shouts of joy from Russ and excited barking from Otis.

Her life was complete. She had everything she'd ever wanted, everything she desired, Russ, the love of her life—she rested her hand on her still-flat stomach—and the new life growing in her womb that they'd created together.

Otis barked and padded to the berth. He lifted his front paw onto her lap and regarded her with wounded eyes.

She chuckled and rubbed behind his ears. "Don't worry, boy. You're part of this adventure. We're a team, right?"

He licked her hand and yipped agreement.

"Hey. What about me? Aren't I part of the team?" Russ's laughter swirled in the air like liquid honey.

She arched her brows. "What do you think, Otis? Should we let Russ into our inner circle?"

Otis barked and spun, his nails scrabbling on the smooth planking.

She grinned. "Looks like the jury's reached a verdict."

The corners of Russ's eyes crinkled. "And? What's the decision?"

"You're in." She planted her mouth on his, expressing the depth of her love in that single deep kiss.

He grinned and faked wiping sweat from his brow. "Phew. I was worried for a minute that you three—" He placed the palm of his hand on her stomach. "—would vote me off the island."

"Never." Her voice thickened with emotion. "We're all in this together."

His eyes glistened, and he lowered his head and kissed her.

Her heart swelled with joy and, as she returned her husband's caresses, a thought struck her. She had Angus Crawford to thank for her happiness. His adopted son loved her, and they were heading to Shelter Island—Angus's island—to start a new life.

Who would have thought?

Someday she'd reconcile her memories of the austere man who'd fathered her with the man who'd sought to protect his daughter at all costs, but for now she'd bask in her happiness and be grateful for Russ's unconditional love.

Life was good.

Life was damn good, and the best part? She didn't want a drink, not even a sip or a sniff of alcohol.

Not today, and hopefully, not tomorrow, nor the next day, or the day after that.

Yes, life was good indeed.

A word about the author...

C.B. Clark has always loved reading, especially romances, but it wasn't until she lost her voice for a year due to a botched operation that she considered writing her own romantic suspense stories. She grew up in Canada's North. Graduating with a degree in Anthropology and Archaeology, she has worked as an archaeologist and an educator. She enjoys hiking, canoeing, and snowshoeing with her husband and dog near her home in the wilderness of central British Columbia.

Thank you for purchasing
this publication of The Wild Rose Press, Inc.

For questions or more information
contact us at
info@thewildrosepress.com.

The Wild Rose Press, Inc.
www.thewildrosepress.com

www.ingramcontent.com/pod-product-compliance
Lightning Source LLC
Chambersburg PA
CBHW050032030726
47506CB00001B/234